"Do you think differently of me now that you know the truth?"

Max stared at her. "I know who you are. You are Ivory Moore. You are the woman who redressed a corpse to save my sister. The woman who kissed me to save me from myself. You are the only one who understands why I can never be put in a prison that was built for me by fate and circumstance."

She swallowed, emotion clogging her throat.

"You are the woman I trust." Reaching down, he caught her hands in his and pulled her to her feet. "The woman I want more than anything."

"Max." It came out like a plea, when she had meant it as a protest.

"I lied," he said. He pressed his mouth to the flesh of her palm, and her knees nearly buckled.

"What?" It was hard to follow the thread of conversation, what with the feel of his lips on her skin.

"I said I wasn't sure of anything anymore," he said quietly. "But that's not true. I am sure of you."

Duke

of my

Heart

KELLY BOWEN

FOREVER

NEW YORK   BOSTON

Copyright © 2016 by Kelly Bowen
Excerpt from *I've Got My Duke to Keep Me Warm* © 2014 by Kelly Bowen

Forever
Hachette Book Group
1290 Avenue of the Americas
New York, NY 10104

HachetteBookGroup.com

Printed in the United States of America

First Edition: January 2016
10 9 8 7 6 5 4 3 2 1

OPM

Forever is an imprint of Grand Central Publishing.
The Forever name and logo are trademarks of Hachette Book Group, Inc.

The Hachette Speakers Bureau provides a wide range of authors for speaking events. To find out more, go to www.hachettespeakersbureau.com or call (866) 376-6591.

The publisher is not responsible for websites (or their content) that are not owned by the publisher.

ATTENTION CORPORATIONS AND ORGANIZATIONS:

Most Hachette Book Group books are available at quantity discounts with bulk purchase for educational, business, or sales promotional use. For information, please call or write:

Special Markets Department, Hachette Book Group
1290 Avenue of the Americas, New York, NY 10104
Telephone: 1-800-222-6747 Fax: 1-800-477-5925

*For my parents, who gifted me
with a love of reading.*

Acknowledgments

Every book is always a team effort, and this one is no different. A huge thank-you to my agent, Stefanie Lieberman, my editor, Alex Logan, and the entire team at Forever for helping to shape each story. And as always, my deepest gratitude to my husband, who has spent many hours convincing the boys that it's best to practice their slap shot somewhere besides my office. At least when I'm writing.

Duke
of my
Heart

Chapter One

London, February 1819

The silk was the color of sin.

It shimmered where the candlelight danced across its surface, its rich crimson and sumptuous garnet hues swirling in the cascading lengths. The silken ribbon was wide, its superior quality was evident, and it must have been expensive, a luxury only the very wealthy could afford. On the brim of a bonnet, it would have been impressive. On the bodice of a ball gown, it would have been spectacular.

Wrapped around the limbs of a dead earl, however, it was a problem.

Ivory Moore pressed her fingers over the pulse point at the man's neck, knowing she would find none, but needing to confirm. Beneath her touch the soft flesh was already cooling, and she let her fingers move to the bindings covering his wrists, tracing the silk to where it was knotted deftly around the bedpost.

"He's dead." It was a statement, not a question, from her pretty associate standing just behind her.

"He is indeed, Miss DeVries," Ivory murmured.

"That is the Earl of Debarry," Elise DeVries hissed urgently in her ear.

"I am aware." Ivory stepped back slightly to consider the tableau in front of her. The naked earl was spread out across the mattress like a marooned sea star, his wrists and ankles tied to the four corners of the bed. His barrel chest rose like an island amid a scattering of rose petals and decorative ostrich feathers and rumpled bedclothes. He was instantly recognizable, even stripped of the wildly expensive clothes he favored, whose absence exposed a body that was just beginning to lose its battle with fine wine and idle living.

The earl was still handsome despite the fifty-plus years of vice he'd enjoyed before this last unfortunate encounter. He was powerful, wealthy, and widowed—and everywhere he went in polite society, he was treated with the deference befitting his title. But privately, behind closed doors, he was known to all as the Earl of Debauchery, more famous for his love of women and his outrageous sexual exploits than anything else. Finding him tied to a bed wasn't a surprise.

Finding him tied to the bed of the demure Lady Beatrice Harcourt, the Duke of Alderidge's eighteen-year-old sister? Now that was more of a shock.

Ivory took another step back, pushing the hood of her cloak off her head, and placed her bag gently on the floor. There was little time to waste, but before she could analyze the potential damage and formulate a solution, there were preliminary matters to consider.

"The door is locked, Miss DeVries?" she asked briskly. Containment was critical.

"Of course."

"Good." Ivory turned to address the woman standing stiffly near the hearth. "Was it you, my lady, who summoned us?"

Lady Helen Harcourt was worrying an enameled pendant at her throat, but at Ivory's question she dropped it, clasping her hands in front of her hard enough to make her knuckles as white as her face. "Yes."

"A wise decision on your part, my lady." Ivory eyed the woman's greying hair, which had been pulled into a severe knot, softened only by a jeweled clip that matched her green ball gown. Deep grooves of distress were cut into Lady Helen's unyielding face, but despite her pallor, there were no signs of impending hysterics.

Ivory felt a small measure of relief. "May I ask who found the body?"

"Mary. Lady Beatrice's maid." Lady Helen unclasped her hands long enough to make a gesture in the direction of a red-eyed maid sitting in the corner, who, at the mention of the word *body*, had started to sob.

Ivory exchanged a look with Elise. The maid would need to go.

"And where is Lady Beatrice at the moment?" Ivory inquired.

"I can't find her. She's just…*gone*." It came out in a rush, the news delivered in a tone barely above a whisper.

Well, that wasn't surprising. Beatrice had very likely fled, and while the girl would need to be found, it wasn't the immediate priority.

Ivory eyed the crumpled bedclothes beneath the body,

and the lavender counterpane that lay in a forgotten heap on the floor. She took in the size of the room, and the pretty dressing table with its collection of bottles and pots. A pale-pink ball gown, embroidered with tiny roses, had been tossed over the back of the chair, layers of costly fabric and lace abandoned with little care. Stockings and slippers, along with Debarry's evening clothes, had been discarded and had fallen in disarray on the floor. Two empty wine bottles rested on their sides at the edge of the rug.

Ivory frowned. If it had been Lady Helen's rooms, she would have had more options. An affair between an aging spinster aunt and a peer of the realm—no matter how unlikely—if properly presented, would cause gossip, but not ruination. A dead earl tied to the bed of a debutante in her first season posed a much greater challenge.

There was very little time to waste. Who knew how long they had before someone—

A sharp banging on the bedroom door snapped Ivory's head around and caused Lady Helen to emit a squeak of shock.

"Helen?" came a disembodied voice through the thick wood. "Are you in there?"

"Who is that?" hissed Ivory, her mind racing through the possible excuses Helen might offer for locking herself in her niece's room.

The older woman was staring at the door, her hand pressed to her mouth.

Another rap sounded, the urgent impatience of the blow making the wood shake. "What the hell is going on, Helen? Is Bea in there with you?"

"My lady!" Ivory snapped in low tones. Whoever was standing on the other side of that door was not going away.

Worse, he would soon draw attention to this room with all his banging. Every servant in the house would descend on this scene, and even Ivory wouldn't be able to contain that.

"It's Alderidge," Lady Helen whispered faintly, as though she didn't quite believe it.

Ivory started. "The duke? I was given to understand he was currently in India."

"He was. Apparently he's decided to grace us with his presence." Lady Helen's words were tight with bitterness. "Too little, too late, as always."

Ivory fought the urge to groan aloud. It was clear there was no love lost between the duke and his aunt. Ivory only hoped the man held his sister in higher regard. She did not need family turmoil to complicate what was already a terribly complicated situation.

"Aunt Helen!" The knob rattled loudly. "I demand you let me into this room at once!"

"Can he be trusted?" Ivory asked, though she feared she had little choice in the matter. Someone was going to have to let him in or risk having the door knocked clean off its hinges.

Lady Helen's lips compressed into a thin line, but she gave a quick, jerky nod. That was all Ivory needed. She flew to the door, twisted the key in the lock, and wrenched the door open. She had the vague impression of a worn greatcoat, battered boots, and a hulking bearing.

"What the hell is going on?" the stranger bellowed. "And who the hell are you?"

"Welcome home, Your Grace," said Ivory, and grabbed the sleeve of his coat. She yanked him into the room. "Please do come in and cease making so much noise, if you would be so kind."

The man stumbled past her a couple of steps before coming to an abrupt halt, but not before Ivory had closed the door behind him and once again turned the key in the lock.

"Jesus Christ," Alderidge swore, getting his first look at the scene in front of him.

Ivory was standing just behind the duke, and she could feel the chill of the night still clinging to his coat. The only things she knew about Maximus Harcourt, Duke of Alderidge, were that he had inherited his title a decade ago and that he spent much of his time overseas captaining an impressive fleet of trade ships. But she knew nothing about his personality, his family relationships, or the motivations that had brought him home to London tonight.

She desperately hoped Alderidge was not going to be a problem. "Did anyone see you come up here?" Ivory asked.

"I beg your pardon?" The duke swung around to face her, and Ivory felt the impact of his icy grey eyes clear through to her toes.

"Is anyone else looking for your aunt? Or your sister, for that matter?" She refused to look away, dismayed to realize an involuntary flutter had started deep in her belly, radiating out to weaken the joints at her knees and send heat flooding through her body.

Good heavens. She hadn't had this sort of visceral reaction to a man in a very, very long time, and she wasn't pleased. Desire was a distraction, and distractions were perilous. Maybe it was because Alderidge was such a radical departure from the long line of polished, simpering aristocrats she'd been dealing with for years. Dressed completely in black, he looked a little like a pirate who had just stepped off the deck of a ship, what with his long, sun-bleached hair, his wind-roughened skin, and at least a week's worth of dark-blond stubble covering his strong jaw. A scar ran along the left side of his forehead, disappearing into his hairline. His clothes were plain, his salt-stained coat meant to be serviceable and warm. He looked dangerous and, at the moment, furious.

"No, no one saw me. I left my ship and crew at the damn docks after a long journey across uncooperative seas and came here, thinking to find some peace and quiet. Instead I find a swarm of gilded strangers packed into my ballroom, and more strangers locked in my sister's room with my aunt and a dead body. Someone damn well needs to tell me very quickly and very clearly just what the hell is going on here." The duke was making a visible effort to remain calm.

Lady Harcourt made little disapproving sounds with her tongue for every curse that erupted from the duke's mouth—and Alderidge flinched, as if on cue, after each of his aunt's tiny clicks and sighs. Ivory might have found this exchange funny in other circumstances. Right now, however, she needed to take control and make sure the duke and his aunt were aligned. Otherwise she hadn't a prayer of extracting the family from this mess unscathed.

"You may call me Miss Moore," Ivory said pleasantly, "and I am from Chegarre and Associates. This is my colleague, Miss DeVries." Out of the corner of her eye she saw Elise make a brief curtsy.

"And Chegarre and Associates is what?" Alderidge demanded. "A solicitor's firm?" He paused, a shadow of uncertainty flickering in his eyes as he regarded her. "I've been away from England for quite a long time, but I feel certain I would have heard the news if a group of women had set up shop at the Inns of Court."

"We are not lawyers exactly, Your Grace."

"Then what—"

"Your sister seems to have gotten herself in a spot of trouble," Ivory continued, nodding at the naked form sprawled across the sheets. "We've been summoned to get her out of it."

"That is not possible. My sister is the Lady Beatrice Harcourt."

"We're aware," Ivory agreed grimly, turning and marching over to the bed. "And the dead man currently tied to her bed is the Earl of Debarry."

The duke's jaw was clenched so hard that Ivory imagined his teeth were in danger of shattering. He turned to his aunt. "Where is Bea?"

"I don't know."

"What do you mean, you don't know?"

Angry color had flooded Helen's face. "I came looking for her when I couldn't find her downstairs in the ballroom, thinking maybe she was feeling poorly. The ball is in her honor. It took *months* to plan. Everyone who is *anyone* is downstairs." She stopped abruptly, as if suddenly realizing the awful import of that fact.

"She's missing?" Horror colored his words.

"The precise location of your sister is not known at this point, Your Grace," Ivory confirmed. "Though I have every confidence that we will locate her shortly."

The duke swung around to face her again, those ice-grey eyes impaling her as if she were somehow responsible for this debacle.

"We have a much more immediate problem that needs

to be addressed, Your Grace, before we can focus our efforts on locating Lady Beatrice. And that is the body currently tied to her bed." Ivory jerked her chin in the direction of the maid still sniffling into her apron. "Your sister's maid, Mary, discovered this unfortunate scene, and most fortuitously, it was your aunt who intercepted her before anyone else could. It was also your aunt who did the sensible thing and hired us."

"Hired you? What the hell for?"

"We manage situations such as the one your sister has currently found herself in."

"And what sort of situation is that, exactly?" His tone was threatening, but Ivory didn't have time for niceties.

"You are a man of the world, Your Grace. I feel certain you are able to guess."

The duke's eyes darkened to the color of an approaching storm, and another unwanted thrill shot through Ivory. She curled her fingers into her palms, letting her nails bite into the skin.

"Have a care, Miss Moore," he snarled. "I assure you, you do not wish to insult my sister's—"

"I deal in facts, not in fairy tales." Ivory cut him off and was absurdly gratified to see shock wash across his face. "There are no signs of a violent struggle, nor are there any obvious wounds or marks on the body. It is likely that the earl died from natural causes induced from the exertions that usually follow being tied with red silk to the bed of a healthy young woman."

Helen Harcourt wheezed. "You can't possibly be suggesting that Lady Beatrice—"

"Further," Ivory continued, "it is also likely that Lady Beatrice panicked and fled the scene once she realized her companion had drawn his last debauched breath. It is a very common reaction, and in my experience, the young woman in question will return when she has had a moment to collect her wits and invent a suitable explanation for her absence. And if Lady Beatrice lacks the requisite powers of invention, Chegarre and Associates shall be happy to supply her with a credible lie that she may repeat to the ton." She paused. "Your loyalty is admirable, but I suggest you save the moral outrage for someone else. I care more about rescuing your sister's reputation than the truth of what happened here tonight. And frankly, so should you. We've got a great deal of work to do if your sister's future is to remain as bright as it was this morning."

The duke's expression was positively glacial. "I give the orders here, Miss Moore, not you. Don't presume that I will ever follow your lead."

Irritation surged. "Take a look around you, Your Grace. Do you see a crew of sailors anxiously awaiting your direction?" She put emphasis on the last two words. "This is not your world. This is mine."

"Get out of my house," the duke said, his voice as sharp as cut glass. "Now."

His aunt made a strangled sound of distress.

"If that is your wish, Your Grace, we will be happy to comply, of course. But I ask that you consider carefully. Our firm has been brought here by your aunt to preserve your good name and honor. Our objective is the same as yours: we want only to protect Lady Beatrice and the rest of your family. And what you must understand is that there is a window of opportunity here that is rapidly closing. Downstairs there is a ballroom filled with some of the most important and influential people in London. Soon those people will begin to wonder where the Earl of Debarry has gotten to. Soon people will start wondering where the comely Lady Beatrice—the guest of honor—is hiding. Soon people will come looking. And should they find a dead earl tied to Lady Beatrice's bed, I will no longer be able to help you. But it is your choice, of course, if I stay or if I go."

"I don't need you to fix my problems," the duke growled.

Ivory resisted the urge to roll her eyes. The duke was in so far over his head that he couldn't even begin to see the surface. Instead she adopted her most neutral tone. "I'm not here to fix your problems, Your Grace, I'm here to fix those of Lady Beatrice."

Lady Helen swayed slightly before straightening her shoulders with resolve. "Don't be a fool. We need help. Neither you nor I can make this all disappear."

The duke was shaking his head. "I can handle this."

"Can you really?" his aunt asked. "How?"

Alderidge blinked, and Ivory suspected the duke was finally getting over his initial shock and was now considering the magnitude of the problem before him.

Helen continued on, relentless. "How will you make certain the honor of the Alderidge family is preserved? How will you prevent this, this...scene from becoming known to everyone? Do you intend to let malicious gossip and baseless slander ruin poor Beatrice's life?"

Ivory rather suspected Lady Beatrice was doing a fine job of ruining things all on her own. But it was not for her to judge. Especially since a little ruin was always good for business.

"You're supposed to be her guardian," Lady Helen said

bitterly. "A lady should have the protection of her brother. If you had ever once thought of anyone but yourself, we would not now find ourselves here, in this sordid and disgusting position."

"My lady," Ivory snapped, sensing that this conversation was in danger of veering badly off track. "Now is not the time to point fingers. If you must lay blame, I would suggest you conduct that useless exercise tomorrow over tea, when your guests are gone and there is no longer a body tied to your niece's bed."

Whatever color had been left in Lady Helen's stoic face fled, and her mouth gaped slightly. Ivory noticed Alderidge's was similarly hanging open.

She put her hands on her hips. "Now, what is it going to be? Do you require our services on behalf of Lady Beatrice or not? Make a decision. Time is running out."

The duke swore again, his expression black. "Very well. Consider yourself hired. My sister can't..." He trailed off, as if searching for words.

Ivory pounced. "You must agree to defer to my instruction and trust in my expertise, Your Grace."

Icy grey eyes snapped back to her. "I will agree to no such thing. I don't even know you."

"And I don't know you, which is irrelevant. But I will not be able to do my job if you get in my way. Dissent will cost your sister everything."

The duke muttered something vile under his breath. "Do what you must." It sounded strained.

"Do I have your word?"

"You heard me the first time, Miss Moore. I do not need to repeat myself."

"A wise choice then, Your Grace." She produced a small

card from a pocket sewn into her cloak and handed it to the duke. "In the event you need to find me in the future."

Alderidge shoved the card in the pocket of his coat without even looking at it. "After tonight, Miss Moore, I hope to never see you again."

That stung a little, though Ivory had no idea why it should. No one in their right mind *wanted* to see her. Her presence in someone's home meant the parallel presence of some sort of acute social or family disaster.

She sniffed. "The feeling is quite mutual, Your Grace. The sooner we conclude this unfortunate bit of business, the better it will be for all involved. But I must warn you before I begin, if I may be so gauche, that the services provided by Chegarre and Associates are expensive."

"Are they worth it?" Alderidge asked in a harsh voice.

Ivory held his gaze. "Always."

Maximus Harcourt, tenth Duke of Alderidge, couldn't remember ever having felt so helpless—or so furious. He had stepped into a nightmare that defied comprehension, and making it worse was the knowledge that he was not the person most qualified to handle it.

Unruly crews could be reformed. He could deal with tropical storms and raging seas. Pirates and smugglers could be summarily dispatched. Max had rarely met a problem he couldn't best. He'd rarely met a problem with the power to confuse him. But this? Well, this was an altogether different sort of beast.

Which meant he was now at the mercy of Miss Moore. A woman who treated the discovery of a dead, naked earl tied to a missing virgin's bed as though it were no more serious than a cup of spilled tea on an expensive rug. As though this sort of thing happened every day.

He'd never in all his life met a woman with such nerve. Or maybe it wasn't nerve at all but simply arrogance. It was difficult to tell how old she was, though certainly she wasn't any older than he. Even beneath her plain clothing and mundane cap, she was striking, in a most extraordinarily unconventional way. Her skin glowed like unblemished satin, framed by tendrils of hair the color of rich chestnut, shot through with mahogany. Her dark eyes were too wide, her mouth was too full, her cheekbones too sharp. Yet all of that together was somehow... flawless.

"Was that the ball gown your niece was wearing tonight?" Miss Moore was asking his aunt, pointing at a pile of abandoned lace and rose silk draped over a chair.

Max wrenched his gaze away from her face and, with a jolt, recognized the embroidered silk that he'd shipped to Bea the last time he'd been in China. He'd been sure his sister would love the detail.

"Yes." Lady Helen pressed a hand to her lips, her face a peculiar ashen color.

"Then she'll not be downstairs," the dark-haired woman who had been introduced as Miss DeVries murmured. "Nor does she have any intention of returning to the ball." She plucked the gown from the chair and held it up to her body with consideration.

Miss Moore nodded. "Let's hope she has the good sense to stay away until we have a chance to speak with her." She paused, eyeing the gown critically. "Can you make it work?"

"Most certainly," said Miss DeVries, replacing the

gown and then inexplicably loosening the ties on her own shapeless woolen dress. Max frowned, perplexed, then horrified, as the top half of her chemise was revealed. It slipped over a shoulder, revealing smooth skin puckered by scar tissue from what looked like an old bullet wound. He gaped before hastily averting his eyes. What kind of woman stripped in the middle of a room full of people? What kind of woman had cause to have been *shot*?

"Excellent." Miss Moore turned to his aunt. "If you wish to preserve your niece's reputation, and your own, you need to return downstairs. Your absence may have been noted by now, so I need you to circulate, smile pleasantly, and ensure everyone is having a marvelous time. If anyone comments on your absence, cite your nephew's unexpected, yet welcome, return. I can't stress enough the value of a good distraction, and the duke's arrival will be splendid."

"My sister is missing and you're telling my aunt she should go and dance a quadrille?" Max could feel a vein throbbing at his temple.

Miss Moore glared at him and then turned her attention back to his aunt. She didn't even give him the courtesy of a response. Bloody, bloody hell.

"Can you do that?" she was asking Helen.

Lady Helen nodded stiffly.

"If anyone asks about the whereabouts of Lady Beatrice, mention you just saw her at the refreshment table. Or near the ballroom doors. Somewhere that cannot be immediately verified." Miss Moore put a hand on the older woman's arm. "Your behavior is critical right now. No one must suspect you are anything but pleased with how successful the ball is. Do you understand?"

"Yes."

"In thirty minutes you will visibly exit the ballroom and make your way to the bottom of the main staircase."

"Why—"

"Thirty minutes. Can you do that?"

"Yes."

He'd never heard Helen so tractable in his life.

Despite himself, Max was grudgingly impressed that Miss Moore had managed to handle his battle-ax of an aunt with a deft touch. That was something he hadn't mastered, nor did he suspect he ever would. She was a good woman, but also a mighty annoyance. She delighted in repeating to him just how much she had sacrificed for *his* family, and it wore sorely on his nerves.

Miss Moore led her over to the door and cracked it open, peering out into the empty hallway. She turned back and softened her voice. "This will turn out all right, my lady. I suspect your niece is rather terrified right now. She'll need you, and your forgiveness, when she comes home."

Helen nodded and met Max's eyes, her expression stony. "Your parents would be turning in their graves," she said coldly. "If you have any regard for your sister, you will help Miss Moore do whatever it takes to find her and fix this."

Max fought the acerbic response that jumped into his throat. As if he were incapable of recognizing that Bea's future was hanging by a perilous thread. He became aware that Miss Moore was glaring at him again with those impenetrable dark eyes, and he swallowed his retort, nodding instead. Arguing with his aunt would get them nowhere.

"Arguing will get us nowhere." Miss Moore stole his thought as soon as his aunt had departed and she'd locked the door behind her. "She's upset, and I need everyone to keep a clear head."

Resentment rose hard and fast. How dare this chit lecture him on maintaining composure in difficult circumstances? He was a sea captain, for God's sake. Every day of his life brought difficult circumstances. The only difference being that he knew what to do with those.

Miss Moore had returned to the bed and was diligently working on the knots that bound the dead man's wrists. Max strode to the footboard and began working on the bindings at his ankles.

"I refuse to believe my sister had anything to do with this," Max said. He wondered for whose benefit he'd made that statement.

Miss Moore straightened slightly, brushing an errant strand of hair out of her eyes. "Your Grace, there is one thing you must understand. I do not get paid to form opinions or pass judgments." She bent to retrieve a cloth bag by her feet and began stuffing the silk ribbons into it. "Frankly, I don't really care if Debarry was your sister's lover or not. What I do care about is ensuring she is not ruined, or worse, because of it."

"Worse?"

"The earl is dead." She was now collecting feathers and rose petals, and they too disappeared into the bag. The wine bottles followed with a loud clink.

Max felt his skin prickle with unease. "You can't be serious. You think she *killed* him?"

"If she did, he went out a happy man," Miss Moore remarked.

Max recoiled. "Bea is barely eighteen. She is beautiful and innocent and—"

Miss Moore had stopped and now turned to meet his eyes. He hated the sympathy that was in them, yet somehow he couldn't bring himself to look away.

"My apologies. My comment was insensitive." She approached him, searching his face. "How long have you been away, Your Grace?"

"What?"

Miss Moore remained silent, simply waiting for his answer.

Despite himself, he couldn't think of a reason not to answer. "I own and captain Indiamen, Miss Moore. I am rarely in England. The last time was two years ago."

"Ah." She nodded, as if this bit of information somehow explained the situation in which they currently found themselves.

"I may not know my sister as well as you think I should, but I know she wouldn't have an earl tied to her bed," Maximus said, ignoring the tiny voice in the back of his head that was telling him he knew no such thing. "And I resent any implication otherwise."

Miss Moore was still studying him carefully, and for the life of him, he couldn't tell what she was thinking. Though he had the inexplicable feeling she was somehow seeing more than he cared for her to see.

"Is there a guest room on this floor?" she asked abruptly.

Max frowned, caught off guard. "There are two of them. At the end of the hall."

"I'll need your help to move his lordship." She left him at the bed, discarding her own cloak, and bent to collect the abandoned clothing strewn about the room. A pair of trousers, then a shirt and a waistcoat. "We'll need to redress him first to stage this properly."

Maximus stared at her. Bloody hell, but this woman was unnerving.

She returned, the clothes draped over an arm, a faint look of annoyance across her face. "Quickly. Time is of the essence, Your Grace." She plucked the ribbons from his unfeeling hands.

Max scowled. "If we're going to dress a corpse together, then at least give me Debarry's trousers."

Miss Moore gazed at him with shrewd speculation.

"I have my limits, Miss Moore."

"A gentleman," she murmured, and he wasn't sure at all that she wasn't laughing at him.

"A poor assumption on your part," Max muttered, but the woman's only response was to toss the trousers in his direction.

"Good" was all she said.

⌒

Ivory yanked the shirt over the corpse's head, careful not to touch the duke where he had the dead man braced. Alderidge had shed his greatcoat, and beneath the bulky winter garment lay a pair of broad shoulders and an impressive collection of muscles in all the right places. His own shirt and waistcoat hid some of them, but not enough to slow the pulse she could feel pounding at her throat.

It was ridiculous, but it was an effort not to simply stare at him.

He looked a bit untamed, Ivory thought, as she jammed a lifeless arm through the opening of Debarry's striped waistcoat. Like a lion that had suddenly appeared amid a clutter of domesticated house cats. She diligently attacked the row of waistcoat buttons, wrestling them into their buttonholes, considering further. It was obvious Alderidge was a man used to power and control, yet it would seem his sister's welfare trumped his disinclination to surrender either. That was certainly a relief—

"Miss Moore?"

Ivory blinked and looked up. "I'm sorry?"

"I asked you if you think I should retie his cravat."

Good God. This was no time for flights of fancy about untamed pirates. They were dealing with the Earl of Debarry here, and she could not afford any missteps. The man had too many powerful friends. The situation at hand required her undivided attention.

"No," she said, gathering her wits. "Leave off his cravat. And his evening coat and his shoes. But bring them with us." She pushed herself off the bed, where she had been kneeling. "Elise, stay here with Mary. Get her to stop sniveling and pick out the appropriate wig from the kit. She'll know what hairstyle Lady Beatrice was wearing tonight. I also need to know if there is anything missing of Lady Beatrice's. Clothing, shoes, jewelry."

Elise, now in nothing but her chemise, nodded, busy examining the rose ball gown. "Of course."

"There's water in the basin," Ivory said, pointing toward the washstand. "I'll need that. Please leave it just outside the door."

"Done. Anything else?" Elise asked.

"No, I think that will get us started. His Grace and I will take Debarry to a guest room." She gestured at the duke to get under one of the corpse's arms.

Alderidge frowned. "Why are we taking him to a guest room?"

"Because he's too big to stuff up a chimney." Ivory pulled a lifeless arm over her shoulder and together they hauled the man off the bed.

The duke's jaw clenched again. "I don't appreciate your humor."

Ivory sighed. "No, I don't suppose you do."

They made their way to the door, Ivory puffing under the dead weight. Thank God the duke and his muscles had shown up when they did. She and Elise would have managed it, but it would have been a struggle. She unlocked the door and cracked it open, peering into the hall. It was still deserted.

"Quickly now."

They made their way down the hall, the duke doing most of the work to support the body. Mercifully, the hallway remained empty, and they shoved their way into a guest room, Ivory pushing the door shut behind them with her foot. The room was dark, the only faint light coming through the window from streetlamps burning below.

She ducked out from under their lifeless load and pulled back the sheets. "Put him into bed," she whispered.

Alderidge dropped the bundle of clothing he had under his other arm and heaved the corpse onto the mattress. Together they arranged his limbs into a pose of peaceful slumber.

"Now what?" he asked in a clipped voice.

"Debarry was feeling poorly when you ran into him," Ivory said, pulling up the sheets and tucking them around the earl. "Though you had just returned home and hadn't even had a chance to change for the ball, you offered to have his carriage brought around. He refused, declaring that he was certain he would feel better with a brief rest.

Being a gracious host, you offered him your guest room. You saw to his needs yourself, as the servants were all busy downstairs."

"Why don't we just take him back to his own house?" the duke hissed. "I don't particularly want him found dead in any of my rooms. People will talk."

"Probably. But Debarry shows no obvious symptoms of anything save a lifetime of overindulgence. His untimely death will be unfortunate but not shocking." She retrieved the earl's pumps and set them neatly by the bed. The forgotten evening coat and cravat she laid out over the end of the footboard, as if Debarry had been planning on redressing. "And the risk of taking him back to his own house is too great. Downstairs there's an army of guests and footmen and coachmen and grooms to get past, and then assuming we arrive safely at our destination, we'd have to navigate Debarry's own servants. It would be almost impossible."

"Almost?"

"I've done it once or twice when there has simply been no other option."

"What the hell does that mean?"

"It means I've helped others out of worse situations than this."

"Worse? How could it be worse? This man is dead, and my sister is missing!"

Ivory winced slightly. There was absolutely nothing she could say at this moment that the duke wanted to hear about Lady Beatrice. "I need you to dress for the ball now," she told him instead. "And you need to hurry."

"Have you lost your mind? I should be out looking for Bea, not prancing around a ballroom." His voice was absolute, and Ivory suspected that he was very good at commanding his crew.

Too bad for him she wasn't one of them.

"And you will look for her. But not right now." She was careful to keep her tone steady but firm.

"You think this is partly my fault, don't you?"

"As I said earlier, I am not here to form opinions, Your Grace. I'm here to make sure your sister returns safely to your protection. And to do that, I need you to trust me."

The duke raked his hands through his hair, creating an impenetrable shadow across his face. Ivory didn't need to see his features to know that furious indecision would be stamped there.

She took a step forward and placed her hand gently on his shoulder. The man might be a controlling ass, but he was clearly worried about his sister. And she needed his full cooperation if she was going to pull this off. "This is what will happen next. You will dress. Go downstairs. Welcome your guests, regale them with tales of your last voyage. Be visible. You are the perfect distraction, and your presence here will doubtless aid your sister tonight. Somewhere over a card game, mention to at least two people, but no more than four, your regret that Debarry is missing the hand because he was feeling poorly. In one hour you will instruct your butler to check on his lordship. Not a footman, but the butler. Butlers are far more discreet." Beneath her fingers his muscles were tight.

"What about Bea?"

"Leave her to me. Just for right now. Now let's get you dressed. Which one is your room?"

Alderidge opened his mouth twice before he managed a response. "You've done quite enough, Miss Moore."

"I will tell you when I've done enough," Ivory said. "You can either tell me which one is your room or I will simply find it myself. But I will remind you again that time is not our friend."

"I don't need—"

Ivory blew out a breath of exasperation and tiptoed to the door. She checked the hallway, but it remained empty, the only sound the muted noise of the music and the crowd below their feet. Silently she slipped from the room and started down the hall. She bent to retrieve the basin that Elise had left outside Beatrice's door, careful not to slop the water on the rug. "Which room, Your Grace? I will open every one of these doors, or you can just tell me."

"Jesus." Alderidge was on her heels, and not happy about it. "This one." He pushed by her and stalked to the end of the hall, opening the last door on the right.

The room was dark, yet the faint musty smell she had expected from a room left unused too long was absent. Though the room was chilled, it would seem the town house enjoyed the attentions of an exceedingly diligent staff. Ivory closed the door behind her and waited for her eyes to adjust, light suddenly flaring as the duke lit two lanterns.

The room was sparsely decorated with the basics, and there was not a personal touch in evidence anywhere. A bed with a Spartan headboard and footboard was covered in a plain white coverlet. A cumbersome wardrobe loomed against one of the walls, and there was a washstand with a porcelain bowl resting empty and cold in the center. A small cheval mirror stood near the washstand, and at the foot of the bed rested a battered trunk, the only indication that this space might belong to somebody.

"No dressing room, Your Grace?" Ivory asked, heading for the washstand. She dumped the water into the bowl and put Lady Beatrice's basin on the floor. Then she moved to the wardrobe.

"A waste of space." He was still standing near the cold hearth and the lanterns.

"Spoken like a man who chooses to live on a ship, I suppose," Ivory replied mildly. "I must assume you have a shaving kit in here somewhere?"

"Of course I do."

"Then I would advise you to get started."

"Are you ordering me to shave? Now?"

"Anything that deviates from an expected appearance will be remembered. Remarked upon. Speculated on. You cannot appear like a barbarous, disheveled pirate on the same night that your ball ends because there is a dead man in your guest room."

"What did you just call me?"

"I didn't call you anything. I simply commented upon your current appearance." Ivory had reached the wardrobe and stopped. "Do you need me to shave you?"

Alderidge's jaw dropped open. "*What?*"

Given his expression, she might as well have suggested she take him on a flying carpet to the moon. "Time, Your Grace, is ticking. I don't know how many more times I need to stress this to you before you understand that we simply must find a way to get done what needs to be done. Either you shave, and make yourself look presentable to society, or I will do it for you."

"No, I don't need you holding a razor to my throat," Alderidge muttered, but at least he was moving now. He knelt before the battered trunk and released the buckles. He opened the lid and rummaged in its interior, then pulled out a leather case. He stalked over to the washstand and started extracting items.

Satisfied, Ivory turned back to the massive wardrobe, just as a terrible thought struck her. "Do you even have evening clothes?"

"Of course I have evening clothes." He stopped. "Somewhere. In there, maybe?"

Dear God. Ivory yanked open the two center doors and nearly swooned with relief when she wasn't met with a swarm of moths. The clothes, like the room, were neat and orderly, folded on shelves, as though the duke had just stepped out for two hours as opposed to two years. When it came to the domestic details, Lady Helen, it would seem, ran a tight ship.

Ivory ran her fingers over a collection of crisply folded linen shirts, waistcoats, breeches, and more formal pantaloons. The drawers below revealed an array of stockings, braces, and pressed cravats, each one separated from the next by a thin piece of tissue. Opening the long door at the side of the wardrobe, she discovered a collection of jackets sorted by function. It had been a very long time since she had had the pleasure of choosing evening wear. Of any sort.

The sharp scent of shaving soap had filled the room, and Ivory could hear the faint swirl of water in the basin, followed by the scrape of a straight blade against stubble. A faint twinge of melancholy struck her, old memories surfacing of the pleasure she had derived from simply watching a man shave. In those memories she sat on the edge of the bed while her husband went about his ablutions, most often preferring to do it himself, as this duke did. In those memories those stolen moments of privacy were always filled with banter and conversation and laughter.

But they were just that. Memories. And they had no place in the present.

Pushing the melancholy and memories aside, Ivory carefully selected a shirt, waistcoat, and tailcoat, draping each over her arm. She stood on her tiptoes and pulled a pair of pantaloons from a shelf. The clothes were all of fine quality and understated in their color, making it easy to coordinate.

"I'll lay your clothes out on the bed," she started, turning around. She had the tailcoat and his shirt spread neatly on the coverlet when she made the mistake of looking up. And found herself staring.

The duke had stripped off his worn waistcoat and shirt, and had his back to her, peering into the cheval mirror as he ran the blade over his skin. He'd moved one of the lanterns to the washstand so that he might see better, and the light created an impressive silhouette, putting his torso in stark relief. The muscles in his arms and shoulders flexed each time he lifted the razor to his face—raw, male, physical power sculpted into beautiful lines. His spine created a valley of shadow that started beneath the ends of his long hair and traveled down through the ridges and planes of his back to dip into the waistband of his breeches.

She couldn't draw enough air into her lungs, and a peculiar light-headedness seemed to have impaired her ability to remember what she was supposed to be doing. He was stunning, and she couldn't even begin to imagine what that power and strength might feel like beneath her hands or between her—

"Am I not doing this fast enough for your liking?" the duke said irritably, and with some horror, Ivory realized he was watching her in the mirror.

"Are you almost done?" she said, and it was a monumental effort to keep her voice even.

"Yes." He picked up his discarded shirt and dried his face.

"Good." She placed the last items of clothing on the bed and turned back to the wardrobe, under the guise of fetching stockings. And while she was fetching him silk stockings, she would try to remember how to breathe normally.

Bloody hell. She needed to pull herself together.

"Get undressed," she ordered, not turning around. "I need you downstairs in ten minutes."

"And I don't need you in here at all."

Ivory jumped, not having heard the duke come up behind her. She turned and was presented with a view of his broad chest.

His broad, shirtless, beautiful chest.

She stumbled backward, only to be caught by a pair of strong hands. She could feel the warmth from his palms on her upper arms.

"I've been dressing myself since I was two, Miss Moore. I do not need further assistance."

"Congratulations, Your Grace." She was pleased that she seemed to have regained her sanity.

His icy eyes bored into her. "And the last woman who ordered me to undress was rather naked herself."

It was meant to shock her, she knew. He wasn't the first man to try to do so.

Ivory snorted. "Congratulations again, Your Grace."

The duke's jaw clenched again. Clearly not the response he'd been expecting.

"If I thought it would get you downstairs faster, you'd already have my gown at your feet," she said, silently cursing her traitorous body and the twist of lust that pooled deep within her at the very thought of her clothes on the floor at his feet. "But I trust that it won't come to that." She had to tip her head up to look at him.

It was he who now looked a little shocked.

Ivory ducked her head. Playing the flirt was entirely counterproductive and unwise, no matter that it felt deliciously wicked. She would leave him to his own devices. "Ten minutes, Your Grace." She turned, slipping from his touch. She had barely a second to miss it before one of his hands caught her own and forced her to turn back.

"I'm trusting you, Miss Moore." He dropped her hand. "Don't make me regret it."

Chapter Two

Max had done a lot of difficult things in his life, but attending the ball held in his own home in honor of his missing sister was one of the hardest. He was welcomed genially, if not a little formally, for he was not often in London, and when he was, it was not to attend parties and balls. His older twin brothers had been much better at this sort of thing, especially Frederick, who had been groomed from childhood to become a duke. Max had never been particularly intimate with either of his brothers. In fact, he'd barely had the opportunity to know them, but he would have given anything to have another soul on his side at the moment.

Miss Moore is on your side, a voice in his head reminded him.

Miss Moore was not on his side, Max thought uncharitably. Not really. Miss Moore was on the side of whoever was paying her. Whoever was following her orders.

He nodded and smiled an empty smile at a group of women fluttering fans and eyelashes, not breaking his stride.

At least none of those women had offered to shave him. Or had chosen his clothes for him. He'd watched her in the mirror, rifling through the wardrobe with the unhesitating authority and detached scrutiny of an experienced gentleman's valet. What kind of woman did that?

The kind who is used to redressing male corpses, he thought.

Given that, dressing a live male didn't seem like much of a stretch.

In the end Max had donned exactly what she'd laid out, because it was expedient, and headed downstairs exactly as she'd instructed. But the entire time, the knowledge that he should be out looking for Bea had gnawed at his conscience. He should not be loitering around uselessly like a helpless child or a puppet whose strings could be yanked at will. And yanked by the insufferable but tempting Miss Moore, of all people.

He was still fuming when a man Max recognized immediately as the Viscount Stafford stepped into Max's path, headed for the offerings on the refreshment table. Max had to check his stride, and he groaned. The rotund man was a known windbag, and Max knew he was going to end up sucked into a gossip-fueled conversation he had no interest in having.

"I beg your pardon," Max said, before the viscount could run right into him.

Startled, the viscount looked up and paled. "My apologies, Your Grace," Stafford stuttered. "Lovely party tonight. Just lovely. My compliments to the Lady Helen.

If you'll excuse me?" The man made some sort of jerky movement with his head and departed abruptly.

Max stared after him, realizing he needed to better school his expression and his demeanor. No doubt his wrath was written across his face, and eventually someone would wonder aloud what could possibly be bothering the Duke of Alderidge amid the festivities.

As much as it aggrieved him to admit, Miss Moore had been right. His behavior was critical.

Max took a deep breath, forcing his jaw and the rest of the muscles in his face to relax. He curled his lips up into what he hoped was a benign smile and signaled to a waiting footman to fetch him a drink. Something stronger than the lemonade and champagne his aunt had supplied. And then he went to work.

He visited the cardroom as instructed and casually commented on Debarry's absence the directed number of times. He had a drink with and answered questions for a number of peers who were heavily invested in the East India Company. He offered his opinion when queried about the conflict between the company and the Marathas in central India.

He did everything Miss Moore had asked him to do, with a smile pasted on his face and while trying not to check the face of his pocket watch too often. Time crawled. Every tick of the watch hands might be marking an increase in the distance that Bea was slipping away from him. Max had no idea what he had been thinking, agreeing to let Miss Moore take charge. He never let anyone take charge if he could help it—he despised not being in control. She had bewitched him, or at the very least bewitched all his good sense.

Perhaps it had been her steady calm and her sensible logic in the face of what anyone in their right mind would call a catastrophic debacle. He would admit that he'd been caught off guard when he'd first walked into that bedroom. But he still refused to believe that Bea could ever—

He squeezed his eyes shut, unwilling to even consider it. The last time he'd seen his sister, she'd been sixteen. Her hair had been in pretty blond ringlets tied back with a blue ribbon, and her round cheeks had been flushed in girlish delight at the ornate seashell he'd found and saved for her.

"Your Grace, I didn't realize you were back in London." The address yanked him from his thoughts. The man standing before him was familiar, with dark hair that was greying slightly at the temples, and a pale complexion made more startling by the severe black of his impeccable evening coat. He was short, with a weak chin and light-brown eyes, and he was looking at Max with an expression of surprise.

Max's memory stumbled before he seized upon a name. "Barlow."

"Delighted to be here, Your Grace."

Edwin Harper, Earl of Barlow, had been a friend of his eldest brother's. Not overly clever, if Max's memory served him well, but affable and well liked. Max hadn't seen him in years.

He forced his mouth into what he hoped was another smile. "Yes, I just returned this very evening, in fact."

"Ah. Welcome home then. Your sister must have been happy to see you."

Max made a noise of agreement, unwilling to pursue any vein of conversation regarding his sister.

"Your timing couldn't have been better," Barlow continued on. "Lady Beatrice will certainly depend on you more than ever now."

"I beg your pardon?" Suspicion flared. "What are you suggesting?"

Barlow swallowed and took an involuntary step back. "Er, I meant nothing by it, Your Grace. Only that Lady Beatrice is a lovely young lady. Her company is very much in demand this evening, as it is at every social gathering she attends. No doubt she will have multiple offers of marriage by the end of the season, and I expect that you, as her guardian, will be instrumental in helping her choose a worthy suitor."

Max forced himself to breathe. Of course. Barlow was only stating the obvious. Bea was beautiful, poised, and charming, and of course she would marry well.

Provided he could find her. Provided he could explain away a dead earl. Provided he could—

"If I may be so bold, I was wondering if perhaps you might consider my suit?"

"I beg your pardon?" This was the last conversation that Max wanted to be having right now.

"I would very much like your permission to call on Lady Beatrice. I think the two of us would get on wonderfully. I would very much enjoy taking her to the theater—in your company too, of course."

Max wasn't at all certain that, when he found his sister, he wouldn't lock her up in a very tall tower with iron doors, a moat, and a fire-breathing dragon to eat the damn key. He certainly wouldn't let her do anything that involved her removal from his sight.

"I secured a spot on her dance card, yet she seems to

have disappeared," Barlow was blathering on, seemingly unaware Max had yet to respond.

This was ridiculous. He was wasting precious time. He should never have—

A flash of green silk caught his eye, and he watched as his aunt made her way with single-minded determination through the crowd toward the tall doors. His heart skipped. Had she heard something? Had Bea returned?

His aunt stopped at the bottom of the curving staircase, staring up, unmoving. His eyes followed her gaze, heedless of the people who brushed by him as they came and went.

Bea!

"I see my sister now," he said to Barlow.

"You do?" The earl blinked.

"If you'll excuse me?" Max left the man staring after him and was already lurching through the guests toward her when he realized something wasn't quite right. Bea was turned away from the crowd milling about below her, only her unique rose-embroidered dress and blond hair recognizable. There was a maid standing at her elbow, chestnut hair pinned neatly under a cap, and she was watching him.

Miss Moore, he realized, with a hollow feeling, belatedly remembering the instructions she had given to his aunt. And the blonde at her side was her associate, Miss DeVries, pretending to be Beatrice. Whatever this was, it was all part of her charade. His aunt was laboring up the stairs toward them, suddenly looking every year of her advancing age. With some surprise he felt a pang of pity and regret. Aunt Helen had stepped in to take care of Bea when he and his sister had become orphans. At the time of his parents' deaths, Max had already been far across a distant ocean, the die of his life already cast.

He caught up to his aunt, placing a hand on her arm. "Please, Aunt Helen, wait here. Let me attend to this."

She hesitated, suspicion touching her face, before both physical and emotional exhaustion won, and she nodded, leaning on the rail.

Max made his way up the rest of the stairs, in plain sight of the guests below, which, he suddenly realized, was the idea. He took his time climbing the last three stairs.

"Lady Beatrice regrets to inform you that she is suffering from a feminine ailment and would like to retire to her room," Miss Moore said from beneath her cap as he drew even with her.

The woman playing Bea put a hand to her forehead as though a headache nagged and held the other hand to her abdomen.

Max moved closer to Miss DeVries and her borrowed dress and blond wig, as though he were in deep conversation with the woman everyone must later believe had been his sister. "Then she should retire immediately."

Miss Moore was grim. "Indeed she should. Please identify the biggest gossips in the room and convey her regrets directly to them." She cast an eye at the people milling below. "When your butler makes his unfortunate discovery, it will, I'm afraid, be the end of your ball."

"Thank God."

"Your sister, along with her maid, will be gone from your home before dawn, should anyone ask. Death is always a distressing business, one that any responsible brother or caring aunt would wish a reasonable distance from their tender charge. I trust you and your aunt to make the appropriate explanations."

"Of course."

"Mary, however, must be eliminated. She is far too volatile and nervous to leave in residence here amongst the staff and trust that she will remain silent."

Max stared at her. What was she suggesting?

"Oh, for God's sake, I'm not going to throw her in the Thames and let her sink, if that's what you're thinking," Miss Moore said, looking annoyed.

"I wasn't thinking that," Max lied.

"I never leave bodies where they might be found. I always bury them."

Max felt the blood drain from his face.

"I'm jesting."

"You. Are. Not. Funny." He could barely get the words out.

"I'm sorry."

"You're not."

"True." Miss Moore tipped her head. "You looked like a bowstring about to snap, Your Grace. I was trying to use humor to help you work back towards normalcy. You have guests to return to."

Max forced himself to take a deep breath. "I'll chalk any deviations in my expression up to an unwholesome conversation of feminine ailments," he managed through clenched teeth.

Miss Moore tipped her head. "That sounds reasonable."

No it didn't, Max wanted to shout. None of this was *reasonable*.

"Your aunt has my direction," she said. "Until this matter is resolved, I am available anytime you require." She was already moving away from the top of the stairs.

"Where are you going?"

She paused, turning back to him. "To do my job."

Chapter Three

Dawn had been threatening in the east when Ivory returned to Covent Square. The square, its glory days long in the past, was never really quiet, being populated largely by actors, performers, musicians, and other manner of entertainers, those of the legitimate and intimate varieties. The piazzas and the coffeehouses were always crowded with people, as was the market that sprawled away from St Paul's Church. But the traffic suited Ivory. She maintained wildly irregular hours, as did most of the residents of the square. Her comings and goings were invisible. Which was always helpful.

Unnoticed, she'd let herself into the town house, being careful to lock the door behind her. She'd eaten a few cold bites of food and then headed for her study. Now, an hour later, Ivory stood up from behind her desk and stretched. She moved closer to the hearth, where a bright fire burned, rubbing her chilled hands together.

The handling of the Earl of Debarry had gone about as well as could be expected, she thought to herself with some satisfaction. Dead aristocrats in beds they were not supposed to be in were always tricky. Explanations had to be airtight, and unfortunately, that usually required the involvement of a civilian.

Like the Duke of Alderidge.

Another shiver of heat snaked through her body at the mere thought of the man. There was no point in denying she was physically attracted to this captain turned duke, and there was little she could do about it anyway. But she had confidence that this fleeting attraction, like everything else in life, would eventually pass. What she could do in the interim, however, was keep the Duke of Alderidge at a safe distance until Lady Beatrice could be located, the Earl of Debarry buried and forgotten, and any residual fires that stank of scandal summarily stomped out.

"I've put the maid in the corner room upstairs." Elise breezed into the room, coming to stand next to Ivory in front of the fire. "She's sleeping with the help of one of my soothing draughts."

Ivory slanted Elise a sideways look. Her draughts were usually enough to knock a rhino out for the better part of a day. Which was just as well.

"Could she tell if there was anything missing from Lady Beatrice's room?"

"Anything that indicated that the lady had packed up and left London for good?" Elise shook her head. "No. There was nothing missing as far as Mary could tell, with the exception of her cloak. And all of her jewelry was still in her room. A lot of expensive stuff. Stuff that could easily have been pawned."

"So Beatrice likely hasn't gone far."

"Not in a chemise with no money," Elise scoffed.

"Mmmm." That might make recovery easier.

"What did you find out about our duke?" Elise asked.

Ivory moved back to her desk, leaning against the side and glancing down at the ledger that lay open. "Born in April 1789. Third son of the late Duke and Duchess of Alderidge. Five years younger than his older brothers, Frederick and Peter, who were twins. Says here he joined the navy when he was thirteen. Went on to become a midshipman when he was sixteen, a lieutenant when he was twenty-one. He left the service after he inherited the title."

"To do what?" Elise asked. "Because he hasn't been in London these last years managing his dukedom."

"It seems he purchased his own ships. The *Aphrodite*, the *Calypso*, and the *Odyssey*. All Indiamen. He commands the *Odyssey* and sails the routes between England and India." Ivory picked up a paper. "Oh, and China."

"The Duke of Alderidge works for the East India Company?" The words were saturated with disbelief. "Why would a bloody aristocrat do that?"

Ivory shrugged. "He's also heavily invested in the company, and it's made him richer than Croesus. Why he would choose to captain the ships himself, I don't presume to know." But the question intrigued her. Why indeed, would a duke, with every imaginable advantage, choose to ignore it all and risk his life out on the open seas? She put the page of notes down. "But it could prove to be useful."

"True. Once located, Lady Beatrice could be taken to India and married to the first British officer with a title who will have her," Elise suggested, twisting the end of her dark hair around her finger thoughtfully. "Gossip rarely travels with any strength across oceans."

Ivory nodded her head in agreement. "I have already noted it as a viable option that I will present to His Grace." It was doubtful the duke would agree to it, but Ivory could be very persuasive when required. It depended on how quickly they could find Lady Beatrice.

"The duke handled it all quite well," Elise commented. "Once he got over the initial shock."

"You could say the same about Lady Helen."

"Aye, but Lady Helen didn't help you redress a corpse." There was amusement lacing Elise's words.

"True. Though he was a gentleman about it," Ivory pointed out.

"The duke is many things, but he is not a gentleman," Elise said, her hazel eyes appraising Ivory.

Ivory ignored another thrill that tingled down the length of her spine, and frowned at her partner. She wasn't sure if she was frowning at the remark, or her own reaction to it.

"Oh, don't look at me like that," Elise chided, and came to join Ivory at the desk. "I didn't say he was a blackguard. I just said he wasn't a gentleman. He is not guided by rules of society, I think. He is a man of action, one who will do whatever is required to get what he wants."

"And you know this after speaking all of three words to him?" Ivory scoffed, pretending a nonchalance she didn't feel.

"*Non, chérie*," Elise replied slyly, slipping into a suggestive French patois. "I know this by the way you looked at him."

Ivory pushed herself away from the desk and stalked back to the hearth. To deny it would be foolish. Elise had been with her for far too long.

"The Duke of Alderidge is a client," Ivory said instead. "I never get involved with clients."

Behind her, Elise made some sort of sound. "The Duke of Alderidge is a man. And once his strumpet of a sister is found, he will no longer be a client."

"Correct. He will be a captain once again, in India. Or China."

Elise sighed dramatically in defeat. "It would do you some good, you know. Knightley would not have wanted you to lock yourself in a nunnery. Your husband, rest his soul, would have wanted you to live. When was the last time—"

"We are not having this conversation."

"Oh, very well." There was the sound of rustling papers. "Anything else of interest in Knightley's notes on the duke or his family? What about the aunt?"

Relieved that Elise had abandoned the topic of Ivory's personal life, or lack thereof, she turned back to face her business partner. "Lady Helen has never been married. She's lived her entire life under her brother's and now her nephew's roof. She collects enameled vinaigrettes and is a current member of the Rare Purple Orchid Society."

"Riveting," Elise drawled. "What about the rest of them?"

Ivory shrugged. "Nothing of import. No outstanding debts, gambling or otherwise, no duels, or at least not one that was witnessed, no noted vices of the late duke or the older brothers. The brother called Frederick supported a mistress for the better part of two years, and it seems they parted on amiable terms. Loretta..." Ivory searched her memory for the name that had been written next to Frederick's. "Ludwig. Her name was Loretta Ludwig."

"Oh, I know her," Elise said brightly. "She used to perform at the old Drury before it burned down. She's a bit too old now to take as many roles, but she is very talented." She paused. "That's it?"

"I've got nothing. The entire family is quite dull, at least on paper."

"Until the duke's little sister went ahead and lashed an earl to her bedposts. And then ran away when he died."

"*Tsk*. Assumptions, Miss DeVries," Ivory reminded her. Though given the evidence, she was inclined to agree. But it fell on her shoulders to find facts. Assumptions could be dangerous.

Elise rolled her eyes.

"Debarry has a file here too, don't forget," Ivory reminded her. "A thick one full of sexual indiscretions of every sort you can imagine and some you shouldn't. A regular Don Juan, that one. Perhaps he cuckolded one husband too many."

"And so someone thought they'd get back at him by tying him to the bed of a debutante?" Elise said with derision. "That would accomplish nothing except giving the gossipmongers something to chew on for a day or two."

"Perhaps they were hoping the duke would call him out. Kill him and do the dirty work for them." Even in her own ears, it sounded farfetched.

"Except no one, including the duke himself, knew for certain that he would even be in London last night." Elise was shaking her head. "No, you're completely over-thinking this. This is a simple case of bed-and-dead if I ever saw one. It's no different than that old bishop we pulled out of a certain baroness's bedclothes last month."

"You're probably right." Ivory pressed her lips together. She still felt as if there was something eluding her. "But I'd like you to speak to your brother. Debarry has undoubtedly patronized Alex's gaming establishment in the past. Get him to find out what he can. Any quarrels, anything out of the ordinary. See if Lady Beatrice's or His Grace's name has come up recently in any circles that Debarry used to mill in. I'd like to be sure."

Elise nodded agreeably and glanced at the clock on the mantel, and then out at the sliver of morning light now struggling through the curtains. "He'll still be up. I'll go now."

"Thank you," Ivory said, and watched as Elise disappeared. She put her elbows on the table, resting her chin in her hand. Silence descended, broken only by the sound of a coal shifting in the grate, and the quiet only served to remind her just how alone she really was. She reached forward with her other hand and ran her fingers over the pages of the familiar neat, slanted handwriting. It was moments like these when she missed her husband the most. Knightley had been so much more than a mentor, and so much more than an irreplaceable friend—

"Miss Moore?" It came with a quiet knock at the door.

Ivory looked up to see a boy standing at attention at the door.

"Yes, Roderick?" She stifled a smile and kept her face suitably grave. Such airs of superiority were usually found in butlers and not seven-year-old boys.

"The Duke of Alderidge is here to see you."

A flutter started low in her belly again. She squashed it ruthlessly.

"Thank you, Roderick. You may show His Grace into the drawing room. I will receive him there in but a moment."

"Very good, Miss Moore." Roddy turned to go, and Ivory's lips twitched despite herself at the untamable cowlick that stood straight up from the back of his head.

Ivory gathered the loose notes on her desk and carefully inserted them back between the pages of the ledger. She closed the tome and returned it to its recessed shelf, amid hundreds of others. Ledgers her late husband had kept for years, and that she had supplemented during their marriage and after. Ledgers that contained the most personal details, secrets, and scandals of almost every prominent society family in London.

There had been no shortage of people to come to her husband for help. Being a duke, and a very powerful one, Knightley had had the ability to manipulate every quarter of society, industry, and government. It had been a happy by-product of his position—every duke of the realm occasionally pulled strings on his own behalf or for those who enjoyed his favor. He had called himself a "fixer of unfixable problems," and he'd attacked the job with a seriousness and professionalism that stole Ivory's breath. It amused him, he had always said, to mete out quiet justice to those who deserved it, just as much as it pleased him to help those who were worthy.

It had been Ivory's own skill at manipulating men that had first captured the Duke of Knightley's attention. Not her beauty, or even her voice, though he had loved it when she sang for him. When he'd proposed, he had told her it was always her cunning that had so infatuated him. As a singer Ivory had navigated the thorny world of opera houses and the private stages of Europe, and her survival had depended solely on her wits and her resourcefulness.

Just as it did now.

When he was alive, her husband had traded their skills for future favor, but upon his death Ivory no longer had that luxury. Instead she traded the skills she had, the abilities that the Duke of Knightley had helped her hone, for currency. And a lot of it.

Because Ivory Moore was very good at her job.

One last time she ran a finger over the spines of the ledgers that had been instrumental in the founding of Chegarre and Associates. Satisfied that nothing had been left out, she moved to the corner of the room and leaned her weight against a heavy wooden partition. With a slight creak, an ornate Chippendale bookcase slid smoothly back into place, hiding the vast collection of ledgers and presenting the unaware with a pretty collection of poetry books and reference texts covering the joys of gardening.

Ivory left her study, locking the door behind her. One could never be too careful with secrets.

Chapter Four

Max paced in the drawing room, impatience and worry vying for his attention. The duke's body had been carted away barely an hour ago, and Max had nearly climbed the walls waiting for everyone to leave his house. He'd seen his aunt to bed with a hot cup of lemon verbena tea, which she insisted calmed her nerves, and a promise to find Beatrice. Then he'd set out, in the dark before dawn, armed only with a list of names his aunt had given him of ladies his sister counted as friends. He knew none of them.

Certainly not well enough to know which one, if any, would be willing to become complicit in whatever it was that had happened in Bea's rooms. He'd gone to one of the addresses and stared at the darkened house and silent square in helpless frustration. He couldn't very well just start pounding on doors, as much as he wanted to.

He'd finally moved away when a watchman turned in

his direction, realizing he didn't know what to do next. He wasn't familiar with his sister's life. Her favorite shops or gardens or parks. He had no idea whom she might turn to for help, and he ignored the voice in his head that was telling him he should know. He should have been here for Bea when she needed to turn to someone for help.

He'd hunched his shoulders into his coat against the chill, shoving his hands deep into the pockets. His fingers had brushed the smooth surface of a small card, and he'd pulled it out, tipping it toward the meager gaslight.

"Chegarre & Associates" was printed in the center, the lettering plain and devoid of the curlicues and looping swirls he normally encountered on cards such as this. The title gave the bearer no clue to the services it represented. It could have been a company of barristers or bakers if he didn't already know better. He turned the card over to find an address, written in the same plain type.

And so, as the sun finally crested the horizon, he'd found himself standing in front of a once grand town house, wondering just what the hell he was doing there.

He raised his hand to grasp the old brass door knocker, but the door was opened before he had the chance. He was greeted by name by a boy who gave no indication that Max's arrival was anything less than expected. Max glanced up at the empty, aged windows and wondered how long he'd been observed before he'd climbed the cracked stone steps leading up to the door. He followed the boy into the bowels of the house, fully expecting to battle his way through a tenement, to find the old rooms of the stately home chopped into pieces and overflowing with people scratching out a living.

Instead he was greeted with silence and the faint smell

of wood polish. He tried not to gape at his surroundings, but it was as if he had stepped back into another century, the grandeur of the past carefully restored. Not in the manner of some of the opulent St James's or Grosvenor Square townhomes, stuffed to the seams with every conceivable object meant to convince visitors of greatness and wealth; this was fine taste tempered with function.

He was shown into a drawing room decorated in subtle shades of blue, the long drapes already pulled back to let the pale wash of morning light flood the room.

"Wait here," the boy instructed him, before vanishing back out into the hall.

Max circled the room, and his gaze fell on a tall clock near the window. Distracted, he stepped closer, noting the gleaming burnish of pearwood inlaid with ebony. The tympanum was a brass relief of the huntress Diana, dogs and hawks and an admiring Apollo at her side. It would have cost a fortune.

Max's eyes skipped over the furnishings, picking out the exotic woods, accented by beautiful brocaded fabrics. A pianoforte rested against the wall by the window, its craftsmanship obvious in the flowing lines. A tall, narrow bookcase grazed the ceiling, a collection of expensive leather-bound tomes standing in neat lines upon its shelves.

Max swung his eyes back to the clock and frowned at the image of Apollo, the god's eyes turned in the direction of the fierce huntress. There was a critical question he'd failed to answer and that was who Miss Moore was. Her accent was that of a lady. Her address was that of a courtesan. Her furnishings were those of a princess. Her occupation was that of a confidence artist. Or worse.

"Good morning, Your Grace." Max spun on his heel to find Miss Moore standing in the doorway of the drawing room.

She'd been nothing if not a woman of her word when she said she'd be available at any time. For if she was surprised to see him at this ridiculous hour, she didn't show it. Nor did she look like a woman who had been up all night. She was dressed once again in a plain grey wool dress, designed to be serviceable and, Max suspected, unnoticeable. Her thick hair was neatly braided and pinned, and at a glance she could have passed for a governess, or a merchant's wife, or one of any number of women who made their way about London daily. Apart, that was, from her uncommon looks. No man with a pulse and eyes in his head would overlook her. She evoked images of dark nights and secret desires—

She stepped into the room, closing the door behind her. "Is the décor to your taste?"

"What?"

"You were examining the clock."

"I was checking the time," he said defensively.

"Ah." Miss Moore had an unreadable expression on her face.

"My father had an Edward East clock similar to this in his study. It was given to him as a gift." Max had no idea why he was telling such an inane detail to this woman.

Miss Moore was looking up at the goddess amid her hounds and hawks, her eyes almost wistful now. "This clock too was a gift."

"To you?" What an unusual thing to gift a lady with. But then again, there was nothing usual about Miss Moore.

"Yes."

"From whom?"

Miss Moore turned her dark eyes back in his direction and considered him. "From my husband."

An inexplicable pang of disappointment assailed him, and he ignored it. She was married? Well, that was a little surprising, since she had introduced herself as *Miss* Moore. Though given what she did, it was less surprising that she wasn't using her real name. A thought struck Max. Perhaps her husband was Mr. Chegarre. "And where is your husband now? Can I speak with him?"

"My husband passed away five years ago," she said, and the wistfulness that he thought he had seen earlier was clearly evident now.

"Oh." A sliver of something that felt like relief needled through him, and Max was horrified at himself. Was he really going to admit to being pleased that this woman was a widow? "I'm sorry." *For your loss and my appalling sentiments.*

Miss Moore raised her shoulders ever so slightly before letting them drop. "Thank you."

"Your husband had good taste," he said.

A smooth brow arched.

"The clock. It's beautiful." *As are you. Your husband was a very lucky man.* Max shifted uncomfortably, uncertain where these thoughts were coming from.

Miss Moore returned her attention to the clock. "My husband said that I reminded him of Diana," she said so quietly that Max barely heard her.

After what he had witnessed last night from this woman, Max was rather inclined to agree with him.

"Chegarre's clients, on the very rare occasion that they have cause to visit these offices, are generally more comfortable when in familiar surroundings," Miss Moore said, the wistfulness gone, and her tone again one of business. "Would you care for a cup of tea, Your Grace?" She glanced at the tall clock as if factoring the hour into her choice of refreshments. "Or perhaps something more bracing?" Her eyes slid to a row of crystal decanters on a small library table.

Max cleared his throat and his mind. "No, nothing." He forcibly reminded himself he wasn't here to socialize and gawk at the beautiful mystery that was Miss Moore. He was here to find his sister.

Miss Moore paused. "Did Roderick not ask to take your coat when he showed you in?"

Max thought of the boy who had shown him to the drawing room. He knew his sort well—he'd recruited two such boys and their sticky fingers to work as surgeon's and gunner's servants within his own crews. It was a wonder his pocket watch hadn't been liberated in between the front door and this room.

"He asked. I declined. I like my coat and the things in it."

Miss Moore's lips twitched slightly, but she didn't rise to the bait, instead moving in his direction. "How can I be of assistance, Your Grace?" she asked pleasantly.

As if he had come to inquire about help in locating a lost cravat pin.

"I would like to speak with Mr. Chegarre directly. Is he available?"

"He is not, I'm afraid." Miss Moore shook her head slightly, her dark eyes betraying only mild regret. "As I told her ladyship, I will be handling your case. You are free, of course, to terminate our partnership at any time, though at this juncture, I would advise against it."

Max wasn't sure he would consider this a partnership. A partnership was something where two people shared equally in the planning and the work and the rewards. But he had found himself adrift in the middle of an ocean, clinging to a life raft, the only chance at rescue coming from the woman standing in front of him.

Max ran a hand through his hair in agitation. "Bea still hasn't returned."

Miss Moore waved Max over to a long sofa and seated herself gracefully in the upholstered chair facing it. "Please, sit."

"I'll stand." He would come out of his skin if he didn't. This feeling of helpless ineptitude was extreme torture.

The woman shrugged, a gesture both accepting and resigned. "You are correct, I'm afraid. I would have heard had Lady Beatrice made an appearance back at your home."

Max stared at her.

"I have a man watching your house," Miss Moore explained. "We could not take the chance of her unplanned return being witnessed by servants or other guests before she could be intercepted and instructed on her expected behavior."

"You have a man watching my house?"

"Two, actually. And I have others out watching any number of houses at the moment," Miss Moore said. "Your aunt provided me with a list of Lady Beatrice's closest friends. People she might turn to for help. Their residences are currently under observation. You'll be the first to be notified should I hear anything."

"I didn't see anyone."

She smiled faintly. "You weren't meant to, Your Grace."

This woman was two steps ahead of him. "If you think I'm going to sit at home and await word from you, you are sadly mistaken."

Miss Moore stood and drifted over to the window to stand in a pool of morning sunlight. The rays made her skin glow, and sculpted shadows into the contours of her striking face. "I do not require your help."

"To be honest, Miss Moore, I don't really care what you require. My sister is my responsibility. I will do whatever it takes."

"Mmmm." She made a noncommittal noise. "I understand that the discovery of the Earl of Debarry went smoothly."

"I'm not well versed in staging deaths, Miss Moore. I cannot comment if it went smoothly or not."

She looked sharply at him. "Were the words *murder* or *poison* used?"

"No."

"Did Lady Beatrice's name come up?"

"No."

"Did the physician who was summoned attribute Debarry's death to natural causes?"

"Thank the saints, but that was his opinion, yes. And he was quite insistent upon it."

"Was he, indeed?" Miss Moore gave him a wry look.

Max blinked. "That had nothing to do with the saints, did it?"

"Well, I suspect the saints are often busy these days. I do what I can to take burdens from their heavenly shoulders and place them on more earthly ones. And ones that take coin and don't ask stupid questions."

"The physician was your man."

"Of course he was. And I am pleased that it all went smoothly. For the record, Your Grace, my physician did report to me on his way home that all signs pointed to an attack of the heart or perhaps an apoplexy." She gave him another half smile and turned back to the window, tracing her bottom lip with her finger.

Max was trying to concentrate on what she was saying but it was infinitely distracting, the slide of flesh against that plump, rosy softness. For one wild moment, Max wondered what she would do if he replaced her finger with his own mouth.

"Mary, Lady Beatrice's maid, has a brother currently toiling in the Earl of Covistan's household as a provision boy. He is the only family she has, and she is extremely devoted to him."

Max's eyes were still on Miss Moore's lips, and it took a moment before her words reached his brain and he looked up. "So?"

A pair of dark eyes gazed at him with what he thought was mild disappointment.

"Leverage," he said, disgusted with himself for letting so slight a distraction cloud his mind. He would attribute it to exhaustion.

"Indeed." The disappointment disappeared. "The only other witness to this incident is Mary, currently lodged upstairs. I have a contact in Kent who will arrange for a new, suitable placement for her. She'll be on a coach late this afternoon. In the meantime you will arrange an anonymous sponsorship that will allow her brother to attend a good school and receive the education he would otherwise never have a chance at. We'll avoid the elite snobbery at Harrow and Eton, but there is a good school in Kent that will be adequate and allow the two to visit. Mary will be made to understand the scholarship will last as long as her silence. I don't anticipate a problem." She arched a brow. "Do you?"

"No."

"Excellent." Miss Moore smiled faintly and turned back to the window, and Max was left with the dawning realization that this woman had done more for his sister and his family in a day than he would have been able to do in a month. If he had even been able to do anything effective at all. And she had done it with a skill and confidence that left him more than a little astounded. "I feel I should apologize," he said suddenly.

Her eyes flew back to him, a crease forming between her elegant brows. "Whatever for?"

"I was rude last night."

"No apology is necessary, Your Grace. You were presented with a difficult situation that most men—most *brothers*—would find intolerable. Your reaction was predictable."

Max frowned. That label didn't sit well. He'd like to think he was better than *predictable*.

"I was the third of three boys, Miss Moore," he said, feeling the inexplicable need to explain himself. "I was sent away to school when I was six, and when I was twelve, my father sent me a letter asking me to choose between the church and military service, as befits an unneeded son in a family with two boys too many."

She watched him in silence.

"What I'm trying to say, Miss Moore, is that I have been solving my own problems since I left home at the age of six. Mine and those of others around me. I have never had to rely on others to manage my affairs, and I find it... difficult to do with any grace."

"I understand. There is nothing easy about the situation in which your family has found itself. Nothing that you could adequately have prepared for."

Max wasn't sure if he felt better or not. "So now what?"

"Do you keep a mistress in London, Your Grace? Or if not a regular mistress, then a lover?"

"What?" Max blinked in shock.

"Someone who might be prone to spite or a jealous rage? Someone who might wish to make trouble for you?"

"I don't have a mistress anywhere," he blurted, taken aback by the question.

"Mmm. Your estate is free from debt and in possession of...ah, considerable wealth and holdings, but are you, personally, indebted to anyone?"

"What? No. And how do you know—"

"Have you made any enemies recently? A card game gone badly? A real or perceived slight? Anything? Think carefully."

"What are you trying to get at, Miss Moore?" Max demanded. He wasn't entirely sure what she might be accusing him of, but he hadn't felt this defensive since a lieutenant had caught him and another boy sneaking filched cognac onboard when he was fourteen.

"Right now I am basing my strategy on the theory that Lady Beatrice and Debarry met in her room for an assignation. When things went awry, your sister fled. But I'd be remiss if I didn't consider other possibilities. It is possible that her disappearance may not, in fact, have been of her own accord."

"Of course it wasn't of her own accord," Max said,

knowing he knew no such thing. But the other option that involved Bea and red silk ribbon was wholly unbearable. "She must have been taken against her will. Kidnapped." He wasn't sure if he'd adequately convinced himself, and he despised himself for that shortcoming.

Miss Moore shrugged slightly in that infuriatingly casual way of hers. "I think it very unlikely though not impossible. There was, after all, nothing to suggest a struggle. It is possible, however, that she was coerced into leaving. The scene we walked in on could have been staged, and Beatrice might have been threatened with exposure unless she complied."

"Threatened. Yes." Max grasped the idea like a drowning man would an extended rope.

"If that was indeed the case, then someone went to a great deal of trouble. Their motivations are likely rooted in greed, control, or jealousy of the most intimate, visceral kind."

Max was aware he was staring at Miss Moore again, but he couldn't help it. She was calmly lecturing him in much the manner his schoolmasters had in his youth. Only she wasn't speaking of geography, Latin, or mathematics, she was speaking of murder, extortion, and sex.

"Aside from the scene last night, I can find no other indications that either Beatrice or your aunt had, or currently has, a lover. And if you are not involved in a dalliance presently, then that leaves only money. As the duke, you are in sole possession and control of an extremely large fortune and a good degree of power."

"You think someone took Bea to get at me? Or my money?"

"While I am still not convinced that anyone took your

sister, if that was, in fact, the case, it is my experience that money makes sane people do insane things."

"If it is a matter of money, I'll pay whatever is required to get her back," Max said coldly. "And then I'll kill the bastards who touched my sister with my bare hands."

Miss Moore didn't flinch. "I can't condone that, Your Grace. Vengeance of that nature gets messy."

"Then I'll hire you to clean up and hide the bodies."

Her eyes held his as if she was weighing his words. "There are other, more effective ways of leveling the scales," she finally said. "If and when that time comes, I would encourage you to consult with me first. Before things get...messy."

Max stared at her, and his pulse kicked, gooseflesh rising on his skin beneath his warm coat. A frisson of...something traveled through his chest and down his spine. Approval? Anticipation? Admiration? He wasn't sure what to make of this woman he'd known for less than a day. He knew she was both intelligent and clever, which were two very different things. She was also practical, logical, methodical. Resourceful, focused, fearless. Dangerous. Bloody hell, but she would've made a magnificent commander.

She held his eyes, a small smile playing around her mouth, as though she were privy to every one of his thoughts and agreed with all of them.

He wondered suddenly if perhaps, at one time, she had been an agent of the Crown. She'd learned her craft somewhere.

There was the sound of a sudden scuffle near the door, and a nondescript man dressed in bulky, nondescript winter clothing loomed within the frame. He was holding a struggling boy by the collar with a casualness that hinted at a terrifying strength beneath all his nondescriptness.

"Picked him up delivering a message to Alderidge's house," the man said, speaking to Miss Moore. "Seemed like a deuced strange hour to be delivering social invitations so I brought him here straightaway—"

She was shaking her head, and the man, suddenly realizing she wasn't alone in the room, clamped his mouth shut.

Miss Moore was already striding forward. "You may take him to the morning room, if you would be so kind—"

"No." Max was faster, beating her to the door. The youth had stopped struggling and was watching them with sullen wariness. "If this boy has information about…anything, I want to hear it."

"I don't think that that is a good idea," Miss Moore said smoothly. "Please, Your Grace, it would be best if I handled—"

"Is this what your clients typically do?"

"I beg your pardon?"

"Wait in their homes until you send them a bill and reassurances that whatever problem they have has been taken care of?"

"Generally, Your Grace."

"Well, be advised that that will not be the case here. You work for me, Miss Moore. *I* hired *you*. I get a say in what goes on here."

Miss Moore's eyes flashed. "In truth, I work for your sister. And it is not in her best interests to have her brother mucking around in matters he knows nothing about and getting in my way."

"Mucking around?" That suggested ineptness, and Max

had never, in all his life, been accused of being inept. "I'm not leaving. And your man here will find that he will have a much harder time manhandling me than he did manhandling this boy."

Miss Moore opened her mouth as if she would argue and then closed it. Max watched as she took a deep breath and then turned on him with an expression he'd only seen nannies use on their three-year-old charges. "Very well, Your Grace. You may have your way this time."

He wasn't sure if he was relieved or insulted.

She turned to the man in the doorway. "Is the boy carrying any weapons?"

"Nothing. Only thing he was carrying was this." He held out a square of folded paper, sealed with a blob of rusty-red wax. "Alderidge" was scrawled across the front of it, along with his address.

Miss Moore took it from his hand and stepped aside. "Thank you. Please leave the messenger with us," she instructed.

The man impaled Max with a hostile stare. "Are you sure? I can stay if you wish—"

"No, thank you. We will be quite fine."

"I'll wait outside."

"Thank you."

The man departed, closing the door behind him, and leaving the youth standing in front of Max.

"You look chilled. Please make yourself comfortable by the hearth," Max said to the boy, who now had his arms crossed belligerently across his chest. He was perhaps ten years of age, though it was difficult to tell amid his layered, slightly tattered clothes and wary-eyed look. "Please rest assured that no one in this room has any interest in torturing you, or otherwise mucking around in your life." He shot a pointed glance at Miss Moore. "But I will have a few questions."

"I ain't got any answers," the boy sniffed, though he was edging closer to the heat from the hearth.

"We'll see," Max said under his breath. He waited until the boy was far enough out of earshot before holding out his hand. "My mail, if you would be so kind."

Miss Moore extended the paper, and Max snatched the letter from her hand and cracked the seal, pulling the paper open. A ring slid out and landed silently on the rug at their feet.

Max bent and retrieved it, a terrible sinking sensation filling the pit of his stomach.

⁓

Ivory watched with a sinking feeling as Alderidge straightened, the color leached from his face, holding a small band of gold in which was set a round amethyst. He clenched it in his fist, his breath hissing out between his teeth.

She was still incensed by the duke and his attempts to wrench away the reins of this investigation, yet her displeasure was mitigated somewhat by the look of fear now stamped on his face.

"Lady Beatrice's?" she asked, though she already knew the answer.

"I sent it to her from Calcutta for her sixteenth birthday." The duke pulled the letter the rest of the way open and scanned the missive.

"What does it say?" Ivory asked.

The duke turned and looked at her, his grey eyes stormy.

"It says, 'Dearest Alderidge, I am fine. Please do not look for me.'"

"That's it?" Ivory frowned and pulled the creased paper from his hands. The brief message was written in the same handwriting as the address on the front.

"Am I supposed to believe this?" the duke demanded beside her.

Ivory examined the note, studying the strange message. "Do you recognize the handwriting?" she asked him. "Is it your sister's?"

Alderidge snatched the paper back from her fingers and examined it. "Yes."

"Are you sure?"

"Of course I'm sure. My sister has sent letters before. I know what her writing looks like." He paused. "But she never calls me Alderidge. She's only ever called me Max, quite improperly, I might add. Annoys my aunt to no end."

"Mmmm. What about the paper itself? Any markings?"

"No." The duke turned it over, but it was of mediocre quality and had no distinguishing marks, something that could be purchased anywhere.

There was no impression in the wax either that gave any clue as to its origin.

"She would never call me Alderidge. Something's wrong."

"There was a dead earl in her bed very recently," Ivory reminded him in a low whisper.

The duke grimaced, but shook his head. "Something's not right."

Ivory wasn't convinced either way. She'd been half expecting an extortion note, but usually extortion notes sent to her clients were detailed, with descriptions of the crime and the amount of money it would take to make the evidence of that crime disappear. Or reappear, in the case of kidnapping victims.

"It is possible it is a simple error. Perhaps she used your title so that there was no chance of the message going astray. It would seem she is trying to reassure you that she has come to no harm."

"I am not overly reassured. And I'm not going to stop looking for her." Alderidge looked up at her. He glanced in the direction of the boy. "Have you ever seen him before?"

"No."

"Then let's find out what he knows. Someone paid him to deliver that message, and I want to know who." He took a step toward the hearth, and the boy hunkered in front of it.

Ivory darted in front of him. "You need not trouble yourself. I will question him."

Alderidge made a rude noise. "I will do it, and you may watch." He held up a hand when she scowled. "Or I can simply fire you, if you prefer. You choose."

Ivory focused on not giving in to the urge to shriek in frustration.

"Glad that's settled." Alderidge wandered over to the hearth, leaned against the back of the sofa, and studied the boy. The duke's body relaxed, his movements almost languid, as if he had not a care in the world, though his eyes remained razor-sharp.

The boy standing in front of him straightened from his crouch and shifted, unsure.

"I am the Duke of Alderidge," he said in a deceptively pleasant tone. "And I am the recipient of the note you delivered to my home this morning. I'd like to know who paid you to deliver this."

"I got paid to forget." The boy crossed his arms over his chest again and raised his chin.

There was pride in that statement, and Ivory wondered at it. The streets of London did not often allow the luxury of pride.

"I'll pay you more to remember." Alderidge's voice was even.

"I don't got much, but I got honor," said the boy with defiance. "Part of my job."

Ivory's brows shot into her hairline as she took a hard look at the youth's lean face and tattered clothes. She gazed at the boy in speculation.

The duke uncoiled himself from where he had been leaning against the sofa, and Ivory tensed. If he thought to harm—

The boy backed up a step. "You can't buy me, like you buy everything and everyone else in your life. Bloody toff. You're all the same."

Alderidge considered the boy, and Ivory couldn't tell what he was thinking. "Ah, but there you're wrong," he said. "I'm not the same at all."

This was met with a rude snort.

"I'm a sea captain."

The boy stared at him suspiciously, uncertain what to do with this information.

"Have you ever seen an elephant?" the duke asked the youth suddenly.

"What's an elephant?" The boy worked the syllables around in his mouth.

A stub of a pencil appeared from the duke's pockets, and he began to draw on the back of the letter still in his hand. "It's an animal. Bigger than the biggest horse you've ever seen. It has thick grey skin all over, and its ears flap out from its head like two enormous rugs. It has a long, muscular nose that hangs almost to the ground, and it can use it to pick up logs, and even people. An elephant has the strength of five hundred men. Yet a single man can tame such a beast and ride it, use it for work and for war."

"You're makin' that up," the boy scoffed, but he edged closer to the duke, craning to see what he was drawing.

Alderidge pocketed his pencil and passed the sketch into a pair of eager, filthy hands. "I'm not making it up." The duke's eyes met Ivory's over the boy's head, and she felt the strength of his gaze all the way to her core. "The place my ships sail is far, far away from England, and it has many elephants. My carpenter's servant, who was not much older than you when I first hired him, finds one to ride every time we are there."

Ivory watched as a grimy finger with a torn nail traced the dark lines on the paper, the boy's initial belligerence fading. She pressed her lips together, knowing what the duke was trying to do, because she had done it a hundred times herself in the past. He was trying to establish a rapport with this urchin, trying to tease out information by establishing a common ground. But he would need to tread carefully—

"I have need of someone like you on my crew. If, of course, you were interested."

Ivory's head snapped up, at about the same speed as the boy's. What in God's name did Alderidge think he was doing? One never made promises, or threats, for that matter, that couldn't be borne out.

"I already got a job."

"Indeed." The duke's eyes considered the boy's thin

form. "Think of this as an opportunity for a promotion. Aside from a wage, I offer regular meals, a bed, a clothing allowance, and the occasional elephant in exchange for a great deal of hard work."

Suspicion was stamped across the captured messenger's pinched features. "I ain't never been on a boat. An' I can't swim."

"If you're doing it right, you don't need to swim," the duke remarked. "We try to keep our ships upright at all times."

"Is there pirates?"

Alderidge tipped his head. "Sometimes." He paused. "Can you fight?"

The boy scoffed. "Not dead yet, am I?"

The duke smiled a lazy smile and crossed his arms. "Then what say you? Will you accept my offer?"

"Why me?"

Why indeed? thought Ivory caustically. She resisted the urge to speak, knowing that the duke was tantalizingly close to a chance at real information, yet his methods were deplorable. Hope was something she never used carelessly.

The duke was grinning now. "Why you? Because you're not dead yet, are you?"

The boy narrowed his eyes. "How do I know yer not just going to sell me to one o' them press-gangs? I don't know you."

"Press-gangs do not buy people, they just take them," Alderidge noted succinctly. "And the good ones do it so cleverly, their victims oft wake up when the sight of land is just a fond memory."

"You know people who do that?" His eyes were wide.

"Unfortunately, yes. But in answer to your question, you're right. You don't know me." Ivory heard her own words from the night before echo in the duke's rich baritone. "You have only my word."

"Can I think about it?"

"No. I need your answer now. But choose wisely. There is no room among my men for those who do not honor their commitments wholeheartedly."

Ivory would kill Alderidge when this was over. This offer was outright cruel.

"Fine. I'll work fer you." The boy scowled. "But I need some coin up front."

"Doesn't work that way," Alderidge said easily. "I will provide you with an address you can report to. There you will be provided with a meal and some proper clothing. Can you find your way to the East India Docks?"

The boy snorted. "Does a dog piss in the streets?"

"'Does a dog piss in the streets, *Captain*,'" the duke corrected.

The youth blinked. "Captain."

"Excellent. As a member of my crew, you are now under my protection, and anyone who takes exception with that can direct themselves to me. And your name?"

"Seth."

"Very good then."

"Do I get a sword?"

"Not yet. Do you have your own knife?"

Seth shook his head.

Alderidge dug into the depths of his coat pocket and produced a small pocketknife, simple and serviceable. He held it out to the boy, and Ivory tensed. Bloody hell, but she wasn't in the habit of giving weapons to strangers standing in the middle of her drawing room, however small. The weapon or the stranger.

Seth reached for the knife, closed his fingers around it, and retreated a few steps, examining his new possession. Alderidge was still ignoring her.

"Then this is yours," the duke said. "Every sailor needs to keep one on his person at all times. It might one day save your life or the life of a mate. Understood?"

"Yes, Captain."

"Excellent." A blond eyebrow rose in approval, and Alderidge once again searched his pockets. The pencil stub reappeared, along with a tiny notebook, and the duke bent, scribbling furiously against his knee. He paused once, adding another note on the back of the page as an afterthought. Once he was done, he pocketed the pencil, ripped out the page, and handed it to Seth.

"You're looking for the *Odyssey*," he said. "When you find her, ask for Duncan and give him this. He'll get you settled."

The boy curled his fingers around it, and for the first time, Ivory wondered if the duke was serious.

"There is one other matter of business to conclude," Alderidge said, "and that is the matter of the letter you hold in your hand. Now, I understand that your honor prevents you from telling me who paid you to deliver it, and I will not ask again, for I admire such. But that same honor demands that you advise your current employer of your resignation. As your captain, I can do that on your behalf."

Seth glanced down at the paper still clutched in his hand and then at the new knife in the other that represented so much more than a simple tool. "Worked at the Lion's Paw." He shoved the letter back at Alderidge. "Until now."

Ivory started. "You're running messages for Gil?"

The boy named Seth suddenly looked nervous. "Didn't say that."

Well, now that was interesting.

"What is this Lion's Paw?" the duke demanded. "And who is Gil?"

"The Lion's Paw is a tavern," Ivory said. "And something of an anonymous communication service. Gil is the proprietor."

"Anonymous communication service? What does that even mean?"

"It means that Gil is not the person who took your sister, if that is what you were thinking."

"That tells me nothing," the duke growled.

Ivory ignored him for the moment, stepping closer and crouching down before Seth. "You must be new there. How long have you worked for Gil?"

"Couple of weeks." The boy met her eyes, looking almost ashamed. "Don't tell that I told you."

"You didn't tell us anything I wouldn't have found out on my own," Ivory whispered. She didn't need Alderidge listening in. "Gil and I do a lot of business together."

Seth's expression suddenly sharpened, and his eyes widened. "You're the duch—"

"Yes." Ivory cut him off before he got too far with that thought. She could feel the duke's stare burning a hole through her.

"Would you be so kind as to stop all the whispering and tell me what is going on?"

Ivory didn't need to look to know that Alderidge was clenching his teeth again. It was a wonder he had any teeth left in his head.

"I'll let Gil know you have accepted another position," she told Seth, and the boy nearly sagged in relief. She stood, smoothing her skirts. "You may go."

The boy looked to Alderidge as if seeking confirmation. The duke jerked his head, and the boy bolted.

"I do hope you are a man of your word," Ivory said the moment Seth disappeared, not giving the duke a chance to demand answers to questions she didn't wish to address. "I know how valuable that information was, but you should only make promises you intend to keep."

Alderidge's eyes went wintry, and he closed the distance between them. "Are you really calling my own honor into question at this moment, Miss Moore?"

Cleanly shaven and dressed in ordinary clothes, he should have made a convincing picture of a town gentleman. At this moment, however, he put her more in mind of Blackbeard than anything Brummel would approve of. He was still staring at her, his eyes traveling over her face, and Ivory felt her heart banging against her ribs at the intensity of his stare. He was standing close enough that she could feel the heat rolling off of him, see the flecks of silver in his irises. His eyes suddenly dropped to her mouth, and desire shot through her, sending liquid fire racing through her veins and setting her body throbbing. All she had to do was lean forward. Go up on her toes and offer her lips to his. God help her, but she wanted this maddening man to kiss her. Kiss her and touch her and—

A coal popped loudly in the grate, and Ivory jerked. What the hell was she doing? She turned away, frantically trying to remember what Alderidge had asked her.

"Miss Moore?" He sounded aggravated.

Ivory balled her hands into fists. His honor. That was

what they had been discussing before he turned his gaze on her mouth and made her wish for things she shouldn't be wishing for. Though perhaps that was what made this man so dangerous. Perhaps he was one of those people who could see into the souls of others and expose their deepest desires, and manipulate them by using those wants. Just as he'd done with Seth.

"You promised that boy a future." There was genuine heat in her words, augmented by self-disgust at her momentary weakness.

"Ah. And now it comes out. You truly have the same opinion of me as the boy did, then?"

"Which is?"

"That I am a useless toff."

"That's not what I said."

"That's exactly what you just said." A muscle was twitching in his jaw. "Let me ask you this, Miss Moore. The men who crew my ships, have you met any of them?"

Ivory frowned. What did that have to do with—

"Have you?" he demanded.

"No."

A deafening silence fell between them. When the duke spoke, it was with great care and restraint. "I'm not sure why I feel the need to say this, Miss Moore, other than the fact that your ill regard is as much an insult to my men as it is to me. Let me tell you where I don't find the men who crew my ships. I don't find them in pretty drawing rooms like this. I don't find them in naval classrooms, placed there solely by the connections their titles and families have provided." He paused. "The boy pretending to be a butler who showed me in—was he recommended to you by one of the grand houses in St James's?"

Ivory scowled. "Of course he wasn't."

"But he works for you."

"Yes."

"Why?"

"You know why."

"I want to hear you say it."

"Because he can have a man's pockets emptied of secrets and possessions in the time it takes for that same man to remove his hat."

"Useful, that, I would imagine, in your line of work."

"What's your point?" Ivory crossed her arms over her chest impatiently.

"My point, Miss Moore, is that any man who sails with me is able to survive in conditions that defy the imagination. He'll fight armed only with his wits and is all the more dangerous for it. He'll die for the man beside him because he is the only family he has ever had." He paused, his eyes narrowing. "Where, Miss Moore, do you think I find such men? Men who aren't needed or wanted anywhere? And what sort of men do you think they become when they are given a place to belong and a job in which they are relied upon?"

Men like you, Ivory thought suddenly. A man who, as a child, was sent away from home to forge his own future because there was no place for him in London. A man who had learned life's lessons the hard way.

"Good men" was all she said, meaning it. "And honorable ones."

"Yes." He looked a little surprised at her response. As if he had expected her to argue.

"And if your new recruit changes his mind?" she asked.

"Then I am out the cost of a small knife, possibly a set

of clothes, and a single meal. A small price to pay. But he won't change his mind."

"And how can you be so sure?"

"For whatever reason, that boy has more principles than many men I've had the misfortune to meet. Though the fact that he holds on to those principles tells me he has no one who depends on him. I offered him coin. He had the luxury of refusing. Had I been in his position with my sister depending on me, there is absolutely no limit to what I would do or take from a man if I thought it might help my sister survive." His face hardened. "No limit."

Ivory knew the duke wasn't talking about Seth any longer. He would be ruthless, this sea captain, if his sister had indeed been put in danger, and that could prove to be either a help or a hindrance. She would have to handle him carefully. She was still mulling this over when she realized Alderidge was striding toward the door.

"Where, exactly, are you going, Your Grace?"

"The Lion's Paw, Miss Moore. My sister is still missing, and I am wasting time standing here. I do not need your assistance."

"Do you know where the Lion's Paw is, Your Grace?"

The duke paused at the doorway. "I am used to finding my way around continents, Miss Moore. I can't imagine it is so hard to find a tavern in London."

Ivory unfolded her arms. "But I—"

"I am not a half-wit, Miss Moore. I am quite capable of having a mutually beneficial conversation with the proprietor of the Lion's Paw, man to man."

"But you should—"

"I thank you for your assistance last night, Miss Moore. I recognize that the quick actions of you and your colleague were invaluable in preventing what could have been a terrible scandal, and I, and my family, are in your debt. Or, at least, we will be until my estate settles with you." He smiled a mirthless smile. "But I am not without my own resources, Miss Moore. If you recall, it was I who was able to ascertain the origins of this letter, the only clue I have as to the possible whereabouts of my sister. I will let you know if I require anything else."

"Are you dismissing me?" Ivory asked. She wasn't sure if she should be appalled or amused.

"Is there any further information you can provide at this moment that may lead to the whereabouts of my sister?"

"No, but—"

"Then good day, Miss Moore."

Ivory stared at the duke's retreating back. Of all the arrogant, idiotic, controlling— She squashed the urge to stamp her foot in frustration and took a deep breath instead. She should let him go. Wash her hands of the Duke of Alderidge and his reckless sister, who might or might not have tied an earl to her bed and who might or might not have found herself in terrible trouble because of it. She should leave the duke to his own devices and wait until he crawled back to these offices for help, his tail between his legs.

Except that was ridiculous. Maximus Harcourt would never crawl back anywhere with his tail between his legs. More likely she'd find herself summoned to Newgate because the idiot had killed someone with his bare hands in an ill-advised effort to get to his sister.

And extracting a person from Newgate was terribly tricky. And she'd hate to see Alderidge take his next ocean voyage chained within the holds of a prison hulk and not on the deck of the *Odyssey*.

Dammit.

"Roddy."

Silence greeted her call.

"Roddy, I know you're listening in the alcove in the hall."

There was a sigh, and Roderick slumped into the room in defeat. "But I was quiet."

"You were predictable." Ivory sighed. "Get your coat. Fetch my cloak while you're at it. We're going out."

Chapter Five

He had almost kissed her.

Standing right there in the middle of that lavish drawing room while she openly questioned his intentions and honor. If Miss Moore were a man, he'd have called her out. He might do it anyway, if only to rid himself of the temptation she presented. He was wildly attracted to her, and it was hard to look at her without imagining what it might be like to kiss her. To taste that soft, wide mouth, to explore the satin of her skin. To do that and so much more.

But Beatrice was still missing, and yet somehow he had allowed his body to lead, allowed himself to fantasize about his own base desires. His hands curled in his pocket around the letter and the ring. Maybe Miss Moore had been right in calling his honor into question. Because right now, his only focus should be on finding Bea.

As he passed Blackfriars Bridge and drew nearer to the

Puddle Dock stairs, the stench from the Thames rolled up in damp waves over the banks and into the streets and alleys. The sunshine of the early morning had disappeared behind a heavy blanket of grey clouds and the wind had picked up, making him shiver beneath his coat. It hadn't been too difficult to find the tavern—he'd had to ask only three watermen before the last had pointed him in the right direction. He turned down the crooked alley, spotting the building immediately. He glanced up at the tavern sign, creaking from its chains under the eaves, and frowned. The sign read *Lion's Paw*, though the picture beneath it made what Max assumed to be the noble beast look more like a starving hyena.

He shrugged, pushed through the door, and ducked into the building. A welcome warmth enveloped him, along with the delicious smells of cooking meat. His stomach growled, and Max realized he hadn't eaten anything since he'd shared a meal with a handful of his crew just after putting into port late yesterday afternoon.

He glanced around, taking in the sturdy tables and the well-swept floor. There were a few patrons already seated, bent over bowls of what looked like stew and generous chunks of bread. At the far end of the tavern, three dozen youths of indiscriminate age and dubious origins were wolfing down their own portions. A couple of heads popped up long enough to glance at Max, before dismissing him in favor of their food.

"Get you something?" asked a young girl with thick red hair pulled back off her face. "Beef stew today. Yesterday's bread, but it's still good for dipping. Best ale this side o' the Channel."

Max slid onto a bench. The serving girl couldn't be

much more than thirteen, but her untouched loveliness was startling, especially in a tavern such as this. A dimple appeared on her fair cheek as she smiled at him and waited expectantly for his order.

"Yes, please," said Max, sliding a coin onto the table. "The stew and ale."

The girl snatched up the coin and flounced away, returning in less than a minute with his meal and a large earthenware cup of ale. "Even got carrots in it," she said as she placed the steaming bowl in front of him and departed, just as a draft of wind heralded another arrival.

Max tucked into his food, letting his eyes wander around the tavern, trying to formulate a plan. He'd yet to see any sign of the man called Gil who was the proprietor of the establishment, but he wasn't leaving here until he'd gotten what he came for. If this man had had in his possession a letter that had a connection to his sister, Max was going to get some answers.

A bell suddenly dinged somewhere in the back of the tavern, and one of the youths sitting at the far end popped up like a jack-in-the-box.

"Not your turn," one of the others still seated complained.

"Is too. An' you know it." The youth shoved what was left of his bread in his mouth as he left the table.

The others watched him go with what looked like envy as he disappeared through the same doorway the serving girl had emerged from. A moment later he reappeared, pulling a ragged hat from the pocket of his threadbare coat. He marched through the tavern and vanished through the front door without a backward glance.

Max eyed the door leading to the back of the tavern.

Downing the last of his ale, he rose and made his way toward the rear.

The young serving girl slid neatly into his way as he approached the door. "You need more food?" she asked, effectively blocking his way. He'd have to shove past her to gain access. And he might yet.

Max shook his head. "I need to speak with Gil."

This did not seem to surprise her. "Gil expectin' you?"

"No."

"Who's askin'?"

Max considered his response. "Captain Harcourt."

The girl's expression didn't alter. "Business or pleasure?"

Max blinked. What the hell did that mean? What sort of pleasure would he seek with a man who owned a tavern? "Business."

"Wait here."

Max was left standing near the end of the tavern, a dozen pairs of eyes now trained on his back. He turned slowly, and all eyes dropped.

"Can I help you?"

Max spun back again to find a petite woman, with the same lustrous red hair and fair complexion as the serving girl, leaning against the doorframe with a calculated nonchalance. Sharp green eyes raked him from head to toe as if evaluating a potential threat. Her hands were in the pockets of a bulky apron, but even the apron wasn't enough to conceal her voluptuous figure. She put Max in mind of a beautiful viper that just might strike without warning.

"I was looking for Gil."

"You found her. What can I assist you with, Captain Harcourt?"

Max tried to hide his surprise, though he clearly failed. The woman named Gil smirked.

Business or pleasure, indeed.

"A boy working for you delivered a message to my house this morning," he said. "That message originated here."

The woman shrugged. "Oh?"

"I wish to know who sent it."

Gil laughed softly, as if this were humorous. "I brew ale and provide meals to paying customers, Captain. That's all."

"You're not a very good liar."

"You wound me."

"I am not in the mood for games. I need information. My sister is missing."

"I am sorry to hear that. Would you like to leave a description? Perhaps I can send word if I see her."

Max shifted. "Name your price."

Gil pushed herself away from the doorframe. "I don't have a price, Captain, because I don't have an answer." The humor had faded from her eyes. Her gaze traveled the length of him, as if assessing anew what she saw. "But the boy you say delivered your message. Can I expect him back?"

Max met her gaze without flinching. "No." She could make of that what she would.

"Then, Captain, I'm afraid I'm going to have to ask you to leave."

Suddenly Max was aware that the barrel of a dueling pistol was pointed squarely at the center of his chest. He was losing his edge. The woman had had it concealed in her apron the entire time, and he had been oblivious. Bloody hell.

He debated his options. He was reasonably sure he could disarm her before she shot him. He was less sure she wouldn't wing either him or one of the other patrons in the process.

"I asked you to leave, Captain." Her expression was cold and detached now, as if she were idly contemplating what color his blood might be when it splattered all over her neat, whitewashed walls.

"For the love of God, Gilda, don't shoot him."

Max closed his eyes.

Gilda's gaze slid past Max, and her eyes crinkled at the corners, her mouth turning up in renewed amusement. "Well, if it isn't the duchess." She paused, her eyes coming back to rest on him. "Why can't I shoot him?"

"Because he's my client."

A red brow arched. "My condolences."

"Thank you."

Max gritted his teeth and turned to find Miss Moore standing behind him, brushing beads of dampness from her cloak. "What are you doing here?" he hissed.

"Aside from making sure you don't end up with a hole through your miserable hide? Having a cup of ale, I should think. Best ale this side of the Channel, you know." She smiled cheerfully at him, smoothing back the damp tendrils of hair that had sprung from her braid.

"You'd be best not to let this one off the leash," the redheaded woman commented, tucking the pistol into her apron strings and gesturing for the young girl to fetch more ale. "All the finesse of a Smithfield bull let loose in a china shop, this one."

Max felt his jaw slacken. "I am standing right here. I can hear you."

"Good," Miss Moore said primly. "Maybe if you do more listening, it will reduce the chance of you getting shot again."

Gil's green eyes suddenly lit up. "Hello, Roddy. I didn't see you there." Max suddenly became aware of the boy's presence behind Miss Moore.

"Good day, Miz Gil," Roddy replied.

"The duchess treating you well?" Gil winked at Miss Moore, and Max wondered at the strange nickname.

"Very, Miz Gil." Roddy grinned at the tavern keeper before drifting in the direction of the youths still watching. He was greeted by name by at least three.

Gilda suddenly swung toward Miss Moore. "Don't tell me you hired Seth too," she said.

"I didn't," Miss Moore said.

A pair of stricken eyes widened, then narrowed dangerously at Max. Gil's hand started to drift to the weapon at her hip.

"He did." Miss Moore jabbed a thumb in his direction.

"What?" Gil looked between them in confusion.

"The good captain here hired Seth on as a carpenter's servant."

"Why would you do that?"

"Because I need a new one."

"What happened to your last one?"

"He got promoted. He's the carpenter's second mate now."

Gil gave Max a long look. "And what did you offer him that made him leave his current job?" she asked suspiciously.

"An elephant," Max replied.

"An elephant," she repeated, clearly perplexed.

"Among other things," he added.

Gil turned to Miss Moore. "And Seth will be well treated at the hands of your captain here?"

It was Miss Moore's turn to give him a long look. "Yes," she said, and Max felt an inexplicable rush of pleasure at her faith.

Gil shook her head before turning back to Miss Moore. "You have to stop taking my best ones, Duchess," she complained, though without venom. "I only had Seth two weeks."

Miss Moore was saved from having to respond by the arrival of more cups of ale. Gil turned to help the girl, and Miss Moore yanked him to her side.

"I need you to wait outside," she murmured into his ear.

"Hell no."

"Your presence here is helping no one, least of all your sister."

"I'm not leaving. That woman knows something."

Miss Moore closed her eyes, and it looked as though she was counting something in her head. "Of course she knows something," she sighed, opening her eyes. "And she's not going to tell you. Gilda has not survived as long as she has by allowing herself to be intimidated by obnoxious sea captains. I think she made that clear, what with the pistol stuck in your face."

Max seethed. "I'm not obnoxious. And I'm not leaving."

Miss Moore said something terrifically vile under her breath. "Then for all that is holy, Your Grace, keep your mouth shut for the next five minutes. Understand?"

Max was so shocked by her vehemence that all he could do was nod.

"Look," Miss Moore said, making an effort to sound more conciliatory. "I don't presume to tell you how to manage your ships or your business. I would appreciate the same consideration when it comes to mine. Is that fair?"

There was no way to argue with that reasoning. "Why are you helping me?"

"You mean now, after you dismissed me like an errant page boy?" The conciliatory note slipped.

Max might have winced. "Yes."

"Honestly, I have no idea."

Both women slid onto a bench, far away from prying ears, and Max followed suit, sliding in beside Miss Moore, unwilling to sit next to a loaded pistol and unwilling to be left standing awkwardly by the table.

Miss Moore took a long draught of her ale and nodded appreciatively. "A good batch."

"They're all good," Gil snorted.

"True."

"You didn't come to compliment me on my ale."

"No."

Max was fully aware he had been relegated to the role of spectator. He chafed and shifted, his thigh brushing Miss Moore's. She ignored him.

"You're here looking for a girl." Gil's eyes slid to Max. "His sister."

Miss Moore's beautiful mouth turned down in displeasure, and she slanted him a sharp look. "He told you."

"Yes. About the same time he implied Seth had met an unfortunate end. He should choose his words with more care next time."

Miss Moore sighed. "The captain is distraught. His sister is missing."

Distraught? Distraught! Max came halfway out of his seat. She was making him sound like a fragile, swooning maiden.

Under the table Miss Moore's hand came down on his knee, her fingers biting through the fabric of his breeches. He sat back down with a thump. Gil smirked again.

"I need to know who sent that message," Miss Moore said evenly.

Gil shrugged. "There's no way of being certain. You know that. I wouldn't have a business if I couldn't guarantee anonymity and confidentiality."

Max frowned. None of this was making sense. And Miss Moore's hand on his knee was becoming all he could concentrate on. Her grip had relaxed, and the heat that was trapped between her palm and his leg was sending all sorts of impure thoughts to fog his brain.

"Doesn't mean no one saw."

The redhead shrugged again. "Maybe."

"I would be in your debt."

Gilda leaned back from the table, a gleam in her eye. "A fine offer if I ever heard one."

"I'll not offer again."

"Very well, Duchess. Collette was working last night. I leave the back door open for her to come in and warm up from time to time. Can't say for sure that she saw anything, though."

"Thank you."

Gil tipped her cup and swallowed the last of her ale. "Pleasure doing business, as always, Duchess." She stood, straightening her apron, and wandered to the other side of the tavern, collecting used crockery and plates as she went.

Max reached down and covered Miss Moore's hand

where it still rested on his leg, lifting her fingers slightly. If he was going to be able to think clearly, Miss Moore could not be touching him. She snatched her hand out from under his, and he was gratified to see a pink stain climb into her cheeks.

"'Distraught'?" he growled at her, trying to establish some distance.

"Would you have preferred *foolish*?"

Max exhaled. This was better. He felt safer behind battle lines.

"Why can't she tell you who paid her to have that message sent to me?" He gestured at the youths, who were starting to drift away from the table. "And who is Collette?"

Miss Moore looked at him for a moment before rising, pulling her coat more closely around her. "Follow me."

Ivory ducked under the low lintel and wove her way through the back room, where kegs of ale were stacked to the ceiling and a wood fire glowed in a large hearth. A medieval-looking cauldron full of stew hung over the heat, simmering. A wooden tub of greasy bowls sat on the floor, a tabby mouser licking the spoils off the edge of the nearest one. The cat gave Ivory a baleful glare as she passed, but didn't budge. There were no windows in this back room, making the light dim, and when Ivory stopped, the duke ran into her back. By reflex he caught her shoulders to keep her from falling, but she twitched out of his grasp as though he had pressed hot coals to her skin.

Another blush threatened. She'd thought to keep him

from folly when she'd shoved her hand on his knee under the table, but it had been clear the folly was all hers. Beneath the fabric of his clothing, she'd felt the power of him, muscles like steel flexing under her hand. The desire to explore the rest of his body was threatening both her sanity and her professionalism.

"This is why Gil cannot identify the person who sent you that message," Ivory said, taking another step back for good measure. She gestured to a heavy iron box mounted to the wall near the back door. The top of the box was hinged, but the lid was secured by an oiled padlock.

She pushed open the back door, was suddenly engulfed in a blast of chilled air, and stepped into a deserted, narrow lane. There were empty barrels stacked along one side of the wall, waiting to be collected, along with a number of broken crates containing refuse. On the other side of the door, however, in the spot where the iron box was bolted onto the interior wall, a narrow slit had been cut into the rough exterior.

"It's a depository," Ivory told the duke. "Messages can be dropped here anonymously. They must be wrapped with two shillings and have a clear address on the front. Only Gil has the key. She retrieves them—"

"—and sends boys like Seth out to deliver them." His voice was flat, and she couldn't tell what he was thinking.

"Yes. One coin is for the messenger, while Gil takes the other." Ivory paused. "Though I suspect a good portion of Gil's earnings are eaten by her messengers."

"A paragon of virtue." The sarcasm was sharp.

"No," Ivory said. "You'd be a fool to believe that. But she does what she can."

"Your boy—Roddy—he used to work for her?"

"Yes. He's talking to the rest of the messengers right now. If any of them know something, he'll find out, though it's doubtful. The system works incredibly well."

"Who the hell needs to send messages anonymously?"

"Besides your sister?"

The duke scowled.

"People who don't want to be found, Your Grace. People who don't want things traced back to them." Ivory gestured around her. The walls of the buildings on the other side of the alley stared blankly back at her. Looking to her right toward the end of the alley, she could just make out the grey surface of the Thames. On the other end, daily traffic passed blindly by as people went hurriedly about their business.

The duke was looking at her strangely. "Like you?"

She met his eyes unapologetically. "Sometimes."

"But why would Beatrice need to do that? Hide behind anonymity?"

Ivory avoided his gaze and started up the alley toward the street. "Have you ever considered that your sister doesn't want you looking for her?"

"That's ridiculous."

"Is it really?"

"Yes, it is. My sister is young. She has her whole life ahead of her. Between her title, her beauty, and, if I may be so vulgar, the dowry that my fortune will provide, Bea will have her choice of husbands. She will marry well and become an important part of society."

Ivory sighed.

"Are you disagreeing with me, Miss Moore?"

Ivory stopped and looked up at him. "Is it possible that

your sister might not wish to carry on as everyone expects, and marry as everyone expects, and become the perfect society wife as everyone expects? Is it possible that she may be running away from a life she never wanted?" Elise had told her that nothing had been missing from Beatrice's rooms that might be pawned for quick coin, but that didn't mean that the girl hadn't been secretly squirreling away pin money for a long time. For all Ivory knew, Beatrice could have enough coin on hand to flee London. Or to flee England altogether.

"What are you implying?" Alderidge had his hackles up again. "That I somehow failed to provide for her? Though I may not have been home often, I can assure you she had the best tutors, the best instructors, the best clothing. She's had music lessons, painting lessons, riding lessons, dancing lessons. She's never wanted for anything. Ever."

The duke was missing the point entirely. Ivory asked a different question. "Is it possible that she might be seeking something different out of life? Something beyond material needs?"

"Like what?"

Ivory stared at him and jabbed a finger at the lapel of his coat. "You tell me, *Captain*. You're a peer who has chosen a far different life than is expected of a man with the title of duke. You don't seem overly interested in selecting a bride and settling into a predictable life of comfort, the passage of time marked by annual balls, games of cards at your club, a good bottle of brandy, or the occasional shooting party at a country home."

Alderidge shuddered. "That may be true, Miss Moore, but I don't see what my lifestyle has to do with Bea's."

"Maybe she too would like to discover what may lie just beyond the next horizon. Maybe she too craves the same life of adventure that she thinks her brother has."

Alderidge's face was a mask of stony horror.

Finally.

"She's asked you to take her to India, hasn't she?" Ivory asked softly.

"Many times," he croaked. "How did you know that?"

"I guessed," she admitted.

"But I explained to her why it was impossible. Just the journey alone is perilous. And then there are diseases and all manner of danger in such a place. I would never put Bea's life at risk like that."

"Yet you put your life in danger all the time."

"That's different."

"How?"

"Because—" The duke stopped, his icy grey eyes locked on hers.

"Because you are a man? Because you are free to make your own choices?"

"I— That's not—" Alderidge stopped. "You're twisting my words."

"I'm not twisting anything, Your Grace. I'm merely suggesting that your sister may have made her own choices and struck out on her own."

"But why would she do that?"

Ivory sighed, realizing the conversation was now going in circles. She started walking again.

"She never said she was unhappy," the duke said, almost desperately, hurrying behind her.

"I think she did, but you just didn't hear her. Why do *you* suppose your sister wanted to go to India?"

Alderidge fell silent, only the sounds of their boots slapping against the wet muck on the pavement breaking the quiet.

"I don't know." They had reached the end of the alley and the sounds of humanity and hooves and creaking equipages were constant now.

Ivory turned, catching Alderidge's sleeve. "Once we find her, I suggest you ask her."

The duke only nodded, suddenly looking exhausted.

She almost reached up to touch a hand to his face to smooth away the lines of worry that were carved deep into his features. She imagined herself going up on her tiptoes to catch his lips with her own, to make him forget his troubles, if only for a brief moment. How long had it been since she had wanted to offer a man such a simple gesture? How long had it been since she had admitted to herself that such a simple gesture was not simple at all? That it was only the start of darker, deeper desires?

Ivory pulled her hand away from his sleeve and shoved it safely beneath her cloak. She was fully aware she was walking on very thin ice. Her reputation, her very livelihood depended on her success. And if she wanted to preserve any of that, her only priority should be finding the Lady Beatrice.

And not imagining kissing Maximus Harcourt.

~

She found Collette in the doorway of St Timothy's Church, barely a stone's throw from the alley. The small building could hardly be described as a church, lacking any soaring stonework and instead boasting listing, rotting beams and a collection of kind clergymen who did their best to aid those who came seeking shelter.

The woman might have been beautiful once, but years of living on the streets had exacted a heavy price. Her dark-blond hair was thin, as was her face. Dark circles ringed tired, faded eyes. Collette was crouched at the top of worn wooden steps, a tin mug of steaming broth in her hands and a vacant expression on her face. A few others were scurrying away, protecting their own tins, as if afraid Ivory had come to steal their meager nourishment.

"Good day, Collette," Ivory said, making her way up the stairs. She was aware of the duke on her heels, his presence impossible to ignore. The vulnerable worry he had worn so recently on his face had been replaced by a hard, remote severity, making it easier for Ivory to concentrate on business.

Collette's eyes shifted and focused slowly on Ivory. "Duchess." She smiled in welcome, keeping her lips carefully pressed together so as not to expose the fact that she had very few teeth left. "Been a long time."

"Is the soup good today?" Ivory asked, glancing at the door of the church. On most afternoons the church served a hot broth, but some days it wasn't much more than thinly flavored water.

"Got some turnips in it today." Another tight-lipped smile. "Would you like some?" She offered her tin, shivering under her threadbare cloak.

"No, thank you," Ivory said gently, coming to crouch next to the woman. "But I might have a bit of business for you."

Interest sparked in Collette's jaded eyes before they lifted to peruse the duke where he stood stiffly, waiting.

"He don't look like the type to pay for a midday tumble. In fact, he don't much look like the type that pays for any sort of tumble. Though sometimes it's hard to tell."

Ivory suppressed the urge to glance back at Alderidge, if only to see if his jaw was clenched as hard as she suspected. "Not that sort of business. Information."

"Ah. He your client then?"

"Yes."

"My condolences."

A giggle escaped Ivory, taking her by surprise. "Gil said the same when she almost shot him."

"That would've been a shameful waste. Did she swive him first?"

Ivory grinned again, though she couldn't stop the heat that was climbing into her cheeks. "No. But Gil also said you were working last night. Behind the Lion's Paw."

"Might have been." Her reply was guarded.

"Someone dropped off a message early this morning. Probably around three or four o'clock."

Collette gazed into her tin. "It was dark." She pulled her thin cloak around her more tightly with her free hand.

Ivory drew out a small purse of coins and pressed them into Collette's hand.

The streetwalker raised her head. "But there was a moon, of course."

Ivory made a sound of encouragement.

"A gentleman," Collette said. "Dark coat, scarf, hat, silver-tipped walking stick. Couldn't see his face, on account of the scarf, though. Average in build. Came from this end of the alley, left the same way. Looked mighty pleased. He was humming to himself."

"Humming what?" Alderidge spoke up from behind Ivory.

Collette shrugged. "Don't know. But it sounded nice." She began to hum with a surprisingly strong, pretty tone, and it took Ivory a few moments to identify it.

"'V'adoro, pupille,'" Ivory said. "From Handel's *Giulio Cesare*."

Collette looked at her blankly.

Ivory sang the opening of the aria softly, remembering the rise and fall of the notes. It was a shame, really, that *Giulio Cesare* had become a nearly obscure piece, having long since given way to more popular operas.

"Yes." Collette was smiling again, and Ivory was aware that the duke was staring at her. "Do you think you could sing—"

"Maybe another time," Ivory interrupted softly. "Anything else you can remember?"

"When I asked him if he wanted to keep his good mood rolling, he told me to sod off—that he had all he needed waiting at home for him," Collette scoffed.

"Did you see if he had a carriage? Or a horse?"

"He was on foot. Whatever he was traveling in would been left up on the road here. I never saw anything."

"Did you see a woman with him? She might have been blond?"

"No. He was by himself."

"What about a lady by herself?" It was the duke who asked.

Collette scoffed. "No lady foolish enough to come down here at night on her own. Never saw no lady. Last night or any other."

A silence fell, and when it was clear the woman had nothing else to offer, Ivory stood. "Thank you."

Collette nodded, and the purse disappeared under her cloak. "Always a pleasure, Duchess."

"I don't suppose I can convince you to come back with me for a night or two?" Ivory asked carefully. "Just in case you remember something else, of course."

Collette's lips thinned, and her chin rose, as if she saw right through Ivory's words. "Doing just fine on my own."

Ivory sighed inwardly. One day Collette would surprise her and say yes. She pulled at the ties of her woolen cloak and swung it over the thin woman's shoulders, not giving her a chance to refuse.

"Don't need your charity," Collette protested, though it was halfhearted.

"Not charity," Ivory assured her. "Part of your payment. Besides, my client here has promised me a new velvet cloak trimmed in satin and ermine when I find what he is looking for."

Collette looked up suspiciously at Alderidge.

"Blue velvet," he said behind Ivory, not missing a beat. "Though it is to be trimmed with fox and not ermine. It's warmer, and I am rather partial to function as well as beauty."

The streetwalker turned back to Ivory and gave her a long, speculative look.

Ivory willed herself not to blush. "Thank you again, Collette."

The woman raised her tin of soup, and Ivory retreated back down the church stairs, her arms wrapped around her waist against the cold. She'd barely made it two steps back in the direction of the Lion's Paw when a blissful heat enfolded her.

Alderidge swung around to stand in front of her, tugging the lapels of his greatcoat gently together across her shoulders.

"What are you doing?" Ivory asked, startled.

"Baking a cake."

She stared at him.

"What the hell does it look like I'm doing? You'll freeze to death wandering around in a dress in the middle of winter." He pushed a stray strand of hair from the side of her face and pulled the collar of the coat up around her ears.

Ivory stopped breathing. "But—"

"If you freeze to death, it will take me much longer to find Bea," he cut her off gruffly.

And if she couldn't remember to breathe, she might suffocate before she froze to death.

"But I can't wear your coat," she finally managed.

"You're already wearing it. I regret that it is not blue velvet with ermine trim."

"Yes, but—"

"Do you think you could simply say thank you and not argue?"

Ivory blinked. "Thank you."

"You're welcome." He was looking down at her, a strange smile on his face.

Ivory slid her hands against the interior of the coat, wrapping it as close to her body as she could. The unfamiliar lining slid against the skin of her shoulders. She closed her eyes and drew in a deep breath, the scent of wool, salt, and something exotic filling her nose. It was like having the duke wrapped around her, she thought, with his heat and his touch and his scent. Just that thought set her skin on fire, her nipples hardening beneath her bodice where her breasts rubbed against the heavy coat. She wasn't cold any longer. Instead she was fevered, her mouth dry and her body throbbing.

Bloody hell, but she was in trouble.

Once upon a time, she had been one of the most desired women in London. Men had vied to possess her. They'd sought to buy her favor with flowers and perfumes, poetry and jewelry. They'd offered her expensive homes, obscene allowances, and silk and satin clothing fit for a princess. And though she was sometimes forced to accept some of these gifts in order to survive, none of it had interested her.

But here, standing in the middle of a dirty London street, she had just been thoroughly, completely, irrevocably seduced by a worn, salt-stained greatcoat. Ivory swallowed with difficulty, knowing that if the Duke of Alderidge so desired, he could push her back up against the church wall and have his way with her right here, right now. And she would, undoubtedly, enjoy every second.

Except he had no interest in possessing her. Nor had he sought to seduce her.

And maybe it was that knowledge that had her so captivated. So tempted. What Alderidge had done just now had been an act of kindness. It had not been a ploy to secure her preference or her company for the night. His only interest in her was in her ability to help him find his missing sister.

And she would do well to remember that he was a client who had come to her for help, not for a tumble, as Collette had so delicately put it. Ivory had spent years cultivating a reputation as the best at what she did, and being the best required her to be professional at all times. Yet somehow, when it came to the Duke of Alderidge, all it took was a simple act of kindness to make her want to throw all that into the wind for a fleeting taste of this man.

"Are you all right?"

Ivory's eyes snapped open to find the duke watching her, his expression unreadable.

"I was just..." She trailed off, second-guessing the wisdom of what she had been going to say.

"You were just what?" He was close enough for her to see the blond tips of his lashes, the jagged edges of the scar that ran across his forehead near his hairline. Close enough to study the way his lower lip tightened as he watched her and imagine what it would feel like to run her tongue along its edge—

"Miss Moore? You were just what?" he repeated.

"Surprised. Most people don't do me favors without expecting something in return." She hated the words the second they were out. They made her sound like a petulant child. Or worse, weak.

Those incredible grey eyes darkened again. "Do not make the mistake of labeling me 'most people,' Miss Moore," he said.

Ivory couldn't look away.

"So it was a gentleman," he said abruptly.

It took Ivory a second to get her bearings.

"That proves that my sister did not deliver that message," he prodded.

"True," she said, grasping at her wits and his statement with alacrity. It was much easier to deal with this man when he was abrupt.

And not gentle and kind.

"But it doesn't prove she didn't write it and have someone deliver it for her. And I'm afraid that Collette's description will not be helpful in identifying the individual. Who she described could have been any of a thousand gentlemen in London."

"Just a ray of optimism, aren't you?" Alderidge grumbled.

"You did not hire me to be optimistic," Ivory replied. "You hired me to be logical."

"Then *logically*, Miss Moore, is it not obvious to you that Bea's been kidnapped? The man said he had everything he needed at home. Whoever he was, he must be holding Bea prisoner in his house."

Ivory's nostrils flared. "Or alternatively, Captain Conspiracy, the gentleman is a faithful husband and was referring to his *wife*."

His eyes slitted. "I do not appreciate being mocked."

Ivory met his gaze evenly. "Again, we have no evidence to suggest that your sister has been kidnapped. What we do have evidence of is that this unidentified gentleman knows your sister, though in what context, I cannot guess. He may be a friend, someone she trusts and someone who is helping her. At the very least, he seems to have her best interests at heart. Otherwise we'd be reading about the scene last night in the *Times* right now. We must not discount the possibility that the gentleman could also be her lov—"

"No."

Ivory rolled her eyes. They were getting nowhere. She began shrugging out of the duke's coat. "Go home, Your Grace. The both of us standing here in the middle of the street accomplishes nothing. Be assured I will not rest until I am satisfied with the outcome. I still have people watching and asking questions. I will send word immediately if I discover anything else."

Alderidge yanked the lapels of his coat back around her, his hands resting just below her chin. "Keep the coat on. And you can't send me home like a disobedient child."

Ivory blew out a breath of exasperation. "Then do as

you wish, Your Grace. But make sure that whatever you do, it isn't out of the ordinary—"

"Hullooo! Your Grace!" The enthusiastic shout came from behind Ivory. The duke dropped his hands and turned. Over his shoulder Ivory could make out a well-dressed man leaning out of the door of a carriage that had stopped in the middle of the street.

Alderidge swore under his breath before returning the man's wave of greeting.

Ivory was already edging away, unwilling to give this stranger any reason to ask Alderidge awkward questions about his companion.

The duke turned back to her. "Where are you going—"

"I say, Your Grace, why have you not got a coat on?" the man in the carriage shouted. "You'll catch your death! You're in England, not India, in case you've forgotten." Laughter at his own jest drifted across the street. "Come, let me give you a ride."

The duke turned back toward the waiting carriage and said something Ivory couldn't make out. She wasted no time darting into the nearest alley, and by the time Alderidge turned back, she was long gone.

⁓

The Earl of Barlow beamed at Max as he sat opposite him in his carriage. As much as Max wasn't in the mood for idle small talk, he couldn't argue that the carriage at least provided a reprieve from the cold winds that blustered outside. Since he no longer had his coat. Since Miss Moore had vanished in front of him.

He shifted, not pleased with the ache that had settled in

his chest, nor the one that had settled in his groin. The sight of Miss Moore wrapped in his coat had been disturbingly intoxicating. What he'd intended as a simple act of chivalry was inspiring all sorts of lustful imaginings, far beyond what a woman wrapped in a coat ever should. He pictured Miss Moore wrapped in one of his shirts, wrapped in his sheets. Wrapped in him—

"What good fortune, happening upon you just now," Barlow said happily. "Too cold to walk anywhere today. Especially dressed as you are." His forehead crinkled. "What were you doing down here?"

Max frowned at the bumbling intrusion on his privacy. "A trifling business matter. Nothing more."

"I see. Was that a woman you gave your coat to?"

Max's frown deepened. So Barlow had seen that. He wasn't particularly pleased with that either.

"Yes." He kept his answer short, unwilling to discuss anything that had to do with Miss Moore or why he had been standing in a London street with her.

"Was she an acquaintance of yours?" Barlow asked curiously.

"No." The answer was out before he had time to consider it. "Just a woman down on her luck who needed a coat more than I."

"How magnanimous!" Barlow exclaimed with delighted approval. "More gentlemen should aspire to such goodwill."

It was not lost on Max that he had given his coat to a woman who had first given her own cloak away without a second thought. "Indeed they should," he murmured.

"Perhaps you might wish to make a stop along Bond Street, Your Grace?" Barlow suggested with a great deal of animation. "I know a wonderful shop where you might purchase a fabulous new coat. Such fabrics and finishings! I recommend that you demand ivory buttons—"

"I have another coat," Max said, his head already beginning to pound. "But thank you," he added hastily.

Barlow looked deflated for a brief second before he sat up again. "I must offer my condolences," he said, his voice dropping to almost a whisper, as though someone might hear them.

Max almost snorted at the mention of the word *condolences*.

"A terrible thing, last night. So unexpected. And in your own house, no less."

For one horrifying moment, a vision of the scene in Bea's bedroom flashed through his mind, before he remembered that Barlow had no way of knowing what had really happened.

"Indeed." Max was abrupt.

"And to think that you were the last one to see the earl before he breathed his last." Barlow sucked in a breath of air through his teeth. "One can never take anything for granted, certainly not the time one has on this earth."

"Indeed."

"I must ask how Lady Beatrice is faring amid all this misfortune." Barlow's face was a portrait of concern.

Max could feel his body tense. "My sister was most distraught," he said, borrowing Miss Moore's word.

"Of course. Any lady would be incapacitated with shock and grief."

Unless her name was Miss Moore, Max thought grimly. Then she managed corpses tied with silk ribbon the way most women managed their daily shopping lists.

Barlow shifted against the squabs. "About Lady Beatrice—"

"My sister is not in town at the moment," Max interrupted before he had to fend off more invitations to theaters or museums or exhibits.

Barlow blinked owlishly at him. "Then where is she?"

"In the country," Max said vaguely. "Recovering."

"Oh. Of course. And when do you expect her back?"

"I don't know," Max said, wishing he could escape the confines of the carriage immediately, coat or no coat. The man's good intentions were starting to wear and the pounding in his head was increasing. The truth was, he barely knew Barlow and had no interest in getting to know him further. He reached for his watch, only to realize it was in the pocket of his coat. On Miss Moore. As were the letter and Bea's ring.

Dammit.

The carriage slowed, and Max pulled the curtain back, relieved to see that they were almost in front of his home.

"I thank you for your kindness, Barlow," Max said, trying not to appear too eager to get out of the equipage. "But I must be hurrying on."

"Of course, of course," Barlow said. "Perhaps, Your Grace, if you have a moment, there is a matter of business I'd like to discuss with you—"

"Can you stop by tomorrow?" Max asked, desperate to get away from the earl.

"Absolutely," Barlow said with a toothy smile. "Would noon be suitable?"

"Yes, yes." Max would have agreed to anything. He snapped the door shut and almost sprinted across the street and up the stairs to his town house.

He yanked open the door and ducked inside, then closed it and leaned against the cool surface. Letting his eyes drift shut with weary exhaustion. He wasn't going to be able to do this. Pretend that everything was fine and perfect when men like Barlow trapped him in conversation.

He would be expected to show up at a few clubs while he was in London. He would certainly be meeting with a number of company men to talk numbers and shipping and contracts for the coming season. He had holds to provision, men to pay, cargo to load, bills to review, ships to repair. How was he supposed to do all of this when his sister was simply...gone? When the woman who was supposed to help him find her was somehow turning into a temptation he no longer wished to resist?

When he didn't have the first clue what to do about any of it?

"Have you found her?" Helen's voice cut across the silence.

Max opened his eyes. "Not yet," he said dully. The pounding in his head was not improving.

His aunt was standing in the hall, dressed immaculately as usual, though her hands were clasped together as if in prayer. At his answer she made a noise of distress and wobbled.

Max went immediately to her side and guided her into the drawing room, where he seated her on a long settee.

"Where is she?" Helen asked, though Max knew she wasn't expecting an answer.

There was an untouched tea service arranged on an end table, and Max poured and pressed a cup of tea into her thin hands. He wandered over to the door and closed it firmly. He sat down on the other end of the settee and regarded his aunt.

"Was Beatrice unhappy here?" he asked with no preamble.

Helen's fingers tightened on the handle of her cup and her saucer clattered. "Who told you she was unhappy?"

"No one," Max said with resignation, knowing he sounded like Miss Moore, but needing to ask the question anyway. "But I can't not consider the possibility that Beatrice has . . . left."

"You mean run away? Like an ill-bred country girl yearning for a big-city adventure?" Helen's voice was harsh.

Max sighed. He would keep the message he'd received to himself until he knew something more. Telling Helen that he had received a message suggesting Bea might very well have fled would only serve to upset her more.

"She wanted for nothing," Helen whispered. "I made sure of that."

"We both did. But maybe I failed to give her what she needed most." There, he had said it. Had said what had been pressing on his conscience ever since he walked into Beatrice's room last night.

"Beatrice worshipped you," Helen said, putting her teacup aside.

"Beatrice didn't even know me."

His aunt stood and retrieved a pretty wooden box, whimsical birds carved across its surface. Max recognized it immediately as a gift he had sent to her from Bombay. She brought it to Max, placed it in his lap, and resumed her seat.

"What is this?" Max asked.

"Every letter you ever sent her. She kept every one. And for each one you wrote, she wrote you four."

"I know." Sometimes he would find a dozen letters waiting for him at the offices in Bombay or Calcutta, brought to port by another ship.

Very slowly he opened the box, finding a stack of worn letters, the paper soft from constant handling. On the top of the pile, a pretty pink seashell rested.

"She knew you through your letters. Through your tales of adventure."

Except his tales of adventure were often just that. Tales. He never wrote of yellow fever. Or cholera. Or any of the other diseases that ran rampant and felled men like flies. He never wrote of wounds that festered and seethed until they drove a soul to madness before taking his life. He never wrote of the men who waited, just as eager to kill for a chance at taking a purse as for a chance at taking an entire ship.

"Still, I think we both know that she needed her brother. Not a pile of stories." There was accusation in Helen's words.

"She had you," Max said, a heaviness settling in his gut.

"And it would seem I wasn't enough." Helen shook her head. "She's all I have. I'm so afraid—"

"She'll be fine. I will find her and bring her home."

"How do you know that?" his aunt cried. "My God. After what we found upstairs…" She put a hand to her mouth.

Max couldn't think of anything to say to make her feel better. Helen had seen everything he had. "Did she ever mention anything about Debarry?" he asked. "Did the earl ever call—"

"No," she mumbled miserably. "She never once mentioned Lord Debarry. I didn't even think she knew him until...until last night. I've never even spoken more than a dozen words to the man."

"Had she done anything unusual recently?"

"No." Her aunt paused, as if a thought had stuck her. "She asked to have a miniature made."

"And that was unusual?"

"She had always refused to sit for a portrait before."

"Who was it for? The miniature?"

"I assumed it was for you." Helen's eyes widened.

"Do you have it?"

"Yes." She stood and went over to the mantel and took a tiny framed portrait from the ledge. "It came this morning. It was being set."

Max also stood. "May I see it?"

Helen returned to the settee and passed it to him. The artist had been incredibly talented and had captured her features perfectly. But gone were the ringlets and the girlish blue ribbon he remembered, and in their place was a somber seriousness. "Can I keep this?" he asked.

Helen hesitated, girding herself to argue.

"I should show it to Miss Moore and her associate. I think it important that they know what she looks like. They are still working on our behalf."

His aunt deflated, and she nodded.

A thought struck Max. "How did you know to hire Chegarre and Associates?" In hindsight, how had he not asked this question earlier? How had his upright, unbending aunt been familiar with people with...the skills that Miss Moore possessed?

"Every member of the ton knows about Chegarre and Associates," she muttered.

"I didn't." Though he supposed he wasn't really a member of the ton. He never had been. "What do you know about Miss Moore?"

Helen shrugged. "Nothing. Nor do I care to. All I need to know is that Chegarre's people can make certain Beatrice still has a future when this is all over. Because that is what they do. Make scandals disappear. And everyone knows it."

Max didn't like that Helen could not provide any more information about Miss Moore than he already knew. The lack of knowledge was beginning to nag, and he would rectify it as soon as possible. But it made sense that Helen had known about the firm. In his absence she had stepped into the void left by his parents. Made decisions, took care of details that he had never given a second thought to.

"I never thanked you for what you did for Bea," Max said, suddenly. "And everything else you've done for me. For us." He said it awkwardly. "I know it was not without a price."

Helen looked away. "Do you?"

Max frowned. "You filled a hole when Father and Mother died."

"Because you refused to." She stared into the fire. "I would have gone with him to Boston, you know," she said dully. "He asked me to go with him."

"Who?" Max had missed something in this conversation.

"Edward. He even asked me to marry him."

"Wait, what?" Max felt his forehead wrinkle in confusion. "Who is Edward?"

"Edward Shelby. He is a barrister. I met him at a conservatory. We share an interest in orchids. We have a great number of things in common."

"And you were engaged?" Why was this the first time Max was hearing of this?

"Not officially. He asked me to marry him before he left. He had a brother there who also practiced law. The two of them set up their own firm." She sounded infinitely sad. "He wanted me to come with him as his wife."

Max stared at his aunt. "You didn't go."

"Your parents had just died. You were in India. Someone had to look after the estate. Someone had to be here for Beatrice. I couldn't just take her away with me."

"I didn't know."

"He still sends me the occasional letter. Apparently orchids do not grow well in Boston." Her voice sounded far away.

"Why didn't you tell me earlier?"

"What was the point? I asked you over and over to stay when you first came back after their deaths. When you first assumed the title. You refused. And if you wouldn't stay for your own sister's sake, why would you have ever stayed for mine?"

Max felt a stab of guilt, which was ridiculous. How could he be held accountable for thwarting a dream he'd never known existed? "I could not stay, Helen. I do not belong here."

Helen gazed at him, her mouth twisted slightly. "You never wanted to belong."

"That is not true. But Father and Mother made it clear to me from the time I was six that I was not needed. My only duty to this family, in whatever occupation I chose, was to not tarnish the Harcourt name. I was expected to find my own path, build my own life. I did that, and have continued to do that. And it's kept the coffers filled and provided every necessity."

"And is that what you expect from Beatrice? And from me?"

"I beg your pardon?"

"That we simply stay out of the way and not tarnish the Harcourt name?"

Max clenched his teeth. "No. And it's not the same."

"Isn't it?" Helen sank back down on the settee as if the fight had gone out of her. "When we find Bea, will you stay then?" she asked Max without looking at him. "Will you stay here as the Duke of Alderidge?"

I can't. The answer was immediate. He didn't belong here in London now any more than he had when he was a child or an adolescent. His life, the one he had carved for himself, by himself, was across an ocean. The only life he had ever known, built on his own blood and sweat, was not something that he would or could simply abandon. Yet somehow he couldn't bring himself to say it.

Helen seemed to take his silence for the answer she had expected. "I thought so."

Max rubbed his hands over his face. "I'm sorry," he said, though he wasn't entirely sure what he was apologizing for. Lost family? Things that fate had commandeered and directed? Things that could not be recovered any more than time could be recaptured?

He looked down at Helen. "I think you've made a far better duke than I ever would have."

She met his eyes then, and all he saw was disappointment. "That is probably so. Since you never even tried."

Chapter Six

Ivory woke from a fitful sleep as the shadows were starting to get long. She sat up on her bed, rubbing her eyes. Her braid had come loose, and her hair rioted around her shoulders and down her back. She pushed it back from her face impatiently, thinking it rather perfectly represented how she was feeling right now—undone and scattered.

Ivory had returned to a silent house—Elise had not yet returned, presumably out escorting Mary to the coaching station and making sure she was safely on her way out of London. There was no message from Alex, Elise's brother, indicating he had come across anything helpful within his network of informants, nor was there word yet from any of the men she had employed to watch the homes of Lady Beatrice's friends. Knowing she needed a few hours of sleep to stay sharp, Ivory had climbed the stairs to her room and lain down on the bed, still wrapped in Alderidge's coat.

She'd told herself it was because the room was chilled

and because she was too tired to rebuild the fire that had died to embers, but she knew better. If anything, her body was flushed and feverish, yearning for things that she had long ago decided she could live without.

Her husband had been thirty years older than she when they'd married, his children from his first marriage already grown. Their physical relationship had been very much secondary to the bond of friendship that had grown between them. In that last year, when Knightley's health had declined, and then in the first years of widowhood, physical intimacy was something she hadn't even had time to consider, much less miss. But now...

Now she was acting like a lovesick, besotted schoolgirl. It was humiliating.

What did she even know about the Duke of Alderidge, anyway, besides the sparse facts that had been carefully recorded in the ledgers? She knew Maximus Harcourt loved his sister to a fault. He could be hardheaded and stubborn. He'd placed his trust and his faith in a street urchin because he saw honor beneath the rags. He could be controlling and arrogant.

He was a duke. Sometimes. He was a captain. Sometimes. He was a gentleman.

Sometimes.

She stood, struggling out from the heated cocoon of wool. She was feeling restless and sorry for herself, and if she had learned anything these last years, it was that such indulgences accomplished nothing.

She hurried downstairs, Alderidge's coat folded over her arms, darkness already painting the windows black. Someone had lit the lanterns in the drawing room, and Ivory ducked in and dumped the coat on the back of the long sofa. She'd intended to repair to her study and review what notes she had on Debarry, but she stopped as her eye fell on the pianoforte that sat silent against the far wall. It had been a long time since she had played. Since she had sung. Collette's mention of *Giulio Cesare* earlier had awakened another longing she had long since thought safely buried. Bloody hell, what was wrong with her today?

Yet she found herself powerless to keep from approaching the instrument, unable to stop her fingers from drifting across the keys. She struck a note, finding the right key, and suddenly she was singing, her voice rusty at first from lack of practice, but gaining strength and confidence as she went. She closed her eyes, immersing herself in the music, her memory supplying every word and every note. And as the last of the aria faded away, she realized she was smiling like an idiot, and perilously close to tears.

"Why did you stop?"

Ivory uttered a strangled shriek before whirling.

The Duke of Alderidge stood motionless at the door, a peculiar expression on his face.

"You scared me," Ivory snapped.

"I'm sorry," he said, not sounding sorry at all. "That was beautiful."

"How did you get in here?" she demanded, ignoring his compliment. "The door was locked." And that aria hadn't been for anyone but herself. Worse, while her identity wasn't a secret, it certainly wasn't something she advertised.

"No, it wasn't. And no one answered when I knocked."

Ivory frowned. Had she been distracted enough to forget? She shoved that to the side for the moment. "I wasn't expecting you—"

"Where did you learn to sing like that?"

Ivory relaxed fractionally. There were benefits to having a client who had spent almost no time in London. It was clear the duke was clueless as to who she had been in her former life. Which was just as well.

"Here and there," Ivory said ambiguously. It wasn't a lie.

"Why aren't you performing somewhere with a voice like that?"

Ivory laughed, though it sounded forced even in her own ears. "Why? You have an opening for a soprano on one of your crews? I confess, Your Grace, I will not be swayed by an offer of an elephant."

Alderidge's brows drew together. "I'm serious."

"That might be the understatement of the year," Ivory muttered.

"What does that mean?" he asked, stepping into the room.

And just like that, the duke was no longer examining her past.

Ivory exhaled a sigh of relief. "It means, Your Grace, that I have yet to see you smile since I met you."

"Pleasure has been in rather short supply as of late, don't you agree, Miss Moore? I haven't had anything to smile about."

She had all sorts of ideas about how to remedy that, none of them appropriate. All of them wicked.

"No, I suppose not." Ivory crossed the room and went to stand behind the sofa, putting a safe, physical barrier between the two of them. Self-consciously she tried to smooth her hair back. "What can I do for you, Your Grace?" There, that had come out normally. "Is there something that you require?"

The duke was circling the room now, his hands behind his back, his eyes roving over the papered walls, the painting that hung above the pianoforte, and the narrow bookcase with its collection of titles. He seemed restless.

She waited, allowing the silence to stretch.

"Who are you, exactly, Miss Moore?" he asked, pulling a volume from the shelves and examining the binding.

"I beg your pardon?" Dammit, they were back to this.

"You asked what I required. What I require, Miss Moore, are some answers. As your client, I am quite certain I am entitled to a few basic facts about the person I have hired."

"What do you wish to know?" She kept her voice pleasant.

"How long have you been working for Mr. Chegarre?" He opened the volume in his hands.

That seemed simple enough. "I have been with Chegarre and Associates for five years now, Your Grace."

"And what did you do before that?"

This answer was thornier. "I did a number of different things."

"Like what?"

I sang on some of the grandest stages in England. And France. And Italy. "I traveled."

"Where?"

"Around Europe." She always tried to use the truth whenever possible.

"Were you a spy for the Empire?"

Ivory felt her jaw slacken before a tickle of laughter rose. She choked it back. "And if I were a spy? Do you think I would actually tell you?"

The duke scowled.

Ivory took pity on him. "No, Your Grace, I was not a spy."

"And I'm just supposed to believe that?"

"Bit of a conundrum, isn't it?" She couldn't help but tease.

Alderidge sighed and closed the book. "What is your name? Your first name."

"Why is that important?"

"Because I want to know." He replaced the book on the shelf and approached the sofa. "You are privy to a secret that has the power to destroy my entire family. You hold everything I hold dear in the palm of your hand, and I know nothing about you. I don't even know your name."

"I am privy to a great number of secrets, Your Grace. None of which will ever be shared with anyone. Ever. But I don't see why—"

The duke's hands came down on the back of the sofa, making it shudder. His head was bent in frustration. "Please."

"Ivory," she whispered.

The duke lifted his head. "Ivory," he repeated, and the sound of her name on his tongue sent a wave of heat licking through her veins. "Thank you."

He hadn't shaved, and his jaw was once again darkened by blond stubble that begged to have her fingers explore the texture of it. His hair was still pulled back into a queue, and it was begging almost as loudly for her fingers to pull the leather thong from it and bury themselves in its thickness. He'd found another coat, this one lighter and more suited to the city, and the breadth of his chest and shoulders strained the seams. His hands, still gripping the back of the sofa, were strong, scarred, and callused.

He pushed away from the sofa then, coming around and advancing on her. She stood her ground, not knowing if it was pride or recklessness that was preventing her from backing away. He stopped in front of her and caught her chin with his fingers, tipping her face up toward his. "Why do your friends call you Duchess?" he asked. "How did you get that nickname?"

Ivory struggled to formulate a plausible answer. But it was impossible to think with the duke's hand cupping her face, his eyes searching hers. His hand moved from her chin to her hair, pushing the curls back gently, his eyes following the path of his fingers. And when he looked at her again, the desire that she saw reflected there nearly made her whimper with need. It would be so easy, she thought, to tell this man everything. To unburden herself on his strong shoulders and free herself of the layers and layers of half lies and hidden truths that surrounded her. It was an irrational, emotional need, she knew, born of the physical desire that had suddenly been awakened within her.

"Does it matter?" she asked. This man weakened her defenses like no other.

"I haven't decided," he said, and she wasn't sure if he was still talking about her nickname. His eyes dropped to her mouth, and the flutter in her lower belly turned into a steady throb.

"When will you decide?" she whispered.

"After this," he said, and then he kissed her.

It had been a lifetime since she had been kissed like this. No, she amended, she had never been kissed like this. Not by a man so powerful, his restraint a living, breathing thing, fraying the edges of her own. He pressed into her, deepening the kiss, and Ivory felt her legs go nearly boneless with her sudden need to have this man. She was shaking, for God's sake, and if she had been able to think, she might have been embarrassed.

Through a haze, she wondered if he would take her on the sofa. Or perhaps on the expensive Aubusson. Or against the wall. Or maybe all three.

"Ivory," he murmured against the skin at her throat, and there was a question in his voice. As if he were seeking her permission to do everything she wanted him to do.

Something she couldn't give him.

Ivory drew away from him, her breath coming in shallow gasps. "I can't do this."

His forehead came to rest against hers.

"Your sister..." She trailed off, a cohesive string of words eluding her at this moment. "You are a client."

"You're right," he whispered, and regret rang clearly. "I'm sorry. This...I shouldn't..." He couldn't seem to find the words either for what had flared between them.

"We shouldn't," she repeated.

His fingers tangled in her hair, and he forced her head back, her eyes meeting his. "Not right now," he said, his voice hoarse. "But when this is over, when my sister is safely at home, I am going to kiss you again, Ivory Moore." He dragged his thumb gently over her bottom lip. "And then you can tell me why your friends call you Duchess."

Ivory closed her eyes, knowing that a confidence like that was unlikely. This man was a captain more than he was a duke, and once this was over, he would return to his life at sea. Whatever existed between them might be incredible and passionate, but it would also be temporary and fleeting. And there was little room for secrets in such a relationship.

Alderidge straightened, his hands sliding from her, and

he stepped away. Ivory hated the acute feeling of loss that washed over her. He paced to the far side of the room, as if distance would cool the heat that had risen. As if distance might help the conversation return to more mundane matters.

He cleared his throat. "Can you at least tell me how my aunt was able to find you?"

That question was easy. And safe. She took a deep, calming breath. "The same way everyone finds us. She simply sent an anonymous message."

"Through the Lion's Paw."

"Of course." Her heart was starting to slow somewhat. "Sending a fleet footman to the Lion's Paw is far less incriminating than sending one to Covent Square. No one will ever admit to hiring Chegarre and Associates. To admit that is to admit that they have something to hide. That a skeleton or two has fallen out of one of their closets. Or more often, their beds. If you were to ask any of my former clients about me or this business, they will tell you that they have no idea what you are talking about. It's quite…liberating. I simply don't exist."

"Oh, Duchess, but you do," drawled a voice from the doorway.

⌒

Max spun to find a long, lean man just inside the study door. He was propped against the doorframe, his arms folded across his chest and his booted feet crossed as though he were casually waiting for a ferry. His hair was dark, curling at the collar of his coat, his eyes the color of dark amber. A long scar started at his upper lip and ran over his right cheekbone, disappearing just over his ear.

"Alex," Miss Moore said warmly, moving to greet him.

The man pushed himself off the frame to meet her, caught her hands in his, and bent, pressing his lips to her knuckles with a flourish. "It's been too long, Duchess," he said.

Max had to look away at the sight of another man's lips on Ivory Moore's skin. Skin that only a few minutes ago Max had explored with his own mouth and his hands. He had never, in all his life, wanted a woman the way he wanted this one. She had somehow slipped into his veins, like a particularly potent drug that had the ability to alter his perception of everything around him. He would have taken her on that sofa, had she not stopped him and reminded him that he was here in this room not to satisfy his lust, but to locate his sister.

The part of him that was still clinging to honor told him that he should be ashamed of himself. The rest of him just wanted to kiss her again.

"I saw you three days ago, Alex," Ivory was saying dryly.

"Like I said, too long." The man smiled up at her. "What was that? That you were singing? For it has been too long also since I heard your voice the way your voice was meant to be used."

Max watched Ivory freeze, his own reaction equal to her distress. Bloody hell, had this man been privy to their entire conversation? Had he witnessed their kiss? Heard the impassioned promise Max had made her?

"It was Handel's *Giulio Cesare*." She cleared her throat.

"It was very . . . provocative." The man's odd amber eyes flickered toward Max.

Ivory sniffed. "It was supposed to be. It's the aria Cleopatra uses to seduce the toga off Caesar."

"You don't say?" It was said with a smirk.

"I try to keep my doors locked for a reason, you know," Ivory said pointedly.

Alex made a sound of amusement, as if a locked door were merely a hiccup. "I was hungry, and didn't want to wait outside. Busy out there tonight. Your neighbors are rather forward with their attentions."

"My neighbors run a brothel, Alex. You're a man with a pulse. And all your teeth. What do you expect?"

"Some distance?" he suggested.

Ivory snorted.

The man straightened, the warmth fading from his eyes as he swung toward Max. "The Duke of Alderidge, I presume."

Max suddenly found himself the object of intense scrutiny, not for a minute liking the fact that this man knew his identity while Max remained ignorant of his. "You presume correctly." Everything about the man put Max on edge. He could see the sharp intelligence in his eyes and could sense the ease with which he moved. Had he met this man near a darkened wharf, he'd have already drawn his weapon.

"This is my associate, Mr. Alexander Lavoie," Ivory offered Max. "He owns a...gentleman's club."

The owner of a gentleman's club? The man looked more like an assassin.

"Why are you here, Your Grace?" Lavoie's eyes were hard.

"I am not sure what you're asking." Max met his challenge coldly.

"Most people who have cause to seek our help avoid unnecessary involvement. They distance themselves. They most certainly don't seek out this address. Nor do they seek out our...company."

So Lavoie had witnessed more than he should have. Max had no idea what this man was to Ivory, but the challenge was poorly veiled. Perhaps he really was an assassin. No matter. Max had dealt with more than one. He had the scars to prove it.

"My sister is missing, Mr. Lavoie," Max said, keeping his voice controlled. "Though it seems you already knew that. Miss Moore has committed to assisting me in my quest to discover her whereabouts."

Lavoie's lip curled slightly.

"Alex." Ivory was frowning, and the provocation in her voice was unmistakable. "There is a reason that you are here. Please be so kind as to share that with us."

Amber eyes slid to Ivory. "Perhaps His Grace should leave at this juncture."

"I'm not going anywhere," Max barked.

Lavoie frowned. "I don't think it's wise to—"

"He stays." Ivory's words rang with finality. Max felt something in his chest squeeze.

Lavoie's brows disappeared under the shock of hair on his forehead, and he watched Ivory with speculation. Ivory stared back impassively.

"Very well. There is a wager recorded in my betting books," the man said, his gaze returning to Max. "For five hundred pounds."

"Go on."

"It challenges Debarry to . . ." Lavoie hesitated.

Max stiffened, and his heart lodged in his throat. "To seduce my sister," he finished for him.

"Yes, though a different term was used. And it was not your sister who was named."

"Then who?"

"Lady Helen."

"My aunt?" Max was trying to wrap his mind around the possibility of Debarry in passionate pursuit of Helen. He failed. "But that's absurd. My aunt barely knew the man. Are you sure?"

From a bag he'd left near the door Lavoie produced a red leather-bound book that looked like an accounting ledger. He held it out to Ivory. "Take a look for yourself. I've marked the page."

Ivory accepted the book and opened it to a page that had been marked with a piece of leather string. "With whom was the wager made?" she asked, and her voice was all business.

"The Viscount Stafford."

It was no wonder Stafford had fled from Max at the ball. The wager might have been absurd, but it was certainly grounds for Max to call him out.

Ivory was running her finger down the page, stopping when she found the entry. "Was this bet public knowledge?"

Lavoie shrugged. "It's in my betting books. The use of them must be privately requested, and I do not keep them on display for casual perusal. But I can't guarantee that someone else besides the viscount and the late earl was not aware."

"When was the wager made?" Max asked, coming to stand next to Ivory.

"A month ago."

Ivory was frowning fiercely at the page. "This makes no sense. The earl was known for his love of younger women. In Debarry's file, I have an entire list of young..." She trailed off, a peculiar expression on her face. "Are there more like this in here, Alex?"

"More what? Wagers?"

"Yes. Wagers between Debarry and Stafford. Wagers like this that name older women as the object of a planned seduction."

It was Lavoie's turn to frown. "Perhaps. I can't say that I study every asinine wager some drunken idiot makes in my books, but I do try to stay informed." He reached for the ledger and flipped to the front. Pages snapped as he leafed through them. "Here," he said after a minute. "There is one from October. A wager between Debarry and Stafford that challenges Debarry to, ah, seduce—"

"Lady Marsden." Ivory said it flatly. "The widow of the late Earl of Marsden."

Alex started. "Yes. How did you know that?"

"Because in October, I smuggled Lady Marsden's eldest daughter out of a coaching inn just outside of London before anyone could recognize her. A very inebriated, tearful girl, who kept insisting she was going to be the next Countess of Debarry."

Max understood immediately, and a black rage was slowly rising and starting to blur his vision. It was just as well the earl was dead. And Stafford would soon be joining him, Max thought hazily.

"They couldn't name a young woman in these pages. But no one would care about a wager made on a widow or a spinster," Ivory said.

"The bastards." Lavoie looked furious. "I didn't catch it."

"You had no reason to," Ivory told him.

Lavoie didn't look any happier. "*Hmph.* Well, as I understand it from Elise's account of the scene, your sister got the upper hand on the earl, Your Grace."

Max jerked. Ivory's hand found his arm, preventing Max from reaching for the blade at his hip.

Lavoie missed none of it, and a faint gleam of what looked like approval sparked in his eye as he regarded Max. "Can't say I'm not glad."

"Are you trying to be an ass, Alex?" she asked.

"No, I'm trying to make you understand you're going to have to scrape up the viscount's remains if you let the good duke leave here alone."

Alex Lavoie spoke the truth. Max would take the viscount apart piece by piece.

"He will not be alone."

Max couldn't look at Ivory, afraid of what he might see. Lavoie was considering her again. "Has the Lady Beatrice been located yet?" he asked into the silence.

Ivory shook her head. "No."

"Hmm." Lavoie ran a hand through his dark hair. "It is possible that Stafford may know something. It is also possible that he knows too much. You may wish to have a word. Or if you prefer, I can do it for you. He'll be at my club tonight."

"And you know this how?" Max was pleased with how steady his voice sounded.

Lavoie turned those strange eyes on him. "Because it's Thursday. And the viscount is nothing if not predictable."

"You need not speak to him. I am quite capable of having my own conversations."

"Of course. But I don't suffer fools gladly, Your Grace. If you plan on killing this man, please be kind enough to make arrangements that don't involve my establishment. I do not enjoy entertaining the law. And blood is devilishly hard to get out of my upholstery."

Max was beginning to like this man. "Fair enough."

"No one is killing anyone," Ivory snapped. "A dead viscount who made a foolish bet will not help us find your sister, Your Grace."

"It would make me feel better."

Ivory scowled.

Lavoie smirked.

"Don't you have somewhere to be, Alex?" Ivory asked. "Gentlemen to swindle, fortunes to make?"

"I don't swindle. I…encourage."

Ivory rolled her eyes.

"Can I expect you tonight then?" Lavoie asked as he moved to the door.

Ivory opened her mouth to answer.

"Yes." Max did it for her.

Ivory made a sound of displeasure. "The duke and I will discuss it and come to an accord before we do anything."

"Hmmm. Well, if you do patronize my establishment tonight, or in the future, Your Grace, remember what I said about the upholstery."

"Go," Ivory said rudely.

Lavoie grinned at her and left as silently as he'd arrived.

"Let's go." Max was already moving.

"You're not going anywhere right now."

"Like hell I'm not." Max spun.

"Think," Ivory said, coming to block the doorway. "The wager that the viscount and the earl made was made in a betting book at a gaming club, and was by no means wholly private. Others may know about it. It is even possible that others may know the true nature of the wager."

Max was trying to concentrate on what she was trying to tell him, but all he heard was the word *others*. He felt another wave of fury crash through him. If that was true, then there were others who had done nothing. Others who had sat back to watch—

"You returned to London the same night that Debarry died. You tell me what conclusions some might draw."

Max froze, the anger draining out of him, to be replaced with something else entirely that made the hairs on the back of his neck stand up. "That I found out about the wager and killed him."

"Yes. You did seem rather enamored of killing his companion a moment ago."

"Oh, I still am."

Ivory pursed her lips in disapproval.

"Oh, don't look at me like that. If I had killed Debarry, I wouldn't have done it in my damn guest room and left him there for the damn butler to discover," Max said, beginning to pace the confines of the room. "I would have called him out properly and run him through. Or shot him. Either one would have done nicely."

Ivory sighed. "Regardless, that wager provides motive."

"And if someone accuses me of killing the earl because of it? Then what?"

Ivory was worrying her bottom lip again with her finger, and Max had to make an effort to concentrate. "I don't think anyone will if they haven't already." She paused. "It is a bit of a double-edged sword, Your Grace. A gentleman cannot openly accuse you of any possible crime without first admitting that he too knew of the wager, and long before you could have possibly become aware. Not only would he dishonor himself by admitting such knowledge, who's to say that he then might not be accused of exacting retribution from the earl himself? Who's to say he wasn't a champion of your sister, determined to defend her honor?"

She paused, her brows furrowed in thoughtful concentration. "At the very least, I could definitely portray it that way if it comes to that."

"Perhaps that is exactly what happened." Max was trying not to sound hopeful. "Someone discovered Debarry's diabolical intentions and hurriedly spirited my sister away before she could be innocently caught in a scandal that was not of her making."

"Mmmm."

"What does *mmmm* mean, Miss Moore?"

"Aside from the flower petals and ostrich feathers and empty wine bottles and red ribbons, your sister left her ball gown behind. That is not a garment that is easily removed if one is in a hurry. Why would she have taken the time to change unless she—"

"Are you trying to be an ass, Miss Moore?" He turned Ivory's words back on her.

"I know you refuse to hear this, Your Grace, but it's quite likely your sister was complicit in what happened last night, wager or no wager. The evidence suggests—"

"Until I have proof otherwise, Miss Moore, I will continue to believe the best about my sister."

"Mmmm."

Max clenched his fists. "Stafford was at that ball last night. I saw him there. He avoided me, in fact, and now I know why. He knows something."

"I agree."

"You do?"

"Yes. I think Alex is right, and we need to have a discussion with the viscount. But from here we're going to need to proceed with a little more flair than the last time a Smithfield bull crashed into a china shop."

Max stopped. "You said *we*."

"I did. There is little point in me believing, even for a second, that you will do the sensible thing and return home and let me handle this."

"You're getting smarter, Miss Moore."

"That wasn't the word I had in mind," she grumbled.

"What did you have in mind then? Regarding the viscount."

"You're actually asking me?"

"I've come to the conclusion that perhaps you have certain information and skills that I do not. At least here in London. And I've recognized that I need you—*them*," he corrected his slip, "if I want to help Bea."

"You're getting smarter, Your Grace." She smiled at him then, a genuine smile that wreathed her face and reached her eyes, and it did terrifying things to his insides. "Wait here."

She disappeared, only to return a few minutes later with a ledger that looked very much like the one Alex Lavoie had carried.

"What is that?" Max asked. "More wagers?"

"No," she said. "Just a less messy way to deal with Stafford."

Chapter Seven

Ivory swept into the club, and immediately her cloak was whisked away by a silent footman. A second footman appeared, bearing an engraved silver tray upon which glasses of champagne bubbled in the muted light. Ivory selected a glass and took a delicate sip, the golden liquid tickling her mouth. Heavens, this was a good vintage. Alex must have some high marks in the club tonight.

She put a hand to the bodice of her gown, resisting the urge to yank it up. It had been a long time since she had worn a gown like this, and she had almost forgotten the way cool air could so thoroughly and indecently caress one's bared shoulders and chest. The jewels at her throat were warm, though. The dark pearls had been one of the last gifts Knightley had given her, and it always gave her pleasure to wear them. She ventured farther into the interior, taking in the decadently papered walls, the heavy silk draperies, and the intricately patterned rug beneath her slippered feet. The gaming tables were full of men dressed in expensive evening wear, interspersed by aristocratic ladies in elaborate gowns.

Like her, every woman was masked. A ridiculous charade, because the identities of many of the aristocratic ladies were obvious even with the fine filigreed and decorated coverings. But an effective one, nonetheless, for without the pretense of anonymity, the club would not be as popular as it was. Ladies were free to flirt and indulge in all manner of things barred to them by daylight and etiquette.

"Duchess." Alex was suddenly beside her.

"Alex." Ivory took another sip of her champagne, the cool liquid sliding down her throat.

"I would suggest you don't breathe too deeply in that dress. I can't afford a riot."

"Flattery at its finest."

"I try." His tone changed. "Third table from the back. He's been playing for an hour. Not entirely sober, but not drunk as a wheelbarrow either."

Ivory let her gaze drift over the crowd to where a pot-bellied, silver-haired man was clutching a sloshing drink with one hand while the other squeezed the rear of one of Alex's serving girls.

"He gets marks for persistence," Alex remarked mildly.

Ivory watched as the serving girl slipped deftly away from the viscount's pudgy hands. The man tipped his chair back to watch her go and said something to his companions that resulted in a round of ribald laughter.

"Where's Elise?" Ivory asked.

"Fleecing a duke, a viscount, and two earls." Alex jerked his head in the opposite direction. Ivory caught a glimpse of a masked redhead in a risqué emerald gown, immersed in a game of vingt-et-un. Ivory could barely recognize Elise, even knowing who she was.

"Perhaps you should pay my sister more so she doesn't feel the need to empty aristocratic pockets here. She's too clever," Alex said with fondness.

Ivory snorted. "A girl needs her amusements."

"Is that what the good captain is to you?"

Ivory had just taken another sip of champagne and nearly choked. "I beg your pardon?"

Alex slanted her a sideways glance. "The captain. Or duke. Or whatever it is that he calls himself. Is he an amusement?"

Ivory cleared her throat, having never been more grateful to have a mask covering her face than she was at this moment. She could feel her cheeks burning. "I already had this conversation with your sister. Alderidge is a *client*."

"Who would have had you across that sofa—"

"I'm not going to dignify that with a response." She gritted her teeth. "And why were you spying on me?"

"That's what I do, Duchess." He cocked his head at her. "What's different about this man?"

Ivory fought to remain impassive. "There is nothing different about this man," she lied. "He requires my expertise. I require his money. He is a client, and is to be treated like any other client."

"No, he's not."

"Are you trying to pick a fight?"

"No." He crossed his long arms over his chest. "But if he is to be treated like any other client, I am wondering why the Duke of Alderidge just walked into my club."

Ivory's head snapped around to follow Alex's gaze, and

her fingers tightened convulsively on the stem of her glass. Her mouth went dry and her heart stuttered. He was dressed entirely in black again, from the well-cut coat that showed off the bulk of his shoulders and chest, to the tips of his boots. Even his shirt and waistcoat were black, and a cravat was nowhere to be seen. The severe simplicity was a marked contrast to the colorful, foppish attire of many of the gentlemen, and to add to the effect, he'd left his hair loose, letting it brush his shoulders carelessly. Not quite correct and not quite civilized. A little unpredictable. A little untamed.

The men closest to him were watching him with wariness. The women were watching him with something else entirely.

His eyes were skimming over the crowd with deceptive laziness, and they settled on Alex before sliding to her. Only the tightening of his jaw betrayed the fact that he had recognized her. And just like that she was transported back into the heat of her drawing room, when he had kissed her witless and promised her more.

"Why is he here?" Alex asked again.

Ivory was jerked out of her trance. "Because I asked him to be here."

"Since when do you ask clients to do anything besides deposit reams of cash into your coffers?"

"Since when is it your business?"

"Do you think that's wise? His presence, I mean?"

No, this isn't wise at all. Because in the moment when he had walked in and captured her eyes with his, she hadn't been able to remember why he was here. Why *she* was here. She hadn't been able to remember the viscount, or the duke's missing sister, or a wager that had the potential to bring the law down on Alderidge's head. All she had been able to think about was how it had felt when he had kissed her and touched her and said her name and—

"For the record, Duchess, I think I might like him." Alex had obviously given up on a response. Or, more likely, he had gotten all the response he needed.

Her cheeks flamed anew.

"But I'll like him less if anyone dies in here tonight." The last was said in a warning tone. "I hope you know what you're doing."

"Of course I know what I'm doing."

I have no idea what I'm doing.

⁓

Max watched Ivory walking toward him, trying to reconcile the vision in deep burgundy silk with the woman he'd left in Covent Square hiding in a shapeless grey dress. Trying also to control the instant lust that spiraled through his belly to pool uncomfortably in his loins. She was utterly breathtaking in the club's soft light, in a way that made every other woman in the room fade to nothing. Her hair had been pulled away from her face and pinned at the back of her head, though soft curls drifted down around her face and over her shoulders. The deep color of her dress and the exotic pearls at her throat made her flawless skin glow, her generous breasts creating a deep valley of shadow where they strained against the top of her bodice. She was the embodiment of sin and every unholy thing a man would do to possess it. And right now, every man in this room was picturing her in his bed. Or across a drawing room sofa—

"Who is that?" someone whispered in awe. There were a group of young men just behind Max, and the raw, licentious interest that had hushed their conversation was almost a palpable thing.

"Does it matter who she is?" Another voice joined in, slurring in snide jest. "A woman like that—you're not fit to kiss her feet."

"Wouldn't be her feet I'd be kissing," snarked his companion. "I'd put my tongue—"

Max backed up and stepped on the toe of the nearest man. The dandy was wearing dancing pumps of all things, and a chartreuse waistcoat so bright that it likely glowed in the dark. He leaned on the heel of his boot, and the man yelped like a wounded corgi.

"I beg your pardon." Max turned slowly.

"Bloody big oaf—" the young man started, only to have whatever he had been about to say next die in his throat.

Smart man.

The injured dandy limped off resentfully, his companions shuffling behind him, and Max watched them go for a moment before resuming his observation of Miss Moore. Ivory was almost even with him now.

Her eyes flickered to his face, though it was difficult to see her expression, hidden by her golden mask. "Your presence is a novelty here tonight, Your Grace. Remember you are being watched."

"If I'm being watched, it is because I am next to you." It was the truth. "You are stunning."

"Thank you."

He watched, fascinated, as a faint blush touched the parts of her cheeks visible below the mask.

"Stafford is at the third table," she said as she passed

him, pausing only briefly to take a sip of what looked like champagne. Her head tipped back, exposing the long column of her throat.

He looked away. He needed to focus. And not on Ivory Moore.

"Pink-striped waistcoat. Take the empty seat across from him. But give me two minutes." And then she was gone, winding her way through the tables.

Her words had the effect of channeling his attention away from his overwhelming desire for her and on to the man who had so unwisely used his sister's honor as a means of entertainment. His hands clenched at his sides.

He watched Ivory as she approached the table in question, running her fingers over the back of a carved chair as one might caress a lover. She said something he couldn't hear, but every man, including the rotund viscount in the pink stripes, suddenly seemed to sit up a little straighter. She bent slightly, as if to better hear a response, and the occupants of the table were treated to a spectacular view of her décolletage. A young man jumped up and nearly fell over himself to pull out a vacant seat. She was good, Max would give her that. She had four men in her thrall, and she had made it look absolutely effortless.

Miss Moore was now sinking into the offered chair gracefully, and the young man standing just behind her let his hands linger on Ivory's bare shoulders as she sat back in her seat. The sultry smile on her face didn't so much as wobble. In fact, it might even have widened.

Something black ripped through Max, eclipsing everything else, and with some shock he recognized it as jealousy. For a painful moment, Max didn't know what to do. He'd never had cause to be jealous before. Certainly not over a woman. As a seaman he'd never been under any illusion that the pleasure and the enjoyment found in bed-sport were anything other than temporary, nor did he believe they were ever exclusive. Emotion was never invested. Especially a dangerous emotion like jealousy. He had no idea what to do with this.

Max suddenly became aware he was no longer alone. He tore his eyes away from Miss Moore, only to have them collide with those of Alexander Lavoie. The man was watching him watch Miss Moore, a knowing look in that hooded gaze.

"Lavoie," Max said smoothly, all the while feeling as if he had been caught doing something improper. "Can I help you with something?"

Lavoie raised a single brow. "I simply came to welcome you to my club," he said smoothly. "*Bonne chance*, and all that."

Max made a rude noise.

"And to remind you that I am fond of my upholstery."

"I already promised Miss Moore not to kill the viscount in your club."

"Ah, but it wasn't the viscount I was worried about. It was the young pup with his hands on all that bare skin I was fearing for."

Max ground his teeth. Beside him Lavoie signaled a serving girl, and in seconds Max was sipping expensive Madeira.

"Don't ever make the mistake of believing she can't take care of herself," Lavoie said in a low voice, and then he was gone.

Max took a healthy swallow of his drink, the liquor burning a trail of fire down the back of his throat. It cleared his head as well. He started forward, forcing his body to relax. He needed all his wits. And all his restraint.

"Good evening." Max was standing next to Ivory, across from the viscount. He was careful not to look at her, and instead addressed the gentlemen. He was reasonably sure at least two of them had been at his ball last night. "Is there room for one more?"

The Viscount Stafford looked up and visibly blanched. Max resisted the urge to sneer. Or simply break his nose and shatter his teeth. Instead he kept his expression pleasant.

"Er—" Stafford was blinking rapidly.

"Of course there is, isn't there, gentlemen?" Ivory positively purred from her seat. "I have just joined the game myself, and we have yet to begin." She ran her fingers over the pearls at her throat, letting them drift toward her cleavage.

"Yes, yes." The young pup who had helped Ivory into her chair was mesmerized, and Max suspected he had no idea what he was agreeing to.

"Please sit…" She gestured at the chair beside her, letting her voice trail off as if expecting an introduction.

"Duke of Alderidge," Max obliged her, settling himself next to her at the table.

Across from him Stafford was shifting uncomfortably. He couldn't get up to leave right now without committing the unpardonable sin of cutting his social better. No one else at the table seemed to find anything amiss, however, and the mood was one of inebriated joviality. Pleasantries and introductions were exchanged, and the cards were dealt.

"A rough homecoming for you last night, as I understand it, Your Grace," remarked the man on the other side of Ivory. He was clearly foxed, and though his comment earned him a couple of mildly disapproving looks, everyone leaned in eagerly to hear Max's response.

"I beg your pardon?"

"I heard that the old Earl of Debarry danced one too many reels, and his heart gave out."

"Ah. You heard about that unfortunate occurrence."

"*Everyone* heard about that," the man said, and he was met with a round of knowing nods.

"It was quite distressing," Max replied, putting an appropriate amount of regret into his words.

"Heard you saw the earl before he turned his toes up. That true?" asked the young man with the wandering hands, emboldened by Max's apparent willingness to answer questions.

"I did. And I can't help but think that, if I had ignored his protests that he was fine and summoned a physician when I first saw him, perhaps Debarry still might be alive." He sighed heavily. "I partially blame myself for his death."

The players at the table all scoffed in unison, save the viscount. "Can't blame yourself, Your Grace. No one knows when your time might be up," someone offered.

Max met the viscount's eyes across the table. "No, you certainly don't," he agreed. "In fact, perhaps it's better if you never see it coming." He smiled.

Beads of sweat had broken out along the viscount's hairline, and the man reached for his glass, only to find it empty.

"I did not know Lord Debarry well," Ivory suddenly spoke up, smiling wickedly. "But I have heard from a number of ladies that he lived a very...fulfilling life." Insinuation oozed.

This brought another round of bawdy laughter to the table.

"That's true. And we should all be so lucky," someone commented with the same intimation.

"Then perhaps we should take a lesson from his example," Max suggested. "Do everything we can to enjoy life before we lie cold in the ground. Leave no pleasure untried and no unfinished business behind. Lord Stafford, don't you agree?"

"Yes?" It came out an uneven warble.

"Tell me, Stafford, if you could choose any meal at all, knowing it was your last one on this earth, what would you choose?" Max placed a card in his hand casually.

The viscount's eyes were darting nervously. "Ah..."

"Good heavens, but that's an impossible question," Ivory giggled beside him. "There are simply too many choices."

"What about a drink then?" Max asked. "If you were making a last toast to all you had *wagered* upon in life, what would you wish to be drinking?"

Stafford went grey.

"Brandy." The pup grinned as he raised his own glass.

"A good claret," someone else chimed in cheerfully.

"Stafford?" Max fixed him with another pleasant smile. "Pick your poison."

"Poison?" Stafford croaked.

"Liquor," Ivory clarified unnecessarily, rolling her eyes.

"Whiskey," the viscount whispered.

Max raised his hand and waved a serving girl over. "A whiskey for the good viscount then, if you would be so kind. His glass is empty."

"Of course, Your Grace." The girl gave Max a smile that

promised more than a glass of liquor, should he want it. She disappeared and was back in a flash, a full glass of whiskey in her hand. She offered it to Max.

Max pointed to the viscount. "That would be his."

She pouted but held the glass out to Stafford, who reached for it with a shaky hand. He promptly dropped it, the whiskey splattering all over the table and down the front of his clothes. The viscount shoved his chair back with a loud scrape and jumped to his feet.

"Good heavens," he mumbled. "So very clumsy of me."

The other players had pushed back their chairs as well, standing to rescue cards that were soaked with whiskey. The game was clearly over before it had really begun, and their expressions ranged from amused to annoyed at the disturbance.

"I must change," the viscount was babbling, avoiding Max's eye. "Terrible thing. I should go."

"Let me assist you," Max offered, also on his feet now.

"Oh no. No, no. I'm quite fine."

"Is there a problem here?" Alex Lavoie had suddenly appeared beside the viscount.

"Not at all," Max replied smoothly. "Just a little spilled whiskey, though it seems that the upholstery was spared the worst of it. I was just offering Lord Stafford my assistance."

"How very kind of you," Lavoie said with a sardonic edge.

"Come, Stafford, let's let these gentlemen get back to their game. If you will excuse us?" Max stepped back expectantly.

The viscount glanced around, taking in all the eyes upon him, and swallowed. "Of course. My thanks, Your Grace."

"Not at all."

Max fell into step behind the viscount, who was suddenly less anxious to get away from the crowd. "Please, Your Grace, I must insist—"

"You don't get to insist anything," said Max darkly. "Keep walking. Right outside, if you would be so kind."

Stafford shuffled forward, into the foyer of the club, but balked near the entrance, his sense of self-preservation finally surfacing. "Your Grace—"

"Good evening, gentlemen." Ivory slid neatly in front of the two men, blocking the path to the door.

"My lady!" the viscount nearly shouted with pitiable relief, clearly believing he'd found a savior to stall the inevitable violence he knew was coming. "Thank goodness! Would you care to—"

"Lord Stafford, if you have any interest in arriving home in one piece this evening, you would be best to refrain from speaking unless the duke instructs you to do so."

"What?" Stafford wheezed. That was clearly not what he'd been expecting. "Who are you?"

"I am the only person in this room who will make any effort to prevent His Grace from exacting his revenge for a certain ill-advised wager you made regarding his only sister."

The viscount suddenly deflated. "You must believe me when I say I meant no harm. We were drunk and—"

"Whose idea was the wager?" Max asked evenly.

"Debarry's! It was all his idea! He had seen Lady Beatrice at the Prevetts' ball, and she quite caught his eye. You know how Debarry was, always charming the women—"

He stopped abruptly when he caught a glimpse of Max's face.

"Who else is aware of your idiocy?" Ivory asked.

"No one! I swear!"

"Tell me where the earl liked to take his conquests," Ivory asked.

"His conquests?"

"Oh, come now, Stafford, do you think me a half-wit? The seduction of the Lady Beatrice was hardly the first time you and Lord Debarry have made such a wager regarding a young debutante."

"I'm sure I don't know what you mean." The viscount ran a hand through his thinning hair.

"Stop wasting my time." Her voice had an edge.

"I don't know—"

"He's all yours, Your Grace," she snapped, turning to leave. "Do with him as you wish. I can't imagine anyone will come looking."

"Wait!" Stafford wheezed.

Ivory turned back slowly. "You have one chance to impress me with the truth, Stafford."

"He never meant any harm, you see?" The viscount was tripping over his words. "He'd take them to an inn sometimes, outside the town limits and in disguise, so that they wouldn't be recognized. He said the thrill of slipping a chaperone and a clandestine meeting was always more of an aphrodisiac than anything that could be bought. But he treated them like princesses. The lonely ones, looking for adventure. Wallflowers or diamonds, it mattered not. He said all women were beautiful and should be worshipped as they were meant to be."

"And would he take them to his home?"

"Never his home." He licked his lips. "But sometimes the homes of the ladies themselves. The danger of discovery was all part of the grand adventure, he said."

Max thought he might be ill. "And my sister was one of his grand adventures?"

"No! Lady Beatrice was different— Oh God. You killed him, didn't you?"

Max sneered. "Of course I didn't kill him. If I had killed him, no one would ever have found the body." He was starting to sound like Miss Moore. "And I certainly wouldn't have done it in my *house*. I would have chosen a much better location. The back of a gentleman's club just like this one, for instance."

Stafford whimpered and wiped his hand over his perspiring forehead.

"How was she different?" Ivory asked.

"I beg your pardon?" The viscount licked his lips.

"You just said Lady Beatrice was different. How?"

"Debarry fell in love with her!" Stafford rasped. "He wanted to marry her. Ask her yourself! She'll tell you he proposed. More than once. She'll also tell you she refused him."

"That is absurd." Max was trying to make sense of this, but his emotions were churning wildly through him. Horror. Disappointment. Guilt. Anger. It was making it hard to think with any clarity.

"Who else knew about Lord Debarry and Lady Beatrice?" Ivory asked evenly.

Stafford's eyes were wide. "No one. Just me, but I never told anyone. I swear."

"Mmmm." She was tapping a finger on the waist of her gown.

Rage was rising like a fast, hard tide within Max, drowning his guilt and disappointment. He reminded himself that he couldn't afford a scene. After everything, he couldn't afford people asking questions about why the Duke of Alderidge had beaten Stafford to a bloody pulp in the foyer of a gentleman's club.

"Have you ever seen a shark feeding, Stafford?" Max asked.

The man's breathing was labored as he shook his head.

"They follow my ships from time to time, and it amuses my crew to throw spoiled meat into the water for them. Fascinating creatures, sharks, the way they tear things into tiny little pieces. An entire side of beef the size of a man can just vanish without a trace in less than a minute." He paused. "I'd hate to hear even a breath of rumor that calls Lady Beatrice's honor and reputation into question. Do we understand each other?"

The viscount looked like he might have an apoplexy.

Ivory stepped forward slightly. "Excuse the duke, Stafford. His Grace is, after all, a man used to the unforgiving hardships of the sea and given to barbaric tendencies from time to time." She looked over at Max briefly. "But in the case of his sister, he is not without just cause, wouldn't you agree?"

The man's glistening head bobbed frantically. "Yes, yes. Just so."

"That's good to hear. Rumors can be quite ruinous, indeed. Like one that might bring attention to the large sums of money you've fleeced from various peers in the last decade by selling them fictitious stock in a certain import business. I understand that debtors' prison is a miserable place to live out your remaining years."

Whatever color had been left in the man's face drained, and the viscount staggered slightly.

Ivory had lost Max somewhere in the last bit of the conversation, though he didn't really care. He was holding on to the last remaining shreds of his restraint with desperation. His hands were balled into fists, and he was a little worried that they might be shaking. "Get out of my sight, Stafford."

The viscount stumbled away from the door, back into the safety of the club, crashing past a group of gentlemen on their way in.

"Sharks, Your Grace?" Ivory murmured. "Really?"

Suddenly Max couldn't get out of the club fast enough. He needed to get away from the press of people and the overpowering scent of perfumed, perspiring bodies. He could feel his restraint slipping like water running through his fingers, and he needed some space to collect himself. He needed the icy air to cool the frustration and the fury that had risen. He needed...out. Before he went after the viscount and did something he would regret later. "I need to leave."

"Then let's go." He could hear the concern in Ivory's voice.

"I say, Your Grace!" The familiar voice erupted from the group of men who had just come in and were dispensing with their coats and hats. "Hullooo!"

Max swore. "I can't do this right now." He also couldn't get past the group blocking the entrance.

Ivory's hand was on his arm. "Come with me—"

"Your Grace! How fortuitous to see you again, and so soon!" Barlow was suddenly in front of him, clapping him on the shoulder with enthusiasm.

Max jerked violently away from the touch, but the man seemed oblivious. "Please excuse me. I was just on my way out," he said through clenched teeth.

"No! You can't leave! I must insist you join me!" Barlow refused to move. Instead he dropped his voice conspiratorially and winked at Max. "Now, I don't mean to brag, but I am quite accomplished when it comes to whist. I believe you and I would make splendid partners, Your Grace. I fancy we could do quite well together here tonight, if you know what I mean." He raised his hand to slap Max on the shoulder again. Every muscle in Max's body tensed, and for a horrifying moment he wasn't at all sure he wouldn't simply level Barlow where he stood, if only to escape.

He took a step toward the man, and suddenly Ivory was in front of him, her body pressed against his length, her arms wrapped around his neck, and her face barely an inch from his. She kissed him then, a hot, open-mouthed kiss that wiped his mind of everything except the feel of her lips and her fingers curling into his hair. His own hands came up, one to her waist and one to cradle the back of her head as she sucked at his bottom lip, her teeth grazing his flesh. His body reacted with staggering speed, the blood roaring in his ears and straight to his groin. He covered her mouth more fully with his, seizing control and exploring the depths of the kiss with his tongue. She opened beneath the onslaught instantly, and a growl rose from his throat as she took everything he was giving and demanded more. The world around him dropped away, simply ceased to exist, until Ivory tipped her head, breaking the contact. She turned within his embrace to face Barlow.

"Find another partner," she purred in a throaty voice that would make a saint sin. "His Grace already has one tonight. If you know what I mean." She winked at the man from behind her mask.

The earl had reddened. "Er, I—"

Ivory slipped from Max's grasp, catching his fingers with hers. The crowd at the entrance had since dispersed, and Ivory tugged him in that direction.

He made his way out into the night behind her, welcoming the blast of cold air. She released his hand once they were clear of the door and stopped, turning to face him.

"Feel better?" she asked.

Feel better? No, he didn't feel better. He felt completely out of control. His thoughts and wits had scattered like grapeshot, and his body was on fire. "Why did you do that?"

She was standing there in the darkness, barely a foot from him, looking up at him through the ridiculous mask. "You looked a little cornered in there. I was afraid you were going to do something you'd regret."

He had done something he regretted. He had kissed Ivory Moore again, and now the beast he'd thought he had caged was starting to claw its way out. It was demanding release. It was demanding that he finish what she had just started.

Loose tendrils of hair rested against her cheek and her neck, and the burgundy silk hugged every curve and hollow of her body. Those beautiful dark eyes of hers shone behind the mask, full of calm intelligence. He needed her. He wanted her. Wanted to give her everything, every pleasure that she could imagine and then those that she couldn't. He would have her speechless, he would have her begging, he would have her saying—

"Perhaps we should continue this conversation elsewhere."

Max stepped away from Ivory, trying desperately to disperse the fog of lust that was addling his mind. What the hell was he doing? He was acting like a randy sailor on his first shore leave, and in another minute he would have had her up against the wall of a gaming club like a twopenny whore.

"I'm sorry," he rasped.

"Please don't be," she responded. "I'm afraid I started that. In hindsight I might have been better to choose a different method of distraction." She sounded distant. Cool.

A different method of distraction? That's what she called what had just transpired between them? He needed to pull himself together and focus on what was important.

"How did you get here tonight?" she was inquiring of him, as if she had just encountered him on the street by happenstance. "Do you have a horse? Or a carriage?"

"I hired a hackney." He finally managed a sentence. Why were they speaking of such tedious matters? When everything seemed to have come apart, and all control seemed to have been lost? When he barely recognized himself?

"Ah. As did I. Perhaps—"

"Your Grace?" The voice came from somewhere beyond Ivory.

"Yes?" Max stepped to the side to find a young boy wrapped in a faded coat hopping from foot to foot on the pavement, a little out of breath. He seemed strangely familiar.

"I got a message fer ye, milord." He thrust out a folded paper with Max's name written across the front and the back sealed with a blob of rusty-red wax.

Max snatched at it, recognizing Bea's handwriting instantly. "How did you know I was here?" he asked, turning the paper over in his hands as though the exterior might provide some sort of clue to its contents.

"The man in front of your house said ye weren't home. Said ye'd come here. An' I can't collect my shillin' unless I put the message right into yer hand. Nothin' in it for me tonight if I have to take it back to Gil." The boy held out his own hand. "The man also said there'd be an extra shillin' fer me if I brought this to ye here."

Max suddenly placed the youth as one of the messengers he'd seen at Gil's. "What man?"

"Mine." Ivory had moved beside him. "I still have your house under surveillance." She jerked her chin in the direction of the messenger. "Pay the boy, Your Grace. He's earned it."

"Duchess?" The boy's voice rose. "Oi, I didn't recognize you! Thought you were a ladybird. One o' the expensive ones." The boy suddenly slapped a hand over his mouth. "Er, that is—"

"That is quite all right," Ivory said with a wry note. "That was the idea."

"Right." He seemed to accept this without question and shifted impatiently as Max searched for the requisite coins.

"You in a rush?" Ivory asked.

"Aye. King's having an auction. Lots o' invitations to deliver. If I can get back faster, I might get another delivery tonight."

"Mmmm. When is the auction?" Ivory asked with what sounded like curiosity tempered with distaste.

The boy shrugged. "Dunno. Soon."

"Who is King?" Max asked. Not that it mattered. Not unless he could help him find his sister.

"A . . . businessman," Ivory said. "Specializes in the sale of rare and sought-after objects."

"She means pinched stuff," the boy clarified helpfully.

"Gil says he's got some bloke with a boatload of fancy stuff this time. Old stuff dug out of some cave in a desert or something."

This time it was Max who shifted impatiently. He was uninterested in any of this. He found two shillings and held them out.

"For your trouble," Max said shortly. He would give the boy any amount of money if he would simply be on his way.

"Thank ye." The coins vanished with astonishing speed, and without another word the messenger was running back down the street.

Max snapped the seal, brittle in the chilled air, and pulled the paper open.

"Dearest Alderidge," Max read. "I am deeply sorry for the troubles I have caused, and I never intended any of this to happen. I will be leaving London for a while. Please respect my wishes and do not look for me. I am safe, and I will write you when I am able. —B."

Max passed the letter to Ivory with unfeeling hands. She took the paper with great care and tipped it to the light from the club's window.

"This is Beatrice's handwriting?"

"Yes."

"She called you Alderidge again. Not Max. Does that sound like the sister you know?"

"I think it's pretty clear I don't know my sister at all. She was having an affair, for God's sake," Max said dully, reality finally settling in like a lead weight. "She and the Earl of Debarry were—"

"In love."

That was kind.

Max pinched the bridge of his nose. "You've been saying that since the very beginning. I've just refused to listen."

"I am not always right."

"Don't patronize me."

"Fine. I'm always right. And it's about time you admitted it."

Despite himself, Max felt his mouth twitch. He knew what she was trying to do.

"Cheer up, Your Grace. Your sister, if the viscount is to be believed, and I am rather inclined to do so, turned down a marriage proposal from an earl."

"She also tied him to her bed."

"Perhaps he was *her* grand adventure," Ivory said quietly.

Max should have been horrified. Instead he just felt... sad. "What kind of man asks a woman to marry him without seeking out consent from her guardian first?" Max asked, recognizing the absurdity of his question. Propriety and etiquette had died long before the earl wrapped in red ribbons did.

"A man in love?"

Again, she was being kind.

"I should have taken her to India with me when she asked."

"You still can. She's not dead. But she is going to need your understanding. Just because she turned down Debarry's marriage proposal does not mean she didn't care for him. Wherever she is hiding right now, she is likely grieving as much as she is terrified about the scandal she may have left behind. She'll want to come home, but she shouldn't be scared of you too."

"Why would she be scared of me?"

"You just threatened Stafford with sharks, Your Grace."

"And you threatened him with—"

"Exposure. He's no better than a common thief."

Max stared at Ivory, thinking of the ledger she had held in her hands. *A less messy way to deal with Stafford*, she had said. "How did you know—"

"I get paid to know these things, Your Grace." She rubbed her hands on her arms and shivered. "But see? I am always right."

Max ignored her attempt at levity. "Did you not wear a cloak?"

"I did. It's still inside."

"I'll fetch it for you—"

"I think it's best if we remain out here."

If you remain out here, she meant. Away from Stafford. Max heard it beneath her smooth suggestion.

"I will get my cloak from Alex later."

Max yanked off his evening coat. "Wear my coat."

"You must stop making a habit of dressing me."

Ironic. He had been fantasizing about undressing her since he'd met her.

He swung the coat over her shoulders, trying not to touch her bare skin. "No argument?" he asked.

"I'm getting smarter." She looked up at him, her eyes soft. "Are you all right, Your Grace?"

"Of course I am," he lied.

"You should probably return home."

He didn't want to return home. He wanted to pretend none of this had happened and that his only responsibility right now was the thorough seduction of Ivory Moore. But he couldn't do that. Not yet. "I know. I need to tell my aunt the truth, even if it's the last thing she wants to hear from me."

"Do you want me to come with you?"

Yes.

"No. I'm not twelve years old, Miss Moore. I don't need you to hold my hand through what is bound to be an unpleasant conversation." It probably sounded rude, he knew, but it was better than what he wanted to say. It was better than begging her to stay with him, not just for a conversation, but for an evening. A night. A week. As long as it took to get her out of his system.

"That wasn't what I was suggesting, Your Grace."

Max looked away. "I'm sorry."

"Will you be at your town house tomorrow then?" she asked, and her voice was full of quiet understanding.

"No. I'll need to go back to the docks. To my ship." He would sort out what he could with Helen tomorrow morning. Then he would sort out what needed to be done with the part of his life that he had neglected while he dealt with viscounts and scandals and runaway sisters and tales of star-crossed lovers.

And then he would sort out what needed to be done about Miss Moore.

⁓

Alderidge hired a hackney and gave the driver Ivory's address, climbing in behind her and taking the seat opposite her. He stared out the window, unmoving. Neither spoke. There was nothing to say, at least nothing Ivory wanted to pursue. Though it would seem the mystery had been solved, Beatrice was still gone. The earl was still dead.

And she'd kissed Maximus Harcourt again.

Ivory squirmed and pulled the mask from her face. Her

stays were suddenly suffocating, and the dampness between her legs was becoming an all-consuming distraction. She'd acted on instinct in the club, seeing a man teetering at the edge of his endurance, looking for any excuse to vent his frustration. He would have taken that annoying little man's head clean off if she hadn't intervened.

And a real sacrifice it was for you, a voice in the back of her head mocked. And now, in the dark of a rather shabby hackney, her actions mortified her. She had been reckless and utterly unprofessional. She'd let her own needs eclipse everything that she knew to be right. And smart. And safe.

Again.

Covent Square was a teeming mess of action at this hour—the theater had concluded its evening performance and many of the attendees were now on the hunt for further entertainments. The taverns were positively bursting at the seams, and there was heavy traffic in and out of the many brothels. Someone, somewhere, was playing a horn, though the bleating, screeching noise could barely be heard above the raucous laughter and shouts. Carriages and horses jockeyed for position on the streets, and no one even noticed their arrival.

"Let me see you in." It was the first thing he'd said since they'd left the club.

"No. After everything, you don't want to have to explain what you were doing at Chegarre and Associates should someone recognize you." She was shrugging out of his coat.

"I'll have my secretary settle with you as soon as possible for your services."

Ivory bit her lip. It was bizarre, this ending of their partnership. This official removal of an excuse to see him. To be near him, to work with him. "We could continue to look for Lady Beatrice—"

"No. She has made it abundantly clear that she does not want me searching for her. She likely believes I'll pack her off to a convent in Wales at my first opportunity. Me chasing after her will only drive her further away. If I have learned anything, it is that Beatrice is no longer a child, and I cannot continue treating her like one. I refused to let my title dictate the way I lived my life. Why should it dictate hers?" He sighed. "It is up to Beatrice to choose a life for herself from here. I—well, *you* have made sure she still has choices. But this has to be her choice, and I must respect it."

Ivory nodded, though she wasn't happy that she had not been able to see Beatrice home safely. It chafed, that failure. "It would seem then that our business is concluded."

The duke caught her hand in his under the coat she still held. She could feel the ridges and calluses of his skin tighten against her own. "Do you remember what I promised you, Miss Moore?" His voice was low and fierce.

When this is over, when my sister is safely at home, I am going to kiss you again.

"Yes," she whispered.

"Then our business is not concluded. Not even remotely." He traced the edge of her jaw with his free hand. "But I will not do what I wish in the back of a hackney. Nor will I do it when there are still matters I must attend to."

Ivory shivered beneath his touch.

"When we…conclude our business, Ivory Moore, it will be without distraction. It will be without constraints and rules. I will not be a client. I will not be the man with the missing sister. I will not be a duke, or even a captain. I will simply be ... something else."

Ivory stopped breathing.

"Will you give me time?"

She rather thought she would give this man anything should he only ask, and that admission was terrifying. "Yes."

Chapter Eight

There you are. Thought I might find you down here." Elise strolled into the kitchen, where Ivory was nursing a cup of warmed milk laced liberally with whiskey. "Couldn't sleep?"

"No," Ivory admitted.

A full twenty-four hours had passed since Ivory had last seen Elise sitting at the gaming tables in her brother's club. A full twenty-four hours had passed since Maximus Harcourt left her with promises that had her in a constant state of anticipation and longing.

She might never sleep again. At least not without dreams that left her restless and aroused.

But that was what happened when she let a man like Alderidge get under her skin. And now he was the only thing she could think of. Which was ridiculous and not a little embarrassing. She considered herself a woman of the world. Level-headed, self-possessed, intelligent. Not given to flights of fancy. But what she was feeling right now was unlike anything she had ever experienced. As though she had stepped off the edge of a cliff and was hurtling through space, unconcerned and uncaring where the bottom might be.

"Duchess?"

Startled, Ivory looked up to find Elise waving a hand in front of her face.

"Are you all right? You looked like you were a million miles away."

Not a million miles. Just at the East India Docks with a pirate captain.

"I'm sorry. I'm fine." She flushed and grasped for a change in topic. "Where were you?"

Elise shrugged and moved away, disappearing into the pantry. "At work." Her voice was muffled. She made a sound of glee and emerged with a cloth-covered plate of scones. "In addition to helping you hide bodies, I am also an actress, in case you've forgotten. And some of us," Elise said, uncovering the plate and putting it on the table, "still practice our craft on a stage and not in the middle of a gentleman's club." She sat down across from Ivory on a polished bench, selected a scone, and took an enormous bite with an appreciative sigh.

"What's that supposed to mean?"

A pair of hazel eyes widened, and Elise nearly choked. "Surely you jest."

"I have no idea what you're talking about."

"Let me refresh your memory then. It involved a duke, your mouth, and his hands on your—"

Despite her discomfiture, heat built instantly within her. "You saw that."

"Half the people in the club saw that."

Ivory groaned.

"Well, maybe I'm exaggerating. I doubt very many saw that. But I was watching. Because that is what I do."

"I thought Alderidge was going to kill someone. I was trying to distract him."

"Well, it worked. He didn't kill anyone." She had finished her scone and was reaching for another. "Or did he?"

Ivory shook her head. "Not that I am aware of. Yet."

"Well, if the Viscount Stafford washes up against the bridge pilings in the morning, we'll know you should have taken Alderidge home, tied him to *your* bed, and finished whatever you started."

Ivory willed her expression to remain neutral, yet failed spectacularly, judging from Elise's expression and the grin that was creeping across her face.

"Tell me he wasn't a gentleman, Duchess." It was said with glee.

Ivory wasn't ready to discuss Maximus Harcourt and his promises with Elise just yet. "Don't be absurd. Alderidge understood that what happened in the club wasn't...real. I do not get involved with clients. Ever."

Elise made a rude noise. "You both did a good job of convincing me otherwise. I saw the way he looked at you in that club, Duchess. And there was nothing pretend about it."

"Do you have anything relevant that you'd like to add to this case that isn't your opinion?" Ivory asked. She was not going to discuss what had happened last night. Or what might happen in the nights to come.

"Is the Duke of Alderidge still a client?" Elise asked innocently.

"No, as a matter of fact, he is not. His secretary settled his bill promptly this morning."

"Well then, I have no idea what you're waiting for, Duchess. Why you're still sitting here and not tying His Grace—"

"Stop. Please."

Elise gazed at her, and Ivory knew her face was flaming. "What is different about this man?" she asked.

"Your brother asked the same thing. And I'll tell you what I told him. Nothing."

"Is it because he doesn't know who you used to be?"

"What? Why would that matter?"

"Because he has no interest in the Ivory who once graced great stages and who men competed to own. Because he has no interest in the Ivory who became the Duchess of Knightley. He simply wants...you. Just as you are now."

Ivory stared into her cup. Elise saw too much, which made her unnerving. And made her invaluable.

Elise leaned forward and perused the remaining scones on the plate. "Lady Beatrice was having an affair with Debarry, wasn't she?"

She was giving Ivory a reprieve, and they both knew it. "Yes."

"I was right!" Elise crowed.

"What's more, his lordship had apparently fallen madly in love with her. Even wanted to marry her."

"You don't say?" Elise sobered slightly. "Debarry's death must have been a horrible shock. I can see why Lady Beatrice panicked so completely."

"Mmmm."

"The duke must have been relieved. Well, perhaps *re-*

lieved is the wrong word. No one wants to know that much about a sibling's sexual escapades, believe me."

"Mmmm."

Elise narrowed her eyes. "Stop *mmmm*-ing me. I know that look too well."

"She's leaving London." There was still something about that that bothered Ivory.

"Who?"

"Lady Beatrice."

Elise paused with her hand halfway to the plate, startled. "How do you know that?"

"She sent Alderidge a second message last night. Apologizing for her actions and asking him not to look for her."

"*Hmph.* Well, I can understand that. I wouldn't much want that man hunting me down for indiscretions either." She chose a scone as her eyes narrowed. "And what do you mean second message? When did she send the first one?"

Ivory related the contents of the first note that had been delivered to the duke, and the circumstances of its delivery.

"So Lady Beatrice was lucky enough to have an unidentified gentleman at the ball help her escape from the house and send messages on her behalf. His Grace should probably be sending him a thank-you." Elise paused. "Did you suggest that Alderidge leave London altogether as well? Lady Beatrice might be persuaded to return home earlier if her brother is not ominously lurking in some dark corner of the house just waiting to pounce. You'll have to kiss the duke again once he finds his sister in order to keep him from killing her—"

"What did you say?" Ivory sat straight up.

"I said you'll have to kiss the duke again—"

"No, before that."

"That an unidentified man from the ball had helped Lady Beatrice."

"Why from the ball?"

Elise blinked. "Well, someone must have told her Alderidge was back. She wrote a note to her brother, not to Lady Helen, in the wee hours of the morning. And the only people who knew the duke was in London were the people who would have seen him at his ball. The duke said he came directly from the docks to his house, and it's not like there was a parade organized through the streets of London to herald his return."

Ivory groaned. That was a detail that never should have slipped by her. Why had she missed that?

Because you've been distracted by Maximus Harcourt ever since Maximus Harcourt stepped into your life.

Elise tore a piece from her scone, her head tipped in thought. "Whoever it was likely smuggled Lady Beatrice to his home, or somewhere close. He probably left and came back, but his absence may not have been noted if he wasn't gone long."

"You're right." Ivory stood, stepping over the bench. "I need a guest list. I have a general description of the man, at least enough to exclude a large number of more, er, substantial guests. We can start visiting the mews behind each of their homes. Beatrice did not walk very far in her chemise. Somewhere there is a driver or a groom who saw something."

"Where are you going?"

"To find the duke."

"But it's the middle of the night."

"Which is why I am not going to Lady Helen's." Ivory was already at the door.

"Do you want to take some red silk ribbons with you?" Elise called after her, and Ivory could hear the smirk that lay beneath her words.

⁓

After dropping Ivory at her door last night, Max had considered going straight to the docks, but in the end he'd gone back to his home in St James's. Whether it was guilt or his inability to avoid what was his responsibility, he couldn't run away from the difficult conversation that was waiting for him with Helen. It was best to deal with unpleasantness immediately. Procrastination never did anyone any favors.

He had crept into his silent house and slept a few hours before being wakened by the dawn. He was waiting in the morning room when his aunt came down, and once she was seated, he told her everything as he knew it. There was no point in leaving out any of the details, or trying to soften the blow. His aunt deserved to know the truth. All of it.

She absorbed his words with her usual silent stoicism. He couldn't for the life of him tell what she was feeling. Angry? Disappointed? Or possibly both. At Beatrice and himself. He'd offered to stay to keep her company, but she'd declined. In fact, she'd suggested it would be better if he stayed somewhere else for a few days.

Max had returned to the East India Docks and thrown himself into his work that had been neglected. Luckily, most of his crew were ashore, enjoying their hard-earned money in other pursuits. The few who were keeping an eye on the *Odyssey* seemed to sense his agitation and gave him a wide berth. There was a reason he hired smart men.

There had been customs officials to deal with, supplies

to order, and a full report to be reviewed on the condition of the ship and the repairs required. He'd inspected sails, caulking, and cannons. He'd even spent time unearthing the letters his sister had sent him over the years, skimming the most recent for clues that might tell him where she had fled, but he'd come up empty-handed.

As darkness fell he'd tried to find rest within the familiar confines of his cabin, but sleep had eluded him. The small hours of the morning had found him pacing the upper decks of the *Odyssey*, his thoughts swinging wildly between Ivory Moore and his sister, who was still missing.

He wanted Ivory. With an intensity that unsettled him. Yet how could he allow himself the luxury of pursuing pleasure when Beatrice was still out there somewhere? If he were an honorable man, a good man, a decent brother, he would be doing everything in his power to make sure she was safe. Not chasing his own selfish desires.

He had thought he could give Beatrice her space and trust that she would come back when she was ready. Except, he finally admitted to himself, he couldn't.

Not that he would chase after her or show up somewhere, demanding that she return home with him. He didn't want to spook her further. But he needed to know where she was. Just so he could keep a careful eye on her welfare from a distance. Make sure she had somewhere safe to stay. Enough to eat. Until she was ready to come back.

He didn't care about Debarry or that she'd had an affair with him. Well, he cared, but he certainly wasn't going to disown Bea over it. Her judgment had been horrific—she'd been reckless and selfish and unthinking—but she was still his sister. He still loved her.

The *Odyssey* was moored directly to the wharves, and the ship was unnaturally still. Protected as it was from the currents and the wind, there wasn't even the slap of water against the hull to break up the silence of the night. Tonight it was cold and clear, the moon creating strange shapes and shadows all around him. A light fog drifted around the forest of masts within the basin, giving the illusion of a moonlit fleet flying through the clouds. It was almost eerie.

Max knew that by dawn the docks would come alive, and the sounds of men and beasts starting their daily toils would echo across the basin and bounce off the looming walls of the warehouses that ringed the docks. People would go on about their daily lives.

And somewhere out there, Beatrice still eluded him.

He jammed his hands into his pockets, his fingers finding a square of heavy paper. He drew the card out of his pocket, smoothing out a corner that had been bent. No matter how he looked at it, he still needed Ivory. Not for himself, but for his sister. Needed her cleverness, her resources, her calm assurances. He needed—

"Your Grace?"

Max's heart shot into his throat, and he spun, his hand going to the blade strapped firmly at his waist.

Ivory Moore was standing on the deck, the hood of her cloak pushed back, the moonlight illuminating her hair and her face. It was as if she had appeared, summoned simply by his thoughts. Instantly he found himself fighting the impulsive, powerful part of him that was demanding he simply sweep her up into his arms and carry her belowdecks. The part of him demanding that he take her now and kiss her senseless and make good on every promise he had given her.

"What are you doing here?" he asked instead, the decent, honorable part of him winning the battle. For now.

"Looking for you."

An unholy shiver of pleasure traveled straight down his spine before he froze. "Alone? At this time of the night? Are you out of your mind?"

"You're still up."

"And so are half the thieves and murderers in London."

Ivory smiled faintly. "I know half the thieves and murderers in London, Your Grace. Most of them have worked for me at one time or another."

"So what are you doing here?"

She was silent for a moment. "I'm still worried about your sister."

His heart squeezed. "That makes two of us."

"The person who delivered that note was at your ball," she said suddenly. "Whoever he was who helped your sister, and dropped off her messages, he was there. There is no other way your sister could have known to write that note to you."

Max started. Of course.

"Your aunt will have a complete guest list. Once I have it, I will go through it and make a list of possible candidates. If I can determine who helped Lady Beatrice, I might be able to discover where she has gone."

Max dropped his head, his initial spurt of optimism fading in the face of reality. "Even if you determine the identity of the man who helped Bea, it would seem to me that this individual is solely in her corner. I highly doubt that he will tell me where she has gone."

"You might be surprised at the information I can extract from individuals when required."

Max looked at her sharply, a chill chasing its way across his skin, but she was staring serenely out at the water. He wasn't sure what to say to that, but images of racks and other diabolical torture devices flashed before his eyes.

"I keep them in the basement," she said without looking at him. "In the space behind the kitchen and the pantries."

"Keep what?"

"My prisoners and all of my instruments of torture. That is what you're thinking, isn't it?" She was smiling faintly, and Max realized she was teasing him.

"Your sense of humor is deeply unsettling, Miss Moore," he remarked, though he was grinning despite himself as he said it.

"So you've mentioned." She turned, another smile playing at her lips. "I am a businesswoman, Your Grace, not a Spanish Inquisitor. Information is a commodity, just like anything else." She paused. "Besides, I stopped using the rack months ago."

"I'm glad to hear it."

"I'm sorry," she said abruptly, whatever teasing had been in her voice fading.

"For what?" What could she possibly have to be sorry for?

"For not realizing sooner that whoever helped your sister was at that ball."

"I didn't catch it either."

"Yes, but it is my job not to miss details like that."

Max stared down at her, her eyes glittering in the moonlight. "I'm glad you're here," was all he said.

She reached for him, and he took her hands and gathered her against him. He felt her arms slip around his waist, and her head rested against his chest. It wasn't an embrace of passion, but one of partnership. It was strange, this sudden realization that, for the first time in his life, he wasn't truly alone.

"We'll find her," she whispered. "I promise."

They stood like that for a timeless minute, the silence around them complete. Until somewhere on the starboard side of the *Odyssey*, footsteps could be heard across the deserted docks, followed by the sound of someone singing loudly, at a drunken volume that was enough for the sound to reach them high up on the deck. Whoever was walking beside the sleeping ships was in a very buoyant mood. Max cocked his head as the person drew closer to where the *Odyssey* was moored. He couldn't make out words, but the song that reached his ears was familiar. He'd heard it recently. On the steps of a church. In Ivory's study.

Against him Ivory had gone completely still. "Do you hear that?" she whispered.

"Yes."

" 'V'adoro, pupille.' "

"Coincidence?" Max asked.

She pulled away from him. "There are no such thing as coincidences in my business, Your Grace."

They'd moved silently to the rail, and in the pale moonlight, a man came into view, shreds of dissipating fog swirling around his booted feet. He was wearing a thick coat, and his hair gleamed wetly in the moonlight, having been slicked back from his face. A dark beard covered his lower jaw, and he was weaving slightly, as though he was drunk. Ivory strained to make out the man's features. The docks were dangerous at night. Not many people chose to walk alone. And certainly not while drunk.

The notes of the melody rose and fell. There was no way such an obscure opera aria would be hummed twice in two days by two different men. Well, anything was possible, Ivory corrected herself. Though the odds of such a happenstance were unlikely. And she always deferred to the odds.

"Black," Alderidge whispered.

"What?"

"That man. That's Richard Black. Captain of the *Azores*."

"You know him?"

"Yes." There was a catch of hesitation.

"Who is Richard Black?" The man had drawn closer yet, and Ivory could see that his coat was hanging open. In his hand an old-fashioned tricorne swung, some sort of feather in the brim bobbing with each step he took. Occasionally the man would start to list to one side, before correcting his gait with the extra care of someone who was well in his cups.

"He captains an Indiaman for the company, same as me. His ship will be moored here somewhere."

"He a friend?"

"Sort of. Not exactly."

"What does *not exactly* mean?"

"Black is a bit of an...entrepreneur. He smuggles a fair amount of cargo to England that never makes it onto company manifests. Or any type of manifest, for that matter."

"Like what?"

"Stolen art and antiquities. Opium. Liquor. Persian carpets. Rare fabrics. It changes based on demand."

"*Hmph.*" Ivory absorbed this information. "And yet you look the other way?"

"Black has a web of informants throughout the ports from here to Bombay. He is a trader of information as well as goods—a man who seems to have an ear everywhere. The routes we navigate are dangerous. So long as I have information that allows me to keep my men and my ships safe, what Black chooses to put in his holds is not my concern."

"Ah. This captain—does he know Beatrice?"

Alderidge shook his head. "No. At least I can't imagine so. I've never spoken about her to him."

"Never? Not even in passing?"

"No."

"Not even at the bottom of a good bottle of rum?"

Alderidge scowled at her. "No."

"You sure?" Ivory was searching for a possible connection. This man fit the general description Collette had given them. And he was whistling the same obscure aria. Was it possible that this was the person who had helped Bea?

"Yes, I'm sure." There was an edge to the duke's voice now. "We're not exactly drinking partners."

A thought struck Ivory. "Bea said in her last message that she was leaving London. Do you suppose she might have appealed to this captain for passage to India?"

Beside her she heard Alderidge suck in his breath. "Oh God."

"You said she's asked you to take her to India. Do you think it's possible she decided to take matters into her own hands?"

"She wouldn't," the duke breathed.

"Wouldn't she? If that was her plan and your sister is anything like you, it may be a wonder if she isn't already halfway there by now."

Beside her Alderidge was silent, tension rolling off him in palpable waves.

"Did you ever mention this captain to Beatrice? In a letter? In conversation?"

"Yes," he said tightly. "She loved to hear of the infamous Captain Black and his exploits. I embellished them for her benefit."

"He wasn't at your ball, was he?"

"Of course he wasn't." Alderidge stopped. "At least, I didn't see him at the ball."

Ivory peered out again. The captain had almost drawn even with the *Odyssey*, and his gait was becoming increasingly more erratic. Suddenly Ivory became aware of three men closing in on the drunken captain from behind, and they were clearly not drunk.

"He's got company," Ivory whispered.

Alderidge grunted and the sound of steel sliding from its sheath hissed near her ear.

"What are you going to do?" Ivory whispered.

"I can't stand by and watch while he gets his fool throat slit."

The hunters were drawing nearer to their prey. The sound of blades being drawn finally alerted Black that something was not quite right. He spun, and the thieves checked their speed, spreading out to surround their quarry.

The captain drew his own blade in a fluid movement, suddenly looking a whole lot less intoxicated than he had a second ago.

"The bastard is toying with them." Alderidge groaned.

"What?"

"He's stone-cold sober and obviously looking for a fight," he muttered, letting the tip of his blade drop.

The thieves were edging closer. One of them called out to another.

"Those are the Harris brothers," Ivory said.

"I beg your pardon?"

"Those thieves"—she gestured at the three men now circling like wolves—"are not your average dockside riffraff. All long veterans of Wellington's army. The French never did manage to kill them, though it wasn't for lack of trying. And now they've found themselves without work, like so many other soldiers."

"You know them?"

"Like I told you, Your Grace, half the thieves in London have worked for me at one time or another."

Black seemed to have suddenly realized that he wasn't facing a ragged group of inexperienced thieves. He crouched defensively as the first one came at him. He parried, with the skill of an accomplished swordsman, though he was forced a step closer to the water. The thief retreated, and the second one came at him with the same result.

"The Harrises usually work the Finish by my place," Ivory told Alderidge, making her way down the deck to where long planks connected the ship to the dock.

"The what?" He was on her heels.

"The coffeehouse at the end of the square. Near the market. Where all the drunken aristocrats with fat purses wind up at the end of their escapades, trying to flush the alcohol from their veins with copious amounts of terrible coffee." She shook her head. "Not sure why they are so far afield tonight, though I can only assume that the captain here has enough on him to make the distance worth it. But no matter how good Black is with that blade, I can guarantee that this will not end well for him."

"Idiot," the duke grumbled as the sound of steel clashing against steel bounced off the walls of the warehouses. He and Ivory had reached firm footing on the docks and were advancing, unnoticed. Alderidge reached out and grabbed her arm, yanking her behind him.

"Your Grace," Ivory began, trying to regain her position.

"Don't Your Grace me," he snapped at her, deftly planting his bulk between her and the combatants. "This will get dangerous. I don't want to see you get hurt."

Ivory rolled her eyes, even as something warm and exhilarating rushed through her body. "Your sentiments, Your Grace, are admirable but—"

"Stay," he barked.

"Oh, for the love of God," Ivory muttered. She put two fingers in her mouth and let out an ear-piercing whistle.

Alderidge jerked and swore. "What the hell are you doing?" He glared at her before shoving her behind him again.

She had drawn the attention of all four men, and the three thieves withdrew slightly, the better to assess the new threat. Black regained the ground he had lost.

"Captain Harcourt," Black called out, somewhat breathless, but with his bravado firmly in place. "What brings you out here on such a fine night?"

"The possibility of watching your ego finally get the best of you."

The captain bent and retrieved his tricorne from where it had fallen to the ground. "I'm sure I don't know what you mean."

Ivory shoved past Max. "As competent as you are with that blade, you're not going to fight your way out of this, Captain Black," she said briskly. "I know it, you know it, and they know it." She gestured at the thieves still waiting, giving the tallest a slight warning shake of her head as she saw recognition flash in his eyes. "And so I have a business proposal for you."

Black straightened, staring at Ivory as though she had appeared in a puff of smoke. "You know my name, my lady, but I do not have the privilege of yours. And I always make it my business to know the names of beautiful women." He bowed and swept his hat in front of him with his free hand.

The gesture was ridiculous, and Ivory almost laughed out loud. "Flattery will get you nowhere, Captain. Now pay the men, and go about your business. I suspect you'll find them quite reasonable."

"I will do no such thing," the captain said indignantly. "That is akin to highway robbery."

"It is the price of underestimating your opponents, Captain," Ivory said.

Black gazed at her, his eyes as dark as the night. "Wherever did you find her, Harcourt?" he asked. "She is rather...charming."

Ivory heaved a sigh. "I was told you were usually smarter than this, Captain."

Black's eyes darted to where Alderidge stood. To his credit, the duke was watching the scene unfold with what looked like detached amusement.

"Have you got nothing to say, Harcourt?" he asked insolently.

"Not really." Alderidge shrugged. "The lady has pretty much said everything that needs to be said."

"And since when do you let a woman speak for you?"

"Since she's right."

Ivory kept her eyes trained on the captain, afraid to look at Alderidge.

The captain swore in disgust. "Very well, you bastards." He yanked a small purse from his waist. "This is all I've got." He threw it at the tallest thief, who caught it deftly. The thief weighed it in his hand.

"You're going to have to do better than that, Captain," Ivory said in a bored voice.

"I beg your pardon?"

"The rest of it."

"I'm sure I don't know what you mean."

Ivory shrugged. "Very well. We'll let these gentlemen find it." She crossed her arms.

The Harris brothers advanced menacingly.

Black uttered a string of curses that did justice to his profession. "Oh, very well," he snarled. A second purse, twice the size, followed the first. The tallest thief considered it.

"Enough for the night?" Ivory asked him.

"Aye. It'll do." The thief smiled at her through his beard. "An' a good evening to you, Duchess," he said, before he and his companions vanished into the night.

"You planned that!" Black was staring at her, the thief's address having made him realize that they knew her.

"I most certainly did not." Ivory's lips thinned. "I'm not in the habit of planning small-scale robberies at the East India Docks."

"But you knew them."

"Of course I knew them," Ivory snapped. "What sort of idiot would put herself in between an obnoxious captain and three thieves with swords unless she knew who the winning team was going to be?"

The captain blinked at her a few times before he threw his head back and laughed. He wiped his eyes with the back of his hand and jammed his tricorne back on his head. "I think I'm in love," he cackled. "What would it take to convince you to have dinner with me, my lady? Or breakfast?"

"Sod off, Black," Alderidge said.

"Ah, Captain Harcourt finally finds his voice!" Black sheathed his sword and stepped toward the two of them. "I must confess, I rather thought you'd be at one of your fancy house parties, all dressed up in your fancy clothes. Your Grace." He said the last mockingly. "I didn't expect to see you here."

"I'm looking for a woman," Alderidge said.

"A woman? What, this one isn't enough for you?" Black's eyes touched on Ivory lightly before swinging back to the duke.

"This woman would have been seeking passage out of England, perhaps. Sometime in the last two days."

"And why the hell would I tell you anything, Harcourt?" Black asked. "Information has a price."

"We just saved your life," Alderidge reminded him rudely.

"No, my money saved my life," Black corrected him. "And I have to confess, I am rather peeved that it took so much."

"I'll replace it tenfold if you can provide me with the information I seek. I have money."

"Yes, yes, I know that. Unfortunately, so do I. I don't need your money, Harcourt."

"Dinner then," Ivory spoke up.

Genuine interest sparked in Black's eye. "With you?"

"Unless you'd prefer to spend your time over wine and roast chicken with Captain Harcourt."

"No, I most certainly would not. Too upstanding for my tastes." His eyes traveled the length of Ivory, though she saw only curiosity in his expression. "But you intrigue me. You have yourself a deal."

"There is no deal," Alderidge nearly shouted.

"You were doing better when the lady was speaking for you, Harcourt," the captain said rudely.

Ivory cleared her throat. "Tell the duke what you know. Then we can decide how much that information is worth."

Black was looking at her with delight. "My God, she isn't charming, Harcourt, she's positively enchanting." He rubbed his hands together. "I must insist on a name first. As a show of good faith. Surely that's fair."

"Miss Moore."

"Miss Moore," Black repeated. "A fine start to a beautiful...friendship. And what shall I call you over dessert?"

"Depends what you have to tell Captain Harcourt."

Black's face fell slightly, and he heaved a sigh. "Very well. No woman has been on the docks in the past two days looking for passage."

"Are you sure?" Alderidge demanded.

"Of course I'm sure." Black looked insulted. "I know everything that goes on on these docks. I make it my business to know. I *pay* people to tell me what goes on."

"Dammit," Alderidge swore.

"What were you singing earlier?" Ivory asked quietly.

Black's expression went blank. "I beg your pardon?"

"You were singing." Ivory sang the opening of the aria. "What was it?"

Black shook his head, even as he gazed at Ivory curiously. "I have no idea."

"If you don't know what it was, where did you hear it?"

The captain's eyes shuttered suddenly, as if a wall had come down.

"The lady asked you a question, Black," the duke growled. He was examining the tip of his blade with his fingers.

"Don't remember."

"Think hard, Captain." Ivory raised a brow.

"That might cost you more than just dinner, Miss Moore."

Before Ivory could say a thing, Alderidge had the captain by the throat, his blade pressed to the man's neck. She blinked, both stunned and impressed by how fast Alderidge had moved.

"Bloody hell, Harcourt, what's wrong with you?" Black demanded.

"That song. What is it?"

"Have you lost your mind?" The captain was struggling against Alderidge's superior size and strength.

"The song. What is it?"

"I don't know!" Black snapped, looking just as furious now as Alderidge. "It was something I heard a chap humming. It was catchy. I haven't been able it get it out of my head all day. Now get your hands off me."

"Where did you hear it?" Ivory asked.

"What does it matter?"

"Where?" Alderidge demanded, the blade pressing against soft flesh.

Black winced. "When I was making a delivery today."

"Which was where?"

"Why would I tell you—"

"Where?"

"He heard it at Helmsdale House," Ivory said, everything suddenly very, very clear. Her heart dropped to her toes.

Black jerked in shock and then flinched as Alderidge's blade bit into the top layer of his skin. "How do you know that?"

"The delivery you were making. Stolen antiquities taken from a cave in the desert. You sold them to King, didn't you? For his auction."

Black's eyes were wide. "Who *are* you?"

Ivory ignored him. "The man you heard humming that tune, what did he look like?"

"I don't know. I wasn't paying that much attention."

"You were paying enough."

Black made a noise of frustration. "Average. He wasn't big, like this hulking gorilla here." He strained against the choke hold Alderidge still had him in. "Just another cove making a delivery like me."

"You don't know his name?"

"I make it a point not to know. I just obtain the requested merchandise and deliver it in a timely fashion."

"Where is this Helmsdale House?" Alderidge had been listening, but now it would seem his patience was at an end and he wanted answers.

"Just north of London. Not far from Kentish Town. It is owned by King," Ivory told him.

Alderidge was looking over Black's shoulder at Ivory. "And this King. Who is he? That night at the club, you told me King was a businessman."

Black made some sort of wheezing gasp of laughter.

"And I'm a Russian czar." His laughter stopped with a strangled grunt as the duke tightened his hold.

"I wasn't talking to you," Alderidge growled.

"He's a fence," Ivory said flatly. "Of the most elite sort. He caters to the very wealthy and very privileged. He specializes in stolen art and antiquities, but he will buy and sell anything that will make him a profit. Jewelry, narcotics, horses, even real estate. More than one peer has sought him out, desperate to trade a family treasure for quick cash, or to sell something he never should have had in the first place. King's tentacles reach equally deep into the underworld as they do upward into the ranks of society. The man has no conscience."

"And this auction—what is it?"

"It is how King sells his inventory. His auctions are held annually, at the height of the London season. The event is by invitation only, and the men who attend are collectors with deep pockets and little regard for the law. Because it isn't enough just to sell. He—"

"Pits these men against each other. Each vying not only to possess something, but to ensure another can't." Alderidge finished her thought.

Ivory nodded. "Exactly."

The duke suddenly let the man down with a thump, and Black staggered slightly before righting himself. Alderidge produced a small miniature from his pocket. "This girl. Did you see her there?"

Black straightened his coat and his collar and gave the duke a dark look. "That was entirely uncalled for, Harcourt. I might remember that the next time I get word that there is a fleet of pirates around the Cape waiting to welcome the *Odyssey* and pick her bones clean."

"The girl. Tell me if you saw her there." The words were tight. "Please."

Black drew in a deep breath and held out his hand for the miniature. He tipped it toward the moonlight and frowned. "I can't tell. I need a better light."

Alderidge muttered something under his breath and disappeared.

Black watched Alderidge retreat before he turned to Ivory. "Whatever you think you want with King, Miss Moore, I must, in good conscience, advise that you reconsider and keep your distance. It is true that my business with King has been quite lucrative, but I would no sooner turn my back on him than I would a jackal."

Ivory considered him. "Why are you telling me this?"

"Because, Miss Moore, you seem like a rather... fascinating woman. It would be a shame should anything unfortunate befall you."

"Is this another attempt at flattery, Captain Black?"

"No, it's not. It's a warning. King is mercurial. Unpredictable. And people who complicate King's life have a habit of disappearing."

Ivory held his gaze, silent.

"But you already knew that." Black was watching her speculatively.

"I am well acquainted with King and his business practices," Ivory admitted.

"Hmmm. Do you know, I believe that." Black paused, his eyes shrewd, before he suddenly grinned. "If—*when* you tire of Harcourt, please remember me. Whatever is in my power to give you is yours."

"Do not make promises you don't intend to keep," said Ivory.

"I never make promises lightly, Miss Moore." Black's expression was serious.

"Mmmm. So if I needed you to—"

"To tell us if you saw the girl in the miniature." Alderidge had returned with a lantern, slightly out of breath and frowning fiercely. He held it up near Black and gestured at the little painting still in his hand. "Did you see her there?"

Black looked away from Ivory reluctantly and returned his attention to the miniature he still had in his hand. "Yes. Yes, I believe she was there."

"Thank God." Alderidge blew out a breath. "You're sure?"

Black shrugged slightly, though something about his body language had changed. "As sure as I can be from a little painting."

"She has blond hair, lighter than mine. About your height. Greyish eyes. A mole on the left side of her face, high on her cheek."

"Yes. She was there." The words sounded stilted now.

"Was she there with that gentleman?" Ivory asked into the silence. "The one who was humming?"

"You could say that." The captain was watching Alderidge.

"Please clarify," Ivory said, stepping closer to Black.

"The gentleman brought her there."

"I don't understand. Was she his guest? Is she to attend this auction that this man is having?" The duke's early relief was giving way to confusion. He set the lantern down at their feet.

"No." The captain's eyes slid to Ivory. "She is to be part of the auction tomorrow night."

A cold finger of dread slithered down her spine. "She is for sale."

"Yes. That was my understanding." The captain was edging away from Alderidge, who had gone completely still. Black made a moue of distaste. "A bad business, that."

"You left her there?" The duke's voice was barely audible.

Black held up his hands. "None of my concern what goes on in those fancy rich houses. Men like what they like."

Alderidge lunged toward Black, but this time the captain had anticipated it. He evaded the duke by a hair. "I only saw the girl once before I left. Heard the man say she would be kept where she couldn't cause trouble and brought back to Helmsdale tomorrow night for the auction. She's to be a grand finale of sorts."

Ivory felt bile rise in her throat. "Did you hear her say anything?"

"No. Silent as a church mouse, that one."

"And you left her there?" Alderidge repeated again, and this time there was fury in his voice. "Knowing why she was there?"

"I get paid to provide objects," Black said harshly. "Bits of porcelain and jade and gold. Baubles worn by people who have been dead for centuries. Paintings created by more dead people. Things for men whose pocketbooks are only exceeded by their greed and their desire to own something that no one else can. I grew up in the slums of Liverpool, Harcourt. Every day that I can go to sleep warm and without hunger gnawing at my insides is a good day for me. I've done what I need to do to get here, and I will continue to do so. I won't apologize for it. That girl will survive, because she will have to. Just like I did."

"That was my sister."

Black's ferocious expression slackened. "I beg your pardon?"

"The blonde is my sister. She's been missing for two days." The duke looked like he would happily tear Black in two.

"I didn't know." Black looked genuinely discomfited.

Ivory stepped in between the two men. "Of course you didn't."

"What can I do?"

"You could supply us with details," Ivory said, marshaling her wits. "Captain Harcourt agrees not to slit your throat and feed you to his beloved sharks. In return, you will agree to tell us everything you can remember so that his sister, whom you left to her fate, might be returned safely to his care." She looked between the two men. "Are we agreed?"

Chapter Nine

Captain Black had been able to provide very few details other than what he had already given them, and what Ivory already knew. Helmsdale House, perched in a bucolic country setting outside the sprawl of London, had been sold nearly a decade ago to cover the gambling debts of a dissolute aristocrat. For those who needed to know, it was owned now by a man who went solely by the name of King. There were whispers that he had once been the youngest son of an aristocratic family, but had been cast out and disowned, rumors of murder and betrayal muddying the waters. Ivory had never put much stock in those rumors—she had never been able to verify any of it, but she knew very well just how ruthless King could be in his insatiable pursuit of wealth and power.

Yet she had never heard of a girl's being part of the offerings before. This was something new. Though not that shocking.

Black had departed quickly, and Ivory and Alderidge had returned to the duke's cabin aboard the *Odyssey*. The duke had barely said two words, only staring intensely into a glass of brandy that he refilled more than once. His silence, more than anything, was unnerving. She almost wanted the bull in the china shop back, crashing around and demanding to ride to his sister's rescue. She let her attention roam around the small cabin, her gaze falling on two piles of letters that had been left on the table, bound by string. From where she sat, she could see Alderidge's name written across the front of the topmost letter, in the same handwriting that she had seen on the messages.

"Are these letters from your sister?" she asked with some surprise. There were hundreds of letters between the two piles.

The duke grunted, which Ivory took to be a yes.

"She is a very prolific writer," Ivory prodded. She needed to get Alderidge talking again. Tentatively Ivory reached for the nearest pile. When the duke didn't move, she picked it up. "Is there any mention of anything—"

"There isn't any mention of anything of import in any of those letters," Alderidge said, without looking up. "No mention of a man whom she would trust until he betrayed her in the most heinous of manners. No mention of anything that would have had me turning my ship around and sailing back to England as fast as the winds could carry me. Nothing but anecdotes of garden parties and balls, musical soirees, the latest color of gown that is all the rage amongst her friends. Stories of her favorite cat that stalks the kitchens and her favorite gelding in the mews. Ramblings about her favorite flowers, her favorite scent, her favorite cake." He stopped. "Visions and conjecture of what it would be like if she could travel with me to India."

Ivory bit her lip, seeing an image of a young girl pouring her heart out to a brother who was a world away. "She wrote what she couldn't tell you in person."

The duke closed his eyes briefly, but remained stubbornly mute.

"Tell me what you're thinking," she said finally, when she couldn't stand it any longer.

Alderidge looked up at her, his grey eyes icy and remote. "You don't want to know what I'm thinking." He drained what was left in his glass and reached for the brandy bottle.

Ivory leaned forward and snatched the bottle away. She needed him sober, though if a man had ever had a reason to drink, this would be it. She kept the bottle securely in her hands. "Remember our earlier conversation, Your Grace. About alternatives to hiring me to clean up bodies."

He glared at her. "I hope you have good help," he said, and Ivory felt every bit of the cold rage in his words down to her marrow. "You're going to need it. Those who would sell..." He trailed off, seemingly at a loss for words.

"Will be dealt with." Ivory tried to keep her voice steady.

Grey eyes burned into her own. "I will deal with them." Alderidge stood up suddenly, the small chair toppling back and crashing against the floor. The flame in the lantern flickered, sending strange shadows dancing up the wall. He paced the small cabin, three steps one way and then back. Abruptly he knelt before a heavy trunk near the door and wrenched it open. Digging under a pile of linens and logbooks, he extracted a long, smooth pistol case.

"And what are you intending to do with that?" Ivory asked as he extracted a long, heavy pistol.

"What do you usually do with guns, Miss Moore?"

Ivory still held the bottle of brandy in her hands, and she banged it back on the table with a loud crash, brandy sloshing from the top. "Do not sign your sister's death warrant," she said.

"What's that supposed to mean?"

"Where is Beatrice right now, Your Grace?" Ivory demanded.

Alderidge looked at her, his jaw clenched in the manner she knew so well.

"You can't tell me because we don't know." She pressed her palms to the surface of the table.

"That is why I am going to go look for her."

"Where will you look?"

"Somewhere near Kentish Town. She cannot be so far from this Helmsdale House."

"Maybe. Maybe not."

The duke was loading the pistol now.

"And if you ask the wrong person the wrong question?" Ivory asked. "If King discovers that her presence might cause unwanted complications to his well-planned event? What do you suppose will happen to her then?"

The scrape of the ramrod stopped.

"She will be replaced. Killed first, most likely, and then simply replaced. And then, Your Grace, we will be looking for her body."

The duke put the pistol down on top of its case.

"King is a dangerous man. He puts little value on anything save money and the power it brings him. If something no longer has value, he will simply discard it."

"So then I cut the head off the snake. Go after this King. Then I look for Bea."

"He is too well protected. Helmsdale is like his own private fortress, with a veritable army protecting it. With the exception of the auction, no one ever has access to the property. And once you're in, you cannot leave. It's a brilliant setup. One's very presence in that house makes one complicit in whatever corrupt activities occur."

"How do you know all this?"

"I have been at one of his auctions before."

"Why?"

Ivory cleared her throat. "I was recovering an item for a client."

"So you know this King."

"You might say that."

"Then you can get close to him."

"Yes."

"Can I hire you to kill him then?"

"I am not a murderer."

"No." The duke let out a humorless laugh. "You only clean up after them."

Ivory looked away.

"I'm sorry. That wasn't fair." Alderidge pushed himself to his feet, his frustration evident. "So what now?" He looked at Ivory. "What am I supposed to do next?"

"You can give me a chance to think." She pushed herself from her own chair, unable to remain seated. "I don't know what happened the night of your ball. But I think you're right in that we have to assume that whoever it was who helped Beatrice out of your house is the same person who was with her at Helmsdale."

"The person who sold her."

Ivory winced. "I can only guess that any goodwill he showed her that night hid far darker motivations. Beatrice was vulnerable, scared, and at a disadvantage. Perhaps he seized that opportunity when it presented itself. He might have threatened her. Told her that you or your aunt would be maimed or killed if she didn't cooperate. She was obviously coerced into writing you those messages. No doubt in the hopes that you would not search for her."

Alderidge leaned back against the cabin bulkhead with a thump and ran his hands over his face. "I can't tell Helen this. This will kill her."

"We will find Beatrice. She is safe for now, because she has value. But we need to be smart. A man like King does not respond well to threats. One must appeal to his vanity."

"I liked my idea better."

"And what idea was that? Storm the Bastille and carry out your sister?"

"It worked for them."

Ivory narrowed her eyes. "No, it didn't. It started a disorganized riot, and people died. Innocent people. I will not take that chance, and neither will you. We don't even know where Beatrice is being held. I think it would be best if you let me handle this."

His hands dropped to his sides. "Don't shut me out. Not when we're this close."

Ivory watched him, saw the worry in his eyes. Her heart lurched.

"Arrange a meeting with this King," he demanded.

"With you?"

"Yes."

"Absolutely not."

"Why?"

"Because he will ruin you."

"That makes no sense."

Ivory searched his eyes. "How much is your sister worth, Your Grace? How many of your ships? How much of your company stock? How many of your properties?"

Alderidge stared at her. "All of it," he whispered, his voice raw.

Ivory braced herself against the emotion that was suddenly burning at the backs of her eyes. "And King will know that. He will see the truth, just as I can see it now."

"I don't care. I would trade it all for her. She is my sister."

Ivory believed him. She felt like crying at the sheer intensity of the unconditional love this man was capable of.

She stomped on her emotion before it completely obliterated whatever perspective she was still clinging to. "While that is a gallant sentiment, I would suggest that such extremes are not necessary, nor are they sensible. King will negotiate, if only because there is a possibility that it might be to his benefit. But you have to trust me to do it." She wanted to touch him, but she remained where she stood. This man did not need her sympathy right now. He had too much pride. What he needed was her help.

"Do I have a choice?" he asked.

"You always have a choice, Your Grace."

He looked at her, his expression bleak. "I will do whatever it takes to get her back. Anything I have is his, so long as Beatrice is safe."

Ivory nodded. "Understood."

"Goddammit." A world of frustration and anguish was contained in that one word. Here was a man who commanded men, who was used to controlling every aspect of his life. Who was used to taking action to achieve his ends.

And she was asking him to place that control in her hands. She did not underestimate the significance of that.

"I trust you." He hadn't looked away from her.

"Thank you," she said softly.

He banged a fist against his thigh. "I was the one who was supposed to be able to protect my sister. To keep her from harm."

"And you're doing that, Your Grace."

"How? By standing here?"

"By hiring me." She aimed for gentle levity, needing to break the strange spell that seemed to have fallen in the small cabin.

He dropped his head. "You're impossible," he said, but without resentment.

She bit her lip. "You were right in the end, you know."

"About what?" he said, suddenly sounding weary. "That I didn't know my sister well enough to keep her safe?" Ivory suspected that all the brandy he had consumed was starting to take effect. Which was probably just as well.

"On the contrary. You knew her well enough to recognize that something was amiss. That she was trying to tell you something in her messages."

The duke ran a hand through his hair. "I was also wrong."

They regarded each other in the glow from the lantern. "If I might suggest, Your Grace—"

"Might I suggest you stop calling me Your Grace?"

"I beg your pardon?" Ivory started.

"I want you to call me Max. That is what all the women who extract dead lovers from my sister's bed call me."

"Max." She repeated the name.

He closed his eyes briefly. "That's better." He met her eyes again. "And for the record, I make absolutely no guarantees that I won't kill this King. And the one who already sold Beatrice can measure his life in hours once I discover his identity. Are we clear?"

"Crystal." There was little point in arguing at this juncture.

"Excellent. I will try and give you a little notice, if you like. For body disposal purposes and all."

Ivory grimaced. "That would be nice."

"I don't anticipate there being enough left of them for you to prop up in a guest bedroom."

"Rather bloodthirsty, aren't you?"

"I'd do the same if it was you this man had taken."

Ivory stared at him.

Max cleared his throat, as if realizing what he had just said. "But then again, I've been warned not to underestimate your ability to take care of yourself. I don't expect you'd ever find yourself at a house party on an auction block set to be bid on by any number of men with no moral compasses, would you?" He laughed, though it sounded a little desperate and uneven.

"Is that even a question?"

"I'm not sure. I'm not sure of anything anymore." He sighed, his head and shoulders still resting back against the bulkhead. "My aunt was the only one who was completely right, you know. If I had come home earlier, then perhaps—"

Ivory snorted softly. "Self-recrimination does not become you. Nor is it helpful."

"But perhaps I could have prevented Beatrice from becoming involved with Debarry—"

"You're delusional if you think you would be able to control the will of an eighteen-year-old girl when she's made up her mind about something. If she wanted Debarry, she would have had Debarry. Whether or not you were here."

"How do you know that?"

"Because I used to *be* an eighteen-year-old girl."

That earned a weak smile that faded quickly. They sat in silence, the ship's timbers creaking occasionally around them.

"Did you know my parents and my brothers had been dead for over six months before I even learned that I had inherited the title? And it was a year before I was able to return to London?"

"Do you miss them?" She wasn't sure what made her ask that question. Maybe it was the bizarre circumstances that had brought them to this point. Maybe it was the cocoon of intimacy they had found in his cabin.

"I barely knew them. I was away at school for most of my childhood. Went to sea when I was thirteen. Came back to London only once before they passed away."

"Why didn't you stay?" she asked quietly. "In London, I mean. After you found out that you had become a duke?"

Max leaned his head back against the wall again. "I did. For a while. But I didn't...fit in anywhere here." He looked at her. "Do you remember what you told me that first night when I came home? You told me that this was not my world. And you were right. It wasn't my world then any more than it is now. I came home ten years ago to find that there were stewards and secretaries and solicitors and all manner of men who competently oversaw the dukedom. Bea was eight and was fully dependent on Helen—she certainly didn't need me. Aside from a few signatures from time to time, my presence was superfluous. I was suffocating here. You can't imagine how it feels to be trapped somewhere you don't belong." He abruptly stopped.

Ivory was silent for another long moment. She bent and righted the overturned chair, then sank into it. She reached for the bottle left on the table and brought it to her lips, letting the liquid fire burn down her throat. "I used to be a duchess." It was out before she could consider the wisdom of that statement.

"You used to be a what?"

"You asked me once why my friends called me Duchess. It's because I used to be one."

"I don't understand."

"I need to explain how one becomes a duchess?"

"Yes. No." He frowned slightly. "If you are a duchess, why are you here? On a ship with me? Living in Covent Square? Working for Mr. Chegarre?"

"Because I am not a duchess any longer. My husband died five years ago."

"That makes no sense. A duchess is still a duchess, even if her husband dies."

"Not if she was an opera singer before she was a duchess. Not if she was despised by the duke's family, who took her to be a money-grubbing opportunist." Holy hell, why was she telling him this? And why couldn't she seem to stop?

Max had come off the bulkhead and was staring down at her in the lantern light, and she could almost see the pieces of information falling into place behind his eyes. Even he, who was never in London, must have heard the improbable tale of the opera singer who had become a duchess.

"God almighty," he breathed. "You were the Duchess of Knightley. Your nickname is not a nickname at all." Max came around, dropping into the chair she had vacated, watching her intently.

Ivory smiled a little sadly. "Then you will know, Your Grace, that I too understand what it is like to not fit into a world in which you have found yourself. There was not a soul in Knightley's world who didn't make it clear that I was an imposter, including his family. A charlatan who had forgotten her place and should be punished for it. My place was in a quiet, out-of-the-way cottage, where I could be kept on the side out of sight and out of mind and used as a diversion when the mood struck. I was not the sort of woman a man married. Certainly not a man like Knightley. But he didn't care. He—*we* simply defied them all, because we could."

"Did you love him?"

"Yes."

"And he loved you?"

"Yes."

"Was it worth it?"

"Yes."

Another silence fell.

Ivory finally broke it. "That's all you're going to ask?"

"What else matters?" Max reached for the brandy bottle and plucked it from her unfeeling fingers.

"You surprise me sometimes."

His lips curled slightly, as if this amused him. "Why did you vanish after he died?"

"Knightley's family tolerated my presence out of deference to the duke so long as he was alive. Once he had passed, they made certain that I understood that they would find a way to destroy me should I continue to lay claim to a title that should never have been mine."

"I'm sorry."

Ivory shrugged. "It wasn't unexpected. Opera singers do not marry dukes without their eyes wide open."

"Then why not return to the stage? You're still a legend. You could have any man you wished."

Ivory was silent for a moment, trying to find words to make this man understand. "Do you know how I came to sing on some of the grandest stages in Europe?"

"No."

"When I was thirteen, a man passing by the hovel we called home heard me singing, quite by accident. My family was poor—poor enough that there were stretches of days when we didn't eat. This man gave my parents five pounds—more money than they had seen in their entire lives—and took me with him when he left. Turned out he owned an opera house in London."

"He *bought* you?"

"He would tell you that he invested in me. Taught me to read and write. And in exchange for lessons in Italian and French and proper instruction in music, I became Ivory Bellafiore, and earned him quite a return on his investment." She paused. "But Ivory Bellafiore was not a legend. She was an illusion. She was a femme fatale, a seductress or an enchantress, depending on the night. An illusion men wished to own so that he could boast to his friends that he had done so. An illusion that could be bought. Ivory Bellafiore was no different, really, than the objects Captain Black sells, destined for the highest bidder."

She could see a muscle working along the side of Max's jaw.

"I did a lot of things to survive in my life, things that I cannot apologize for because they have, in the end, brought me here. But I am done surviving that life. Ivory Bellafiore no longer exists, nor will she ever again. I am no longer something to be owned. My destiny is mine to choose, mine to control. Do you understand?"

He was watching her, a turmoil of emotion swirling in the grey depths of his eyes. "Yes. It's the same reason I bought the *Odyssey*. I did not want to be sailing someone's ship with men who weren't my own, plotting courses to destinations that were not of my choosing." He paused. "It's the same reason I can't stay in London. I am not a duke. I never have been."

An ache started deep inside her, at the realization of just how impossible it would be to hold on to a man like this. She saw so much of herself in him.

"Why did you tell me all this? Who you are?" he asked presently.

Because I trust you. Because you possess honor and heart and strength. Because in another life, I could probably fall in love with you. "Because I hold your secrets, and I wanted you to have one of mine."

He tipped his chair forward on two legs, bringing himself closer to her. She held her ground. He was close enough to kiss her. He braced his elbows on his knees, the bottle dangling from his fingers, his ice-grey eyes searching her face. There was a sheen of liquor on his lower lip, the moisture visible in the flickering lantern light. She could taste it on her own tongue, imagined tasting it on his. Her heart seemed to be crashing in her chest louder than it should, and her stomach felt as it would have on heaving seas. Her control was slipping, and taking with it her judgment and her wits. "Do you think differently of me? Now that you know who I am? The things I've done?" The questions slipped out of their own volition.

"The things you've done?" His forehead creased.

"I sold myself, Max." There. She'd said it. "Before I had enough power to control my own destiny."

He stared at her. "I know who you are. You are Ivory Moore. You are the woman who redressed a corpse to save my sister. The woman who kissed me to save me from myself. You are the only one who understands why I can never be put in a prison that was built for me by fate and circumstance."

She swallowed, emotion clogging her throat.

"You are the woman I trust." He pushed himself away from her abruptly, and the chair came back down on four legs with a thud. He stood and set the bottle back on the table with great care. Reaching down, he caught her hands in his and pulled her to her feet. He studied her hands before bringing them to his lips. "The woman I want more than anything."

Desire streaked through her and settled somewhere deep in her belly. Time seemed to have slowed. His lips grazed the insides of her wrists.

"Max." It came out like a plea, when she had meant it as a protest.

"I lied," he said. He pressed his mouth to the flesh of her palm, and her knees nearly buckled.

"What?" It was hard to follow the thread of conversation, what with the feel of his lips on her skin.

"I said I wasn't sure of anything anymore," he said quietly. "But that's not true. I am sure of you."

Ivory searched his eyes, seeing only a raw vulnerability in those clear grey depths.

"You've more courage than anyone I've ever met," he whispered, pulling her closer to him, their hands still joined.

"You're drunk."

"Not nearly enough. But I wish I was."

"What?"

"If I were drunk, it might excuse what I'm about to do."

Ivory didn't have time to even respond before he kissed her.

This kiss was not one of gentle exploration. This was the kiss of a man seeking oblivion and solace. She whimpered beneath the onslaught, returning his desperation with her own. He let go of her hands and ran his own down her back, over the curve of her buttocks and her hips, then up along her ribs and shoulders. She felt his fingers trace the back of her neck and drop lower to stroke her collarbone, and then the side of her breast, his thumb finding her nipple through the fabric of her bodice. He was exploring the recesses of her mouth, his tongue delving and demanding as he covered her breasts with his hands, cupping and stroking and sending currents of pure ecstasy pulsing through her.

He backed her up two steps, until she hit the cabin's bulkhead. She wrapped her hands around his neck, her fingers tangling in his thick hair, and arched into him. He growled in approval, and his hand dropped from her breast to the curve of her backside, his fist crumpling her skirts as though frustrated with the barrier. She could feel the press of his erection against her lower belly through the layers of their clothing, and she too felt an impatience at the hindrance.

Her fingers left his nape, traveling down his back, tracing the valley of his spine that she had admired a lifetime ago. Except now her hands continued where only her eyes had gone before, over his buttocks and the muscle bunched beneath the seat of his breeches. God, but he was hard everywhere. She urged him against her, and he groaned, plundering her mouth with his tongue. She opened herself willingly, letting him assume full control.

His hands moved to her face, holding her steady beneath his kiss, until his fingers slid down, skimming over her breasts, along the edges of her ribs, finally caging her hips within their steely grasp. His mouth left her lips, leaving a trail of scorched skin down the side of her neck and along the tops of her breasts. Her head tipped back, and she tried to catch her breath, but it was impossible. She wanted this man's hands on her skin. His lips on her skin. Everywhere. All at once.

The steady throb that had ignited in her belly and was building at the apex of her thighs was becoming unbearable. She tried to get closer to him, as if she could somehow meld her body with his and find the release she so desperately craved. But there were clothes to deal with, and they were in the way. She made a sound of frustration and suddenly Max's hands dropped to her arse, and he hauled her up against him.

She wrapped her legs around him awkwardly, hampered by her skirts. But it didn't matter because through the fabric she could feel the bulge of his erection *there*, right where it needed to be, pressed against the spot that was already sending sparks of pleasure coursing through every cell of her body. She might have moaned but she couldn't remember because Max was surging up against her. She bore down on him, and her eyes closed, and her head dropped to his shoulder, her fingers tangled around his neck and in his hair, and she gasped, struggling for breath as her orgasm ripped through her like a tidal wave.

He held her tightly as she shook, pressing kisses along the curve of her neck, letting her ride out the spasms and the eddies secure in his arms. When the last tremors had drained from her limbs, she raised her head, never having felt in all her life as lost for words as she was at that moment.

Max didn't give her a chance to find those words. He kissed her hard, letting her down, his hands not leaving her back.

Which was just as well, for Ivory wasn't at all sure she could stand under her own power.

He drew away slightly, searching her eyes again with his own. His fingers were still stroking her back, and his continued touch was making it difficult to put her thoughts into any sort of rational order.

"I promised myself that I would wait to finish this," he said. Against her she could still feel the hard evidence of his need. "I promised that I wouldn't allow myself this until Beatrice was safe at home."

"Max—"

"I can't do this right now. I can't give you what you deserve right now."

What *she* deserved? He had just given her pleasure the like of which she had never, in all of her life, experienced. Pleasure that had tilted her world and wiped everything from her mind except for him. And he hadn't even undressed her.

But what had happened to her own principles? What had happened to her own rules about clients and the distance that should be kept from them at all times? When had she abandoned everything for the chance to be with this man? Because Max was right. They could not do this. She could not do this. Not yet. She had known that once.

God help her, but she was in way over her head.

"Don't think that this is because I don't want you, Ivory Moore." He sounded as if he were in pain.

"No," she whispered. "I don't think that." Her fingers skimmed the sides of his breeches, over his hips.

He groaned and stepped away.

"We should probably get some rest," she said quietly, trying for a tone of pragmatic normalcy. "There is little we can do until morning."

Liar. There were all sorts of things they could do until morning.

"I'll come back first thing." She took an unsteady step toward the door.

"Where do you think you're going?" the duke demanded.

"Home."

"Like hell you are. It's too dangerous out there."

"I'll be fine."

"You're not going anywhere until it's light out. And I'm with you. You'll sleep there." He jabbed a finger at the narrow berth that ran along the far end of the cabin.

"With you?" She regretted it instantly. What was wrong with her?

His eyes darkened to the color of tempered steel, and he was clenching his jaw again.

She was aware that her response seemed to mark her acceptance of his command. As if now they were simply sorting out the details of the whole arrangement.

"Double occupancy in that berth would be most uncomfortable, Miss Moore." His face betrayed nothing. He was trying to do the sane, honorable thing.

Not if I was on top of you. Or beneath you.

"I can't take your bed."

"There are two more berths in the surgery, one in the first mate's cabin, and dozens of hammocks hanging belowdecks. I'll manage." He seemed to have made the decision for her. "There are extra blankets in the trunk if you're cold. You will not be disturbed."

She didn't know which was worse: her relief that sanity and honor had prevailed or her disappointment that they had.

"Max—"

"I couldn't keep my sister safe. Can you find it within yourself to let me keep you safe for one night?" The raw misery in his voice made her breath catch and pierced her heart.

"Of course." She swallowed the lump that seemed to have lodged in her throat.

"I'll fetch you in the morning." He turned from her, pausing only when he reached the door. "And then we'll go fetch my sister."

Chapter Ten

Strangely enough, Max slept.

Perhaps it was because he had real information about Beatrice in his possession, information that would help him get her back. He didn't know how yet, exactly, but he knew that he would. That they would. It was not a resolution, but it was somewhere to start.

Or perhaps it was the brandy. Perhaps he had lied to Ivory when he had told her that he wasn't drunk. And if that was the case, perhaps he did have a reasonable excuse for taking her up against the bulkhead of his cabin in the way he had promised himself he wouldn't, at least until this entire mess had been resolved.

He had wanted so much more. To take off every stitch of clothing until there was nothing left between them. Worship her with his hands and his tongue the way she deserved. Push her underneath him in his berth and tease her and taste her, until she came apart again. Feed her desire and her every want until only his name and his body filled every corner of her being.

He had not been prepared for her passion. He had not been prepared for the way she had come apart in his arms, but it had likely been the most heady, erotic experience of his life. And the thing he had found most difficult to step away from. But he also hadn't been prepared for her confession, and it was that, more than the shattering interlude they had shared, that was stirring up unfamiliar, peculiar emotions deep within him. She had entrusted him with a gift. A piece of her past. A piece of who she was. That single gift was the most valuable thing any woman had ever given him. Ever.

There was so much about Ivory Moore that made sense now. The Duke of Knightley had been one of the most powerful men in England. And not just because of his wealth or his endless connections within government, industry, society, and the royal courts. But also because he made it his business to know people and the secrets that they carried. Max had never met the man personally, but everyone had wanted the duke's ear and his approval. He'd had a reputation as a man who could just as easily grease the right wheel at the right time to make it turn in the direction he wished as he could simply cause it to seize indefinitely should he so choose.

He wondered about the elusive Mr. Chegarre and his firm, for which Ivory worked now. Perhaps Chegarre had been a secretary or barrister for the duke. Someone who would have been privy to the secrets and political maneuverings His Grace had made his stock in trade, and understood how to manipulate them. It would explain how Ivory had come to work for the firm, and the responsibility she had assumed on his behalf. She would have brought infinite resources of her own from her past life on the stage. Connections to people like Elise DeVries and Alexander Lavoie, for starters. People like Gil. And the Harris brothers. No wonder Mr. Chegarre had hired her.

Regardless of how she had come to work for the man, she had certainly learned the business well.

He had told her last night that he would allow her to handle King. He was smart enough to recognize that he would need to trust her, but he fully intended to go with her wherever it was she needed to go. To help her do whatever it was she needed to do.

He'd taken one of the berths in the surgery, simply because it was closest to his own, where Ivory slept, and he'd reasoned that he would hear her if she tried to leave. Though now, as he pulled his coat on, he knew she could have left with a drummer boy leading the way and he would likely not have heard her.

The sun was struggling over a low cloud bank in the east, sending feeble light through the portholes of the surgery, as he ducked out into the dimness. His cabin door was still closed, and he wondered if she was still sleeping. He stood outside the door, straining to hear any sort of noise, but the cabin was silent. A vision of her curled up in his berth left him a little breathless. A picture of her sitting in his cabin, scrubbing the sleep from her beautiful eyes, or maybe re-braiding her hair, left him aching with an unfamiliar longing that stole whatever breath remained.

He suddenly realized he had never brought a woman into his cabin before. Mainly because the berth was much too small for bed-sport. But the knowledge that Ivory was in his space, a space that had only ever been his, made him suddenly want all sorts of things that he had never thought he would want.

A woman who would miss him when he was gone. A woman who might be waiting for him, welcoming him home with a warm smile and a warm bed. A woman who fit into his space. Into his life. Permanently.

Max knocked at the door and heard a muffled response. At least she was up. He knocked again and waited a heart-beat before pushing into the cabin.

"Good morning—" He stopped abruptly.

"Good morning, indeed, Your Grace." Alexander Lavoie was reclining in one of the chairs in his cabin, one booted foot crossed over a knee. In his hand he held a glass of the brandy that had been left on the table last night.

Of Ivory Moore there was no sign. Apprehension pricked.

"What the hell are you doing here?" He didn't care if he sounded rude.

"At the moment? Enjoying a very good glass of brandy. This must be French. My compliments."

"It's not even eight o'clock in the morning," Max snapped, crossing his arms and leaning against the cabin door. "Isn't it a little early to be drinking?"

"Ah, but I'll consider it a nightcap. My hours are some-what different than those of an industrious fellow like yourself."

"Where is Miss Moore?" Max was not in the mood for games.

Alex swirled the contents of his glass. "Did you know, I had the very same question barely two hours earlier when I stopped by Chegarre and Associates and was informed that Miss Moore had come here. At a positively indecent hour. I thought I might stop by on my way home."

Max gazed at Lavoie impassively. "This is not on your way home."

Lavoie shrugged.

"And you came here to make sure that I had not bound and gagged Miss Moore and stashed her in my holds?"

Lavoie looked up from his glass and considered Max, the men measuring each other in the silence. "I didn't think you would have gagged her. And I didn't think she would be in your holds."

"Have a care, Mr. Lavoie."

The man tilted his head and placed his glass on the table with a ghost of a smile. "She told me to ask you to be available this afternoon. At your house in St James's."

Anger rose in Max, both at himself for not anticipating this and at Miss Moore for knowing him too well. "Where is she?" he asked coldly.

"She might have mentioned something about an appointment. Asked to borrow my carriage. I was only too happy to comply, though it has left me here awaiting an hour when I might easily hire"—his lip curled up in distaste—"public transportation."

"She left you here to prevent me from going after her." Goddammit, but she had played him. She had left him here, and she had gone to see King. And he didn't have the smallest idea how to find her. He banged the flat of his palm against the doorframe in useless frustration.

Lavoie dragged a finger around the rim of the glass. "And I can see why."

"King has my sister. He plans on selling her like one would a pretty filly at Tattersalls."

"I'm aware."

"And I'm supposed to sit by and do nothing?"

"No." Dark brows drew together. "You're supposed to trust her."

"It's clear she doesn't trust me!"

Lavoie shook his head. "It is not a matter of trust, Your Grace."

"Then what?"

"She might have mentioned something about you being a dangerous distraction." It was said guilelessly, but Max knew better. "Miss Moore no doubt regrets any perceived insult, but she is fully committed to her job. You should be pleased." The last had a slight edge.

Ah yes. Miss Moore and her commitment to her job. To Mr. Chegarre and his damn firm.

"Why aren't you with her?" Max demanded in frustration, ignoring the heat that rose within him. If he couldn't be with her, then Alexander Lavoie should be. He didn't have to like the man to know that he would protect Ivory if the need arose. Lavoie was both clever and dangerous. Chegarre had chosen well when he had hired this man.

"Miss Moore does not need me, nor anyone else, hovering over her shoulder." The intimation was clear.

A thought struck Max. "Why do you work for him?" he demanded. "Why do you work for Mr. Chegarre?"

"Why do I work for Mr. Chegarre?" Lavoie repeated slowly, stalling.

A spurt of impatience fueled Max's anger. "Miss Moore introduced you as an associate. Yet you are clearly a man of means. You own a gaming club, and a wildly successful one at that. I suspect you are in control of a fortune that exceeds mine, which is saying something. So why would you continue to work for Mr. Chegarre?"

"Ah." Lavoie brushed an invisible piece of lint from his

coat. "Let's just say it is a matter of loyalty. I help whenever I can."

"Why?"

"Why does it matter?"

"Because I like to understand why people do the things that they do. Because I like to know where people have come from, where they'd like to go, and just what they're willing to do to get there."

"You sound like the duchess."

"I'll take that as a compliment."

"You should." Lavoie was silent for a long minute before speaking again. "Chegarre loaned me the capital I needed to get my start. Introduced me to the right people. Helped me make connections that were vital to my success. I have long since repaid the monetary debt in full, but such kindness deserves more than prompt payment and compounded interest. Loyalty deserves loyalty."

Despite his ire, Max felt something relax within him. He might not know this man well, but he knew many like him. He put his life in their hands every day on the *Odyssey*. "Thank you. For your honesty."

"You're welcome." Lavoie steepled his fingers. "Have you taken her to your bed? The duchess, that is?"

Max stared at the man, uncertain if he had heard correctly. "I beg your pardon?"

"While we're being honest with each other, it seems like a reasonable question."

"How is that reasonable?" Max was getting over his shock.

"Have you?" Alex repeated his question.

"Why don't you ask her yourself?" Max narrowed his eyes.

"I did. She wouldn't tell me."

"And neither will I."

Lavoie flattened his lips. "I can see why she likes you."

"Why? Because I refuse to sit like an old harpy, gossiping and using her personal life as fodder for a few minutes of entertainment? I think she has rather endured enough of that in her life, don't you?" Max was angry.

Lavoie's eyes sharpened. "You know who she is."

"Of course I know who she is."

"You recognized her."

"No, I didn't recognize her. Until I walked in on her untying a dead earl from my sister's bed, I had never seen her before in my life."

"Then how did you know who she was?"

"She told me."

Lavoie's brows shot to his hairline. "She told you?"

"Yes."

"When?"

Max crossed his arms. "When she wanted to."

Lavoie was studying him in the manner of a boy who had just turned over a rock and discovered a leprechaun.

"Is there something amiss, Mr. Lavoie?" Max inquired.

"No." Lavoie looked contemplative.

"Is there anything else you'd like to say about Miss Moore?"

"No."

"Then get off my ship."

Lavoie stood. "May I inquire as to your plans this morning, Your Grace?"

"No, you may not."

Lavoie sat back down with a sigh.

Max closed his eyes, searching for patience. "For the love of everything that is holy, I will not do anything to interfere with her *appointment* this morning. I don't even know where she's gone."

"Good to hear." Alex drained the last of his brandy from his glass. "I'd have hated to have bound and gagged you and stashed you in your holds."

Max ignored the jibe. "Will she be safe?"

The glass froze halfway back to the table.

"Will Miss Moore be safe? From this King? Will he hurt her?"

Lavoie placed the glass back on the table. "You care about her."

"Of course I care." *I think I'm half in love with her.* That unsolicited thought stopped him cold. That was ridiculous. He admired her, certainly. And there was no denying the overwhelming desire he felt every time she was near. But those things weren't love.

Horrified, he retreated. "That is to say, I care very much about the woman who has taken it upon herself to negotiate for my sister's release."

"Ah." That single response told Max that Lavoie's sharp eyes had missed nothing. "What did I tell you about underestimating Miss Moore's ability to take care of herself?" Alex asked. "She doesn't need you."

"That doesn't make me feel better."

Lavoie stood and leaned over the table. "My job this morning is not to make you feel better, Your Grace. It's to make sure you don't get in her way."

⁓

The day had started out dark and grey, and it hadn't improved as the morning had crept on. Clouds hung low, threatening snow or rain or something in between, and the wind had picked up, rattling the carriage windows as they traveled north to the outskirts of London.

It had been almost a year since Ivory had last turned down the long drive to Helmsdale House. Underneath the carriage wheels, gravel crunched as they rolled past lines of silent trees, their spindly fingers reaching up to the winter sky. Ivory shifted in the carriage, peering out the window, and tried to concentrate on the meeting ahead. And not the meeting that had undoubtedly gone on this morning aboard the *Odyssey*.

Max would have been furious to find her gone. It would be a cold day in hell before Maximus Harcourt simply waited while she negotiated with King for Beatrice's release. Of that there was no doubt. Whatever trust he had gifted her with last night had undoubtedly been retracted with her deception, and that knowledge created a hollow ache deep within her. But desperate times called for desperate measures, and this was not about her and her feelings. It never had been. The future of an eighteen-year-old girl hung in the balance, and Ivory could not fail. If Beatrice wanted to go home with any of that future intact, Ivory would need to keep her wits about her and her feelings out of it.

As Alex's loaned carriage neared the house, it came to a massive gate flanked on either side by imposing stone gatehouses, built within the last decade. A tall wrought-iron fence fell away from either side of the gatehouses, and Ivory knew that the fence went all the way around the house. Ivy had begun to wrap itself around each pointed bar, but the effect was still ominous. As if they were entering an enclosed prison. King did not suffer trespassers kindly.

Two men stepped into the path of the carriage, and Ivory could hear them exchanging words with the driver. Abruptly the door to the carriage was yanked open, and one of the guards stuck his head in.

"State your business." There were no words of welcome.

"Miss Moore to see King," she said smoothly. "He is expecting me."

The guard leered at her. "I just bet he is."

Ivory stared at him, expressionless. She couldn't even begin to count the number of men just like this one whom she had dealt with. They were all the same, the world over. "He's expecting me," she repeated. "And I'd hate to have to explain why I was late."

The guard faltered slightly under her continuous gaze. "I'll open the gate."

"That would be wise." Her tone was icy.

"He is a very busy man today," the guard said rudely, as though unable to leave her with the last word, and slammed the carriage door.

"I just bet he is," muttered Ivory as the gates swung open, and the carriage rolled toward the house.

⁓

King reminded Ivory of the early portraits she had seen of Henry VIII.

He was fair, with reddish-gold hair and pale-blue eyes set into a face that was unyielding and poised. He was clothed in subdued colors, though he made up for the understated dress with a cravat pin that boasted a ruby the size of a sparrow's egg. Gold and gems glinted from fingers that were curled around the top of an ebony walking stick. He was a physically beautiful man, yet Ivory knew that under those layers a dangerous darkness dwelt.

"Good morning, Duchess!" he exclaimed, striding into the study, his eyes appraising her from head to toe. "It has been much too long since this house has been graced by your stunning presence. Still as beautiful as ever."

"Thank you." She had dressed carefully, her gown elaborate and flattering. Exactly what King would wish to see. Ivory offered him her hand, as he expected, and he took it, squeezing it slightly and pressing his lips to the backs of her knuckles.

"You look well, King," she said demurely.

"I am well, indeed," King replied, waving Ivory to a low chair that faced a massive mahogany desk.

She lowered herself into the seat, forced to look up at King as he perched himself on a heavy leather chair behind the desk. Which, she knew, was not an accident.

"You've decorated since I was last here," she said silkily, glancing around the spacious study. One entire wall was covered from the floor to the high ceiling with books, the higher titles accessible by a sliding ladder built expressly for that purpose. The ceiling was plaster, carved cherubs and creatures vying for space along the edges. The walls were covered in sumptuously patterned wallpaper and were hung with an array of framed paintings depicting scenes of battle or voluptuous women reclining in opulence. Crystal abounded on every lighting fixture, and the furniture was heavily gilded. It was a room meant to impress.

Ivory just felt stifled. "Good heavens." She rose, unable to sit, and wandered over to a canvas mounted on the wall near the desk. "Is that a Rubens?" The painting depicted a woman standing over a supine man, shoving his head back and slicing through his neck with a wickedly curved sword. Angels hovered above the pair in silent observation.

King made a delighted noise. "*Judith Beheading Holofernes.* Is it not the most divine thing you've ever seen?"

"Quite." Despite the grisly scene, the detail was exquisite. "I thought this was lost."

"Nothing is lost when one knows where to look." King rubbed his hands together. "I couldn't bear to part with this one." He gave Ivory a smile that sent an unpleasant chill crawling down her spine. "Look at her expression, Duchess. She knows exactly what she is doing. Breathtaking, isn't it? She reminds me a little of you."

Ivory mustered a smile as if this pleased her immeasurably.

"I can't tell you how much I esteem a woman who appreciates rare talent such as is captured on this canvas. Rubens was a master at his craft." He leaned back in his chair. "Just as you were. Did you know I was sixteen when I first saw you on a stage, Duchess? I've always thought it an endless shame I have not seen you there since."

Ivory shrugged slightly. "The woman you saw on that stage is dead, King. She no longer exists. I've moved on. And I enjoy what I do now."

King's lips twitched. "Because you are good at it."

"I'm flattered."

"You should be. Speaking of which, tell me, did everything work out with that diamond necklace?"

"It did." Ivory returned her attention to the painting. "My client was most relieved to have recovered it."

"He might consider more carefully around whose neck he places it again, yes?"

"Something like that."

"Like I said, nothing is lost when one knows where to look." King paused. "But you have not come here seeking diamonds this time, have you?"

Ivory finally turned from the painting, relying now on years of honed acting experience. "No. Not diamonds."

"Then what?"

"A girl."

King tipped his head, his face unreadable. "A girl?"

"Mmmm. One hears things."

"And just what do you think you've heard, Duchess?"

"I've heard that you recently acquired a lot for your auction tonight of the blond variety. Approximately eighteen, naïve, probably more trouble than she'll be worth in the end."

"But very, very beautiful. There are a lot of men who will pay for that."

Ivory shrugged. "The world is full of beautiful women. I must confess I am surprised that you chose to buy such..." She paused, as if searching for the right word. "Risk. I thought horses were bad enough."

"I admit, the offer did take me by surprise. I had to think on it. But with great risk comes great reward, no?" he said. "And this man who sold her is a desperate one. His father frittered away most of their fortune, and he has decimated what was left. Now he supports himself by bringing me all sorts of treasures from what's left of his estate. Some I buy. Some I do not. But his latest offering was intriguing. He didn't know what to do with her." He smirked. "I, on the other hand, had some ideas."

"What sort of man does not know what to do with a woman?" Ivory scoffed, concealing a very careful fishing expedition.

"One who is cowardly. And not very clever. Did you miss the part about the lost fortune?"

Ivory slanted him a sidelong glance. "You do know who she is, don't you?"

"Of course I do."

"And you bought her anyway?"

King frowned slightly. "What's not to like? She's beautiful, docile—"

"Docile?" Ivory sniffed. "Not the word I might have used for her."

"Who wants her?" King was drumming his fingers on the desk now, the pace matching the gallop of Ivory's heart.

"A client."

King made a sound of displeasure. "Don't be obtuse, Duchess. It is not attractive."

Ivory sighed, signaling her remorse. "Very well. I represent her family."

"Her brother. The duke." King leaned forward just a little too eagerly.

Ivory didn't answer and strolled along the wall, stopping at a painting from which two curvaceous naked women stared coyly at her as they frolicked in a fountain. "Not her brother, really. Her aunt."

. King sat back in his chair. "I would have thought the duke would be anxious to prevent his sister from ruin."

Ivory snorted loudly. "From ruin? Surely you jest."

King's fingers froze, the drumming ceasing abruptly.

Ivory gazed at him. "Jesus, King. You thought she was a virgin? This was what you thought to auction? You were going to sell her virginity to the highest bidder?" She suppressed an inward shudder.

His lips thinned unpleasantly.

Ivory shook her head. "Do you know why her aunt hired me in the first place? It was because the Earl of Debarry expired in the young lady's bed from debauched exertions of the likes I will not detail. Let me just say that she was a little too much for an old man to handle."

A faint, mottled red was creeping up King's neck. "I heard Debarry died at a ball from an apoplexy."

Ivory smiled and returned to the painting of Judith. "Of course you did."

King was frowning. "That was your work."

"Of course it was." Ivory took a deep breath, choosing her words with care. "Look, the duke is an arrogant ass. He has about as much interest in his sister as he does in me. He chooses to spend all of his time in India, as opposed to London, with his family. You tell me how much a promiscuous sister is worth to a man like that." She shrugged carelessly. "The duke would have her back if only to ensure that there is no further stain on the family name. She was ruined long before she was sold to you."

"I don't believe you."

"Then ask her yourself. Ask her what color the ribbons were that she used to tie the earl to her bed."

King was staring at Ivory coldly. He reached behind him and yanked on a gold-tasseled bellpull. Within a minute a hulking brute of a giant appeared in the doorway.

"Bring me the girl," King demanded, and the giant disappeared.

Ivory could feel a bead of cold sweat slide down her back. Beatrice was here. She was so close. Feigning casualness, she wandered to the next canvas on the wall. A Roman general in full armor was in the process of slaying a writhing, scaly beast. His face, like the face of the woman in the first painting, held only cruel determination.

"I must assume that the man who sold her to you was not entirely forthcoming." Ivory was fishing again.

"I will reserve judgment on that," King snapped.

"If you want my opinion, King, in the future, stick to what you know. Paintings. Sculpture. Things that don't dally in the beds of earls."

"I didn't ask for your opinion, Duchess."

"I'm only trying to help. You know I have your best interests at heart."

"You have my best interests at heart when it suits you," he replied with biting sarcasm.

"Touché."

"I had something very special arranged for this girl tonight," King mused darkly. "I don't want to—"

The doorway was suddenly filled with a man, pushing a girl in front of him. She was tall and slender and possessed the same grey eyes as her brother, only hers were redrimmed and full of fear. She was dressed in an ornate white gown adorned with silver embroidery. Her blond tresses had been pulled off her face but left to stream down her back, and a wreath of tiny white flowers had been woven into the crown of her hair.

"Good Lord, King. You went all out, didn't you? All she's missing is a pair of wings."

"Bring her here," King demanded.

The guard moved, prodding Beatrice forward. She came to a halt in front of the huge desk, looking like an errant schoolgirl about to get reprimanded. The guard left the room, and Ivory moved to the side of the desk, standing slightly behind King, so that she could face the girl.

She willed Beatrice to look at her, but she was staring at the floor.

"I have been informed that you are not as advertised," King started.

Beatrice didn't respond.

"Look at me when I'm speaking to you," King snapped, and Beatrice's head finally came up.

"Tell me that you're a virgin."

Beatrice paled.

"Answer me!"

Moisture filmed her eyes.

"Bloody hell, King, stop yelling at her." Ivory made a noise of disgust. "You're terrifying her and hurting my ears. Whoever it was who sold her to you should have disclosed that information, not her." She softened her voice. "But it's a yes-or-no answer, dear. Just tell the man and save us all a great deal of time."

A single tear slid down Beatrice's cheek as she slowly shook her head.

Ivory leaned closer to King. "Did you know that Debarry wanted to marry her?"

Beatrice's eyes snapped to Ivory's. Finally.

"But I can't imagine that will add much value. Too bad the earl isn't still alive. He would have beggared himself to get her back." Behind King, Ivory put her finger to her lips, praying the girl had some sense. "Certainly more than her brother is willing to do."

Beatrice dropped her gaze back to the rug at her feet.

Ivory let out a careful breath.

King had his hands clenched on the desk.

"What do you want for her, King?" Ivory asked in a bored tone. "And be reasonable. She's a ruined sister of an absentee aristocrat. She's a nobody."

King abruptly stood, swinging around to face Ivory. "You have no idea how much this displeases me," he said, and the icy calm with which he said it was ominous. "I had plans for her. Plans I made known to interested parties. Now there are expectations that I cannot meet, and that is never good for business. It's too late to replace her with something of equal quality." He stared hard at her. "You've ruined things for me tonight, Duchess."

Ivory felt cold, even though she was sweating under her gown. To show weakness or fear now would be dangerous. "In all fairness, I didn't ruin anything. You ruined whatever plans you had when you purchased ruined merchandise." She paused. "In fact, I might have just saved you from some embarrassment. For you do not sell forgeries."

"Perhaps." King pushed past her and stopped in front of the Rubens painting. He studied the bloody scene for a long minute. Somewhere a clock ticked the time into the silence. Beatrice sniffled loudly. Ivory held her breath.

Suddenly King turned from the painting, and whatever anger he had shown was gone, replaced with cunning calculation.

"She's yours, Duchess, if you want her."

Ivory felt the hairs stand up on the back of her neck. "How much?"

"Two hundred pounds. It's what I paid for her."

Ivory's mind was racing. There was no way that King would simply give her what she wanted this easily. There was a catch somewhere.

"Two hundred pounds?" She made sure her voice held nothing but cool skepticism.

"Yes. And your attendance at tonight's auction."

"Why?"

"Because it pleases me to have you attend my little soiree."

Why? she wanted to demand. She held her tongue, knowing she would receive her answer only when King was ready to give it.

"There is nothing little about anything you do, King," she said instead, keeping her voice low and faintly amused.

The man smiled. "Indeed there isn't."

Ivory didn't like this one bit. Every instinct she had was screaming a warning. For the life of her, Ivory couldn't even begin to guess what King was plotting, but it was there, hanging over her like a giant guillotine blade, waiting for someone to release it when it was least expected.

"I have a reputation of being a man who can provide the…*impossible*." King waved a hand airily at the walls of his study. "Lost paintings and the like. And you too have a reputation for providing your clients the impossible. Lost debutantes and the like." Brows rose over pale eyes. "I think, Duchess, that this is a superb opportunity for us to help each other. A…trade, perhaps, to make sure we each get what we want." He paused. "Because there is something far more extraordinary that I could offer in her place. You were right—this girl here is a nobody." He smiled then. "But Ivory Bellafiore is not."

Understanding descended, landing like a leaden weight in her gut and forcing the breath from her lungs. King would exact his price tonight, and he would do it by catching her up in the gilded cage she had fled. The cage she had promised herself she would never return to.

"I don't think I like your suggestion." She kept her voice firm with a monumental effort.

King's face hardened. "Then leave the girl. Go back to your duke and tell him you were unable to retrieve his sister. Though my clients will not be pleased, someone *will* buy her, regardless of her flaws. At the very least, I'll get back what I paid for her, which, incidentally, wasn't that much. But it's up to you. You can take her home now, or leave her here."

Ivory looked at Beatrice, who was watching her again, terror and misery stamped clearly across her pretty features. She felt the weight of that grey gaze, so much like Max's that it was a little like looking into his own. She thought of him, and how much he loved his sister. Of how much he had trusted Ivory to do this. To get her back. She thought of the single stupid mistake that an eighteen-year-old girl had made to set off a chain reaction of events that was about to cost her everything. She thought about what might happen if Beatrice was sold to one of King's clients.

Beatrice Harcourt might not be a virgin, but she was innocent in the ways of men.

Ivory Bellafiore was not.

A calm descended then, a perfect clarity that made her next words easy to say. "Very well," Ivory answered finally.

The man smiled and clasped his hands together. "Splendid! I'm so glad to hear it."

Ivory stared impassively at him, feeling as if she were watching this scene play out from somewhere far away. "One night. Those are my terms."

"You aren't in much of a position to demand terms, Duchess."

"Perhaps not, but Ivory Bellafiore is."

King chuckled. "God, Duchess, but you have nerve. I admire that."

"Then we are in agreement?"

"Yes."

"Good. I'm taking her back to her family now." She moved to where Beatrice stood.

"Of course, of course. I'm sure they will be thrilled to have their wayward lamb back in the fold." King joined her. "An earl," he murmured. "Who would have thought? Just as well I didn't know sooner or I might have sampled the wares myself."

Beatrice was cringing, and Ivory grasped her arm and pulled the girl behind her. "Don't be crude, King. It's not attractive."

The man laughed, a dry, empty sound. "Ah, Duchess. You are going to be magnificent tonight. And please don't worry about what to wear, I'll have a little something here for you to slip on when you arrive. Now, I will send a carriage for you at eight o'clock sharp. I do so hope to find you waiting. It would be a shame if your little lamb or someone in her family should find herself the victim of a terrible accident."

Ivory did not think for one second that the man was making an empty threat. "It would," she agreed.

King *tsk*ed. "London has become such a dangerous place these days."

Chapter Eleven

London was a dangerous place.

It was one of the points in the speech Max had prepared in his head that he was bound and determined to deliver to Ivory, whether she wanted to hear it or not. He had rehearsed his words, all reasonably ordered and all logically argued, that explained why she could not hare off by herself without him like that. Ever again.

Though he was smart enough to know what her reaction would be. No doubt she would scoff and remind him that her connections throughout the demimonde and the underbelly of London were exceptionally exhaustive. No doubt she was handling this King with the same aplomb with which she handled corpses.

Yet that didn't make him feel better.

Nothing had made him feel better since he had woken in his cabin to find Alexander Lavoie drinking his brandy and

Ivory Moore gone. And now he was left pacing through his town house like a caged lion, waiting.

Waiting for Ivory to show up. Waiting for news about Beatrice. Waiting for information on this King. Waiting, waiting, waiting. It was not his strong suit.

The servants had wisely found duties that kept them well out of his path, and he was prowling across the empty hall, chasing his smeared reflection across the brilliantly polished marble floor, when he heard the rattle of carriage wheels come to a stop outside. He swerved toward the tall window and yanked back the expensive curtain. A carriage had come to a halt in front of the steps. The driver was still perched atop it and speaking to someone inside the carriage through the vent behind him. The equipage shifted on its springs, and then the door swung open and Ivory stepped out.

Well, it was about bloody time.

Max flew to the front door, taking a minute to compose himself. He would need all of his wits for the conversation he was about to have. Not waiting for her to knock, he yanked open the door.

And stared.

Beatrice stared back at him, frozen on the top step. An intense relief such as he had never known flooded through him, making his muscles a little wobbly. His eyes raked Beatrice from head to toe as if searching for wounds, or some other physical trauma. But his sister was wearing a plain grey cloak, the skirts of a mundane brown dress peeking out at the bottom. Her hair was pulled neatly away from her face, braided and concealed under a bonnet. Aside from the unusual paleness of her cheeks and the slight redness of her eyes, it looked as if she might have just returned from a morning of travel.

"Bea," he said numbly.

She sniffled, and then, in a heartbeat, she launched herself at him and buried her face against his chest. Max started before drawing her to him, emotion swelling within him.

"I'm so sorry," she whispered, her voice full of misery.

"I know," Max told her.

"I was so stupid," she mumbled.

"I know."

"You must hate me."

"I could never hate you," he said fiercely, hearing the truth of that. "You're my sister."

His eyes skipped then over her shoulder to the second figure who waited just behind her, the hood of her cloak covering her dark-brown hair and casting her face in shadow. She was waiting patiently, the way a well-trained lady's maid might until she received further instruction from her mistress.

"Come," he said, carefully disentangling himself from his sister and glancing around the square. "Let's go inside."

Bea nodded tearfully and gripped his arm, allowing herself to be led into the hall. The sounds of hurrying footsteps signaled the arrival of the butler, no doubt alerted by the sound of the front door. Max was well aware that they were now surrounded by unwanted ears.

"Welcome home, my lady," the butler said, shutting the door behind them and hurrying forward to take her cloak. "I was unaware we were expecting you back this afternoon."

"She decided to come home a little early," Max said for her.

"Shall I send for Lady Helen?" the butler asked. "She is resting upstairs."

"No, no, let her rest. I fear she's been quite tired as of late. Dull winter weather makes anyone weary." He shrugged casually. "The ladies will have plenty of time to catch up later." There was not a chance in hell that he would let Helen speak to Beatrice before he did.

"Of course, Your Grace."

Max patted Beatrice's arm. "I imagine you're exhausted from your travels, my dear. And I'm sure the roads were frightful. Might I suggest we retire to the drawing room?"

Beatrice nodded silently.

"Will you require refreshments, Your Grace?" the butler asked.

"No. That will be all, thank you." Max waved the butler off, frantic to be rid of the man.

The butler left and Max glanced over at Ivory, his gaze colliding with hers. It was everything that Max could do not to catch her up in his arms and kiss her senseless. Whatever ire he'd harbored at her deception had drained, leaving him humbled and unsteady. A million questions crowded into his brain, each demanding an answer. But that would have to wait. For now he would have to simply accept that she had done what she had promised to do. She had brought Beatrice home safely.

"Let's move out of the hall, shall we?" Ivory suggested quietly.

Max led the way into the drawing room, ushering Beatrice through. He caught Ivory's arm before she could follow.

"Are you all right?" he asked, searching her eyes. The urge to kiss her was overwhelming. The longing that had been building became unbearably acute. It made him want to give her impossible things. It made him want impossible things.

"I'm fine, thank you."

Of course she was. "Ivory, I—"

"I took Beatrice back to my place before we came here. Cleaned her up, gave her some decent clothes so as not to arouse suspicion that she has been doing anything else in the last days except traveling." She glanced meaningfully over his shoulder in the direction of Bea.

"Thank you." It sounded excruciatingly insufficient.

"Of course."

He stole a glimpse at his sister, who had sunk down on a settee, her expression bleak. "Is Beatrice—"

"Untouched. Well, at least by King." She stopped, looking as though she was collecting her thoughts. "She's also ashamed and embarrassed about what happened and properly terrified about what might have happened."

"Did she tell you who—"

"Yes."

"Who?" he hissed, a cold fury starting deep in his gut. He embraced it, because it was something he knew. Something that anchored him amid the rest of the emotions that were battering at him.

"She needs to be the one to tell you," Ivory murmured. "She needs to own her part in this."

Max let out a breath.

"But you need to get rid of the current expression on your face. It looks like you're about to kill someone."

"I am."

"I do ask that you endeavor to remember what I told you about vengeance," she said. "You can't undo what happened."

"No, but I can make sure that someone pays for it."

Ivory tipped her head, and he was extraordinarily grateful that she wasn't trying to placate him with inanities.

"What— How did you— How much—" He stopped, trying to marshal his thoughts.

"King and I came to an agreement regarding your sister's release," Ivory said, her eyes unreadable.

"What kind of agreement?" Max demanded. Nothing about that statement sounded good.

"The kind of agreement that gets everyone what they want." She smiled strangely again and gestured back in the direction of the drawing room. "You should go to her, Your Grace. She needs her brother."

And I need you.

His hand tightened around her arm. "Stay."

"My place is not with your family, Your Grace."

You're wrong. Your place is with me.

He tightened his hand on her arm. "I want you to stay. Please. If not for me, then for Beatrice."

Ivory bit her lower lip. "Very well."

"Thank you."

Ivory slipped past him, and he closed the door and turned the key in the lock. He would not take the chance of any unwanted eavesdroppers.

Ivory had taken a seat on one of the wing chairs close to the hearth. She jerked her head in the direction of the settee, and Max approached his sister, settling his weight on the opposite end. He gazed at Bea, wondering how she had grown up so fast. She wasn't a little girl anymore. Even red-eyed and pale, she carried the beauty of a woman now, all traces of pretty girlishness gone. When had she stopped being the girl who could be delighted with the gift of a seashell and become a woman who amused herself with earls?

"Tell me about Debarry," he said, unsure of where to start. Debarry seemed like the beginning, which was as good a place as any.

Beatrice looked up at him, dry-eyed now. She glanced in the direction of Ivory as if seeking reassurance. Ivory nodded encouragingly.

"I was a fool," she said.

"I think we've already established that," Max said. "But I am not innocent of doing foolish things in my life either."

Beatrice stared at him, her lower lip trembling slightly. "I didn't love him."

"Debarry?"

She nodded. "That's why I wouldn't marry him."

"But you could tie him to your bed." It sounded harsh, but there it was.

Beatrice flinched but didn't look away. "He made me feel special. He made me feel like I had power. Like I could control my destiny. I loved how he made me feel."

Max stared.

"I never wanted him to die. I might not have loved him, but I cared for him." A single tear escaped, and she scrubbed it away, almost angrily. "He'd been complaining about feeling poorly all week. I should never have..." She trailed off before looking up at him, her eyes beseeching him to understand. "I was suffocating here, Max. You have no idea how that feels."

He could feel Ivory's eyes on him, and he was afraid to look at her. "You're wrong."

"How could I be wrong?" Beatrice cried. "How could you know how I feel? You have all the freedom you could ever want. There is a new adventure awaiting you every day over every horizon. You get to live on your own terms." She paused, making a visible effort to collect herself. "What is here for me? What do I have to look forward to?"

"You have everything to look forward to," Max said. Didn't she? What could she possibly want that wasn't attainable? He was well aware he was deep into uncharted territory now.

"Like what, Max? A loveless marriage arranged by the proper merger of title and fortune? The production of at least one child every two years so that they might be banished into a nursery until they are old enough to be banished elsewhere? A constant parade of visits with the ton, who are more concerned with the cut of their dress than the changes that are happening all around us in the world?" She stopped and took a deep breath. "I don't want that life, Max. And no one seems to understand it."

"I do."

That stopped her cold. "What?"

"I said I understand." He looked over at Ivory, her eyes soft with a gentle understanding of her own. She had understood Beatrice long before he had. She had understood him long before he had.

She blinked. "Then why wouldn't you ever take me with you? Why did you leave me here?"

"Because I thought I was doing what was best for you. I didn't want to see you hurt. Or worse."

Beatrice looked down unhappily.

"Tell me what happened the night of the ball." Max knew he was shying away from a much longer, much deeper conversation that was going to need to take place between Beatrice and him. But not right now.

His sister took a deep, tremulous breath. "I panicked. When I realized Debarry was dead, I ran. My only thought was to get as far away from it all as possible. Childish, I know."

"Then what?"

"I went around back to the mews. I thought maybe I could take a horse or...I don't know what I was thinking. I wasn't thinking. I was dressed in only my chemise and my cloak." She was studying her hands, her fingers twisting the fabric of her skirt.

"And who was there?" Max asked carefully.

"The Earl of Barlow," she whispered. "He was smoking out back."

"Barlow," Max repeated, concentrating very hard on keeping his voice even. He'd been at the ball, had talked to Max that night and then again the next day in the street. Had asked if he could arrange an appointment to discuss a matter of business— Oh God. Max had missed that appointment. And he had a very good idea now what Barlow had wanted to discuss. His stomach lurched sickeningly.

"And what did Barlow do?" It was barely a whisper.

Beatrice swallowed. "He helped me. At first. Smuggled me into his carriage. Took me to his house, said that I could stay there until the talk died down. Promised to talk to Helen and make sure that no one knew what had really happened."

"I see."

"But then he wouldn't let me go. Locked me upstairs. There was no way for me to escape. He told me that there was only one way that he would allow me to leave." The fabric of Beatrice's skirts was completely twisted now, her knuckles white. "And that was as his wife."

Max started. "What?"

Beatrice looked up at him, a fierceness blazing briefly from her grey eyes. "I told him I would rather die than marry him. That he could rape me or ruin me, but that I would never marry a man like him."

"Jesus, Beatrice." Max felt his blood ice over.

"I wouldn't have, you know." Beatrice dropped her gaze again, back to her hands. "Killed myself."

"I'm glad to hear that." Max shifted uncomfortably.

"But that monster didn't know that. He made me write those letters to you, afraid that you would come looking for me. I don't think he planned on you being back in town. I think you terrify him." She said the last with a note of cold satisfaction.

The edges of Max's vision were blurring again. Belatedly he realized that Ivory had left her chair and come to stand behind the settee. He could feel one of her hands on his shoulder, a warm, steadying touch.

"The Barlow estate is in ruin, Your Grace," Ivory said quietly. "It has been for decades. I can only assume that Barlow thought he might force Lady Beatrice to marry him, if only to gain access to her dowry."

Max felt every muscle in his body tense. "That is the most idiotic, preposterous thing I've ever heard. Did he not think that I wouldn't find out the circumstances surrounding their sudden engagement? The fact that he had blackmailed Bea into marrying him?"

"I don't think he counted on you at all. I think he thought you were still an ocean away and that his negotiations would be solely with your aunt."

"Who would have agreed to anything to preserve Bea's reputation."

"Probably."

Max felt her hand move from his shoulder. "Barlow is well acquainted with King. He's been selling off what remains of his estate, piece by piece. It's how he's been raising money to live on."

"So he thought he would sell my sister the same way he would sell a silver tea service?" Max knew his voice was rising but he didn't care.

"He was desperate. Nothing had gone as planned. And he needed money."

"He won't need money for anything for much longer," Max snarled.

"I'm so sorry." Beatrice was looking between Max and Ivory. "I never wanted any of this to happen."

Max reined in his anger. "But it did and we are not done talking about this. God, Bea, you could have—" He couldn't even finish.

"I know." She hung her head in misery. "I've disappointed you."

"Yes. But I might have disappointed you first," Max sighed. "We'll figure this out. Together."

The doorknob suddenly rattled loudly. "Beatrice? Alderidge? Are you in there?" Helen's voice was frantic.

Max stood and hurried to the door and unlocked it, and Helen burst into the room, her eyes swinging wildly about until they came to rest on Bea.

"My maid told me Beatrice had just arrived. That she'd come home early. She was worried about having enough time to press a dinner gown." Helen stood frozen. "I didn't believe her."

"She's all right, Aunt Helen," Max told her.

Helen turned and suddenly Max found himself being

embraced by a woman who had never had cause to do so in the past. "Thank you," Helen whispered, her voice quivering. "Thank you for bringing her home."

"It wasn't me," he said, but Helen didn't seem to hear him, only slipping from his grasp to hurry to Beatrice's side. He looked for Ivory, only to realize that she had drifted silently to the door.

"Where are you going?"

Ivory started, as if she hadn't expected to be stopped. "Home," she said. "It is clear that you and your family have a great deal to discuss. But you no longer need me."

You're wrong, Max wanted to say. *I need you more than ever.*

She paused, one hand on the doorknob. "If you require anything further, please don't hesitate to ask. If I am unavailable, Mr. Lavoie or Miss DeVries will be able to assist you." With every word she spoke, it felt as if she was slipping further and further away from him, and he was damned if he knew how to stop it.

"Ivory—"

"Goodbye, Your Grace. It's been a pleasure working with you."

And with that, she was gone.

Chapter Twelve

When the Duke of Knightley's health had begun to fail in the last year of their marriage, he had secretly bought this place in Covent Square. Had the interior renovated and repaired, an oasis hidden in plain sight. He and Ivory had both known that, despite his best efforts, despite wills and paperwork and heated arguments with his children, he would not be able to protect her once he was gone. Though both had been confident that her resourcefulness and intelligence would ensure that she would be fine on her own. And she had been.

Until now.

Ivory sighed, watching disinterestedly from her window as darkness fell outside and the drunken revelry of the night built in volume. People falling into old habits under the guise of new adventures.

And Ivory would know about that.

She pulled the drapes and lit a candelabrum. The expensive beeswax candles gave off a soft glow and sent long shadows into the corners of her study. On the mantel the clock ticked the time away relentlessly, counting down the minutes until she went back to Helmsdale House and did what she'd sworn she would never do again.

She'd made a deal with the devil, but she would do it again given the chance. If only to see the relief and the love that had suffused Max's face when Beatrice had flown into his arms. It was what she had always imagined a family to be. Devotion and forgiveness. Support and understanding. It had brought tears to her eyes.

Ivory slid down the back of the desk, the heavy walnut smooth and cool at her back, the pile of the carpet thick underneath her. She stared at the glowing coals in the hearth as she stretched her legs out in front of her and took another healthy swallow of the whiskey that was dwindling in the decanter as quickly as the heat was dwindling in the hearth.

She was lost. Everything that had been so carefully planned and patiently executed teetered on the edge of recklessness. Her entire existence—her entire way of life—had been blurred by a gasping, desperate sense of longing so painful she could barely manage her emotions anymore. Because of him. Because of what he'd shown her.

From the depths of the house, she could hear voices. Roddy's, and another, deeper, more urgent voice. Booted feet sounded in the hall, drawing closer until they stopped at the door of her study. She didn't move.

"Ivory? Where are you?" Max's voice came from somewhere near the door on the other side of the desk.

Ivory closed her eyes, not sure if she had the strength to face him. She did not want to lie to him. Nor could she tell him the truth.

"I'm here," she said with resignation, knowing he'd find her in a few seconds anyway. She closed her eyes and took another swallow of whiskey, the liquid sloshing loudly against the crystal.

"Ivory?" She heard the sound of the door closing, heard the click of the lock. And then she felt, rather than heard, Max move around the desk and come to a stop somewhere beside her. "What the hell are you doing?"

She let her head tip back carelessly against the desk and opened her eyes. *Hiding from you.* "I live here," she said instead.

"Are you drunk?" His face was wreathed in shadows and his question was devoid of nuance.

"Not nearly enough," she replied. "Roderick wasn't supposed to have let you in."

"I can be very persuasive." He stood in silence for a long moment before coming to stand directly in front of her. His bulk blocked the meager heat that was emanating from the hearth, and cool air caressed her skin. "Why are you here? Hiding behind a desk?"

Ivory took another sip of whiskey. "You should go," she said quietly.

Max shrugged out of his coat and let it fall carelessly to the floor. Then he dropped to his knees and crawled to the empty space beside her, coming to sit next to her, his back resting against the desk. He unfolded his legs, almost enough for hers to touch should she ever find the courage. Intimate but distant.

The story of her life.

His body warmth beside her had far eclipsed what the struggling hearth provided, and it ignited a wild need that a thousand bonfires couldn't compare to. The same need she had fought against since the moment she had first laid eyes on him. She stared at the tips of his boots, gleaming dully in the firelight. She was terrified that if she turned to look at him, she would do something foolish. For this night, her emotions were being checked by only the most tenuous of holds. Tonight they writhed and seethed, looking for a crack from which to explode.

Beside her Max shifted, yanking his cravat loose with a sigh of relief. He dropped the offending linen to the side and reached for the decanter she still held. Silently she relinquished her hold and heard him breathe deeply before tipping his head back and swallowing. She would not think about his lips on the cool edge where hers had been. She would not think about the way his lips would taste now— of whiskey and desire. She would not think at all.

"This is good whiskey." His voice was roughened by the liquor.

"Life is too short for cheap whiskey."

She heard him take another swallow while she refocused her attention from the tips of his boots to the edge of her skirt that was trapped underneath a muscular thigh. Her own thighs squeezed together to ease the ache that was building.

"Tell me what happened with King. Tell me how you got Beatrice back."

Ivory felt a hysterical bubble of laughter rise in her throat. "I negotiated." She pronounced the word carefully.

"That's not good enough."

"What does it matter?"

"Because I want to know what her release cost."

Nothing she hadn't traded before. And she had survived that just as she would survive this. "Two hundred pounds. What he paid for her."

"That's all?"

"That's all that concerns you. This was a business matter between King and Chegarre."

"I see." He sounded relieved, and she knew he had interpreted her words exactly as she'd intended. She'd given him something he could relate to—an agreement between two businessmen.

Casually he handed the decanter back, the heavy crystal warm in her hand. She stared down at the rim, daring herself to put her mouth where his had been. Instead she placed the whiskey on the floor beside her. "Why are you here, Max? Sitting on a floor in the middle of Covent Square?"

"I believe I asked you that first."

"And I answered."

"You did not. You evaded."

Ivory bowed her head. "Don't be difficult."

"I'm not difficult. I'm concerned." His hands were resting on his thighs. Relaxed. Unaffected. She thought she might scream if she didn't come out of her skin first.

"Don't be concerned, Max. I'm fine."

"Now you're being difficult. And you're not fine. People who are fine do not hide behind desks."

"I'm not hiding. I'm enjoying a good vintage."

"By yourself? On the floor?"

"It's a comfortable floor."

"Ivory." There was a faint question in the syllables.

She bit her lip.

"Ivory. Look at me."

"I can't."

Beside her he sighed and turned his body so that he was facing her. She could feel the weight of his gaze. Her fingers curled into her skirts.

"I'm going to kiss you now." He was so close, his eyes searching hers.

Yes. Do it and don't stop.

He reached out and ran a finger down the side of her cheek, his thumb grazing her lower lip. Her heart was pounding, and the blood was roaring through her veins. She might have nodded. Wants and desires and dreams that she had shut away long ago were suddenly crashing through her mercilessly. She wanted to be with this man, to be by his side, not because he was paying her to do so, but because she could.

The careful barriers that she had built around herself were crumbling like a wall of sand in the face of a rising tide. Maximus Harcourt was no longer just a client, any more than he was an amusement or a distraction. There was no point in pretending anymore, and with that admission a weight seemed to slide away from her. For better or for worse, this man had become something more. "Max—"

"Shh. I'm going kiss you, Ivory. And then I'm going to make love to you."

"But I think—"

"You think too much. Stop thinking. Just feel."

She nodded, even as her body shuddered. Just this once she was going to let go. Choose something for herself. "Upstairs—"

"Too far away." There was a ragged edge to his words as he pushed himself away from the desk on his knees and leaned into her. His hands came to rest on either side of her hips. "I've wanted to do this for too long." His lips grazed her forehead.

The scent of him filled her nostrils. That strange male essence of heat, laced with whiskey. Her hand went to the smooth fabric of his waistcoat, as if that might keep her steady.

His lips slid to her cheek, branding her irreversibly. "I love how you feel," he whispered.

Her other hand rose to the collar of his shirt, sliding along his neck and down his shoulder. Beneath her fingers she could feel his restraint, his muscles flexing and bunching. Max groaned softly and dipped his head to where her pulse thundered along the side of her throat. His lips were gentle and insistent all at once. The stubble from his cheek grazed the underside of her jaw, and she closed her eyes, her fingers tightening on his shoulder.

His fingers were working now at the pins on the front of her gown, and quickly the fabric fell away. He pushed the top off her shoulders, pulling it down her arms, and she wriggled free. His mouth was sliding down her collarbone now, and his hands went to her back, pulling her up and forward so that she knelt in front of him. He was tugging at the laces of her dress and her petticoats, yanking them from their neat bows, shoving everything down her body, his actions becoming more urgent.

Her stays and chemise went next, tossed to the side with a growl of triumph or frustration—it was difficult to tell which. She was naked now, kneeling in a puddle of linen and wool, the cool air sending gooseflesh skittering across her skin. He knelt before her, his hands resting on her hips, his fingers tracing small circles over the bones. Slowly they skimmed up over her ribs, cupping her breasts, his thumbs grazing her nipples that had already hardened to sensitive peaks. Ivory gazed up at him, breathing hard.

"So beautiful," he murmured, bending to kiss her again, his mouth demanding now. Ivory surrendered, her own fingers working at his clothing frantically. It wasn't enough to have his hands on her bare skin. She wanted to feel all of him, the friction of heat and skin and sweat.

She pulled his shirt over his head and was met with his glorious chest, planes of muscle and sinew begging to be explored. Beneath the pads of her fingers was a scattering of blond hair, thickening as it narrowed into a trail that disappeared down the front of his breeches. She leaned forward, trailing kisses along the strong column of his throat, and continuing lower, sucking gently on his nipples, running her tongue over the ridges of his ribs. He groaned, his fingers tangling in her hair, urging her lower. Her hands went to the fall of his breeches and the bulge of his erection straining through the fabric.

She was wet, the intense throbbing in her belly and between her legs eroding her self-control. The need to have him filling her, pushing deeply into her, was overwhelming. It was making her clumsy as she fumbled with his buttons. "Your breeches," she gasped, not caring how desperate she sounded. She *was* desperate.

Max let go of her long enough to rip at the buttons, pushing his breeches along with his boots from his legs. He came at her then, catching her behind her back and lowering her down on the rug in front of the hearth. He crouched between her legs, dipping his head, kissing her hard, a fevered clashing of teeth and tongues. One of his hands drifted past her navel, fingers gliding through the folds of her sex, hissing with pleasure at what he found.

Ivory arched off the floor, every nerve ending in her body on fire. He slid a finger deep inside her, and Ivory gasped before she caught his wrist and pulled his hand away.

"No. I want you inside me when I come," she said. "All of you."

Max made a tortured sound deep in his throat, lowering himself on top of her, his hands braced on her shoulders. She could feel him now, his erection pressing against her opening, and she wrapped her legs around his waist, knowing she was perilously close to falling over the edge. He pushed into her ever so slowly, his head dropping to catch one of her nipples with his mouth. His teeth grazed it, the sensation bordering on the edge of pain, intensifying every touch. A shudder ripped through her.

She rocked her hips against him, the torment nearly blinding. "Max," she whispered.

Her plea seemed to snap whatever threads of restraint remained, and he thrust, sheathing himself deep within her. Ivory closed her eyes against the rush of ecstasy that ignited, gasping as he withdrew slightly and then surged into her again. She tightened her legs about his waist and held on to his upper arms as they bunched and flexed. Pleasure was tightening deep within her, wave after wave coiling and building with each of his thrusts. His hair brushed her cheek, and she could hear his breath laboring in her ear. He was sweating now, and she opened her eyes, turning her head just enough to lick the saltiness from his throat. He moaned loudly, his hips driving forward, and without warning everything convulsed within her, pleasure of an intensity she'd never experienced tearing through her limbs and emptying her mind of everything except the feel of him.

He stiffened, pulsing within her, every muscle in his body straining, braced against the tide of his own pleasure. After a moment he collapsed against her, rolling to the side, pulling her with him. They lay silent on the floor, catching their breath, the air cooling their damp bodies. Max reached behind him for his coat and pulled it over both of them, tucking Ivory's head against his shoulder as he did so.

"You should stop thinking more often," he said presently, staring up at the ceiling. His free hand was caressing the soft skin of her inner arm, his touch warm under the blanket.

Ivory smiled, not sure whether she should laugh or cry. She did neither, only turned her head to press a kiss against his chest. She just wanted to preserve this moment, fix it in her memory. Allow herself the luxury of pretending that things could be different, just for this tiny snippet of time that was still hers.

"You have to admit I'm right." He jostled her gently.

"You're right." She smiled.

"Mmmm. Say that again. That I'm right."

"I'll say it if you can do *that* again," she teased, unable to help herself.

A low chuckle rumbled through his chest against her ear. "What, this?" He levered himself up and kissed her, a long, lazy exploration that left her head spinning. "Or this?" His free hand stroked her breast, caressed her hip and her belly, before parting the folds of her sex and putting a slow, steady pressure against her clitoris.

Ivory sucked in her breath at the friction. "Yes." She couldn't get enough of this man. She should be sated and exhausted, yet already arousal was flooding through her again, her body straining toward him, toward his touch. And he knew it.

Max ran a hand along the inside of her thigh, pushing

it wider. All the humor had fled from his face, replaced by a dark desire that stormed in his eyes. He watched her, his gaze trapping her own, while his fingers delved into her heat and slickness.

"Don't stop," Ivory said breathlessly, feeling a heat build within her again.

"Are you giving me orders again, Miss Moore?" His voice was low and husky.

"Yes," she gasped.

Abruptly he withdrew his fingers, and Ivory made a sound of frustration. But then he was pulling her on top of him, the coat falling to the side, her legs straddling his waist. He grasped her hips and pushed her back, and she was met with the feel of his hard cock straining against her cleft.

A fierce satisfaction intensified her arousal.

"That was quick," she whispered, reaching down between them to grasp the steely length of him.

"You make me feel invincible," he said hoarsely, looking up at her. She was stroking him now, sliding her hand from the base of his erection to the crown. She squeezed gently, circling him, swirling the moisture along the surface of his skin with her thumb. He heaved beneath her with a gasp of his own and caught her hand, stilling her movements.

Very deliberately he guided himself to the folds of her entrance, his eyes never leaving hers. "I want to be inside you when you come."

Lust clenched hard within her, and she sank down on him, feeling him slide so perfectly into her, impaling herself. She rolled her hips, reveling in the feel of him filling her, his thickness pressing against her inner walls. Max groaned and bucked beneath her, his hands clutching her waist.

"Let go," she urged, the power she held over him at this moment making her reckless. She squeezed the muscles deep within her pelvis, and he closed his eyes, fighting for control.

"You first," he managed, digging his fingers into the muscles of her arse, lifting her slightly and then letting her drop, starting a pulsing cadence that she was helpless to stop.

She whimpered and braced her hands on his shoulders, trying to find a rhythm that would afford her some restraint, but her body had taken control, and she slid forward slightly and back and then again, riding the length of him, pleasure roaring through her veins. She closed her eyes, sparks exploding behind her eyelids as she felt her body reaching for the pinnacle.

Max thrust hard up into her, his hands grasping her waist and pinning her against him, and she exploded into spasms, her fingers clutching at his shoulders as she surrendered to pleasure. Max bucked once more, driving hard into the eddies of her orgasm, and found his own release. Ivory sank down on his chest, her face pressed into the hollow of his throat, certain she would never move again.

Eventually she turned her head, her cheek scraping against the stubble on his jaw. Never had a man so thoroughly and completely seen to her pleasure. "You were right," she said simply.

He laughed again, and she grinned, loving that new sound. "Of course I was right." He ran his fingers down her spine and let his hand rest on the small of her back. Neither made any attempt to cover them. "But if you want to say that again, I'm going to need a few minutes."

"Mmmm." With an epic effort, she lifted her head, then crossed her arms over his chest and rested her chin on her hands so she could see his face.

He reached behind him and grabbed her abandoned petticoats, then shoved them beneath his head as a pillow. He brought his fingers to her face, tracing the edge of her jaw. He searched her eyes with his own.

"Are you looking for regret?" she asked.

His other hand tightened on her back. "Maybe."

She dipped her head, pressing a kiss to his chest, feeling the steady thump of his heart. One day she might regret her inability to have kept this man for herself, but she would never regret the time they'd had. "You won't find it."

He smiled at her, and whatever breath she had regained fled. Like this, with nothing between them but the intimate smile of a lover, he was irresistible. Held safely in his arms with him smiling down on her like that—it would be so easy to fall in love.

"Next time I promise we'll do that in a real bed. Well, that and a whole lot of other things."

Ivory felt her heart splinter. She wanted so many more next times than he would be able to give her. But she shoved that thought away, unwilling to let go of the fantasy just yet.

"How did you get this scar?" she asked, her fingers tracing the ridge of white that ran along the edge of his hairline. It sounded so normal, this question. A question a lover would ask.

Max gazed down at her. "I didn't secure a swivel gun properly. And it swiveled directly into my head."

Ivory stared at him.

"What?" Max laughed. "You wanted me to tell you I

narrowly missed death at the end of a Barbary corsair's saber? While I had a beautiful young woman in my arms, winging her across the decks to safety?"

She made a face. "Well, I could do without the beautiful-young-woman-in-your-arms part, but yes."

Max chuckled, a sound deep in his chest that rumbled against her ear. "I am sorry to disappoint then."

"You really got hit in the head by a gun?"

"It was my second week as a midshipman. We had just put into port. Knocked me clean out, or at least that was what I was told later. Split my skull wide open. Spent the next two days lying in a darkened surgery with a vicious headache and casting up my accounts."

"On second thought, let's go back to you winging across the decks with a beautiful woman in your arms. Was she very heavy?"

"It is a preferable story to one that has me covered in my own blood and vomit."

Ivory touched the jagged scar again. It had clearly not been stitched with any expertise. "Did you not have a surgeon?"

"Aye, but he was somewhere in port. Now *he* would have had a woman in his arms at the time. Perhaps two." He sighed. "The cook sutured the gash."

"And was the cook drunk?"

"Usually."

"Good Lord."

"You're starting to injure my ego. First you call me a disheveled pirate and now this. Are you suggesting that my good looks are irrevocably damaged?"

"I'm suggesting it was likely a small miracle you didn't die of infection."

"I suspect there were liberal amounts of rum involved," Max said dryly. "There usually were with the cook."

"Why did you tell me the truth?"

Against her she felt Max still. "What do you mean?"

"Most men would never have admitted their error."

"What have I told you about lumping me in with most men?" he said, his lips curling. "Besides, what does telling you a lie get me?"

"My regard?"

"Oh, I have your regard." He wiggled his eyebrows suggestively.

Ivory smacked him with her hand. "Everyone lies," she said after a moment. "At the very least by omission." As she had.

"Perhaps."

Ivory leaned forward, pressing a light kiss to the hollow of his throat. She drew back to find him gazing at her.

"I've never met anyone like you, Ivory. Ever."

"I'm sure you say that to all the girls," she said, forcing a lightness she didn't feel.

"No." He wasn't laughing. "I want you." He caught her chin and forced her eyes back to his.

"You currently have me. Sprawled on top of you. Naked at that."

"That's not what I mean. And you know it."

Yes, she knew it. "Don't do this, Max."

"Ivory—"

"Why can't you just enjoy this? Why does it need to be more?" She couldn't let herself build expectations.

"Because it already is more."

Ivory pushed herself up off of him, feeling the loss of his touch acutely.

He sat up. "You're not something to be just *enjoyed*."

She bent and retrieved her chemise and her stays, redressing with jerky movements.

"You're a brilliant woman. Clever. Courageous. Resourceful. Beautiful. Kind." He paused. "Stubborn and hardheaded, but then, no one is perfect." He said the last to tease her, but it only made her heart hurt.

Ivory faltered before pulling her dress over her head. She didn't bother with the petticoats still behind Max and scrounged for the pins that had fallen to the rug. She jabbed them into her bodice, securing her dress.

He stood and caught her arms. "Ivory."

She stopped, but couldn't bring herself to pull away. "And what will you do with me once you have me?" Ivory asked.

"What?"

"You want me. How? As a wife? As a lover? As a friend?"

His jaw was clenched, confusion clouding his eyes.

"Where would you keep me? On your ship? In your town house? Or perhaps on one of your country estates?"

And that was the crux of it all. What she had built here in Covent Square represented her freedom. Represented her independence. She'd become her own woman, relying on herself, providing for herself, at the mercy of no man. Knightley had shown her the path. Ivory had never looked back.

There could be no future for her and Max. They were too much the same. Too unfettered by the constraints of a world that would see them tied by tradition and expectation. Neither one could ever truly possess the other. At least for any length of time.

"You are unlike any man I have ever met, also," Ivory said gently. "You are strong and compassionate and honorable. Stubborn and hardheaded at times, but then, no one is perfect."

A shadow of a smile touched his lips. She went up on her toes and kissed him softly. "What exists between us is..." She trailed off, trying to find the proper word. "Magical. Real. It doesn't need to have a label." *And it doesn't need to have walls and bars.*

He blew out a heavy breath. "I can't let you go."

"I'm right here." *For a little while longer.*

⌒⌒

Max had retrieved and donned his clothing, chilled in the cooling air. His entire body felt wrung out after being with Ivory, shaken to the bone with the intensity of the longing that had gripped him as he held her in his arms. And now, as he watched her dress, he could feel her retreating from him again, and he despised his inability to stop it.

"I'm going to need to hire you again." He said the only thing he could think of that might bring her back to him. That might halt this inexorable retreat she was now in.

"For what?"

"The Earl of Barlow," he said. It was becoming easier to say that name without blackness crowding the edges of his vision.

"Ah. Is there a body you need me to deal with?"

"No, there is not a body. Yet. I've learned a few things from you."

"Like what?" She sounded surprised.

"Like patience."

"Then you are going to hire me to do what?"

To stay with me.

"I haven't decided what I will do with Barlow. I'm going to take some time to think about it."

She folded her arms across her body. "Murder is messy."

"So you've said." This was ridiculous. Barlow's fate was not Ivory's responsibility.

"You'd be best to keep Beatrice out of sight until you've decided on a course of action."

"Agreed."

From the mantel a clock chimed. Ivory looked up, as if suddenly remembering where she was. "I'm sorry. I have to go."

"What?" Max could feel his forehead furrow in confusion.

"I have another appointment."

"At this time of night?"

"I usually work at night." Her answer was expressionless.

"Let me take you to wherever you need to go."

"No need. My client is sending a carriage."

"Ivory, what's wrong?"

"Nothing." She was already moving toward the door. Dammit, why did she always do this?

"Please let me come with you. I can help."

"This is a matter that doesn't concern you," she said as if she hadn't even heard him. "I'm quite fine on my own."

Of course she was. Until very recently, Ivory Moore hadn't even known he existed. She did not need him. She didn't need anyone.

And that wasn't good enough for him.

He moved then, a few quick strides that caught her at

the door, and suddenly his hands were cradling her head and he was kissing her with a desperation that he felt in his bones. Her hands went to his chest, curling into his shirt, and he felt her respond.

The kiss ended as abruptly as it had started, and he pressed his forehead to hers, breathing harshly. "I'll wait for you," he whispered.

He felt her hands tighten in the fabric against his chest. "Please don't." She raised her head, kissing him with such a poignant gentleness, it left him shaken.

Ivory pulled away from him, her eyes filled with an incomprehensible sadness. "Goodbye," she said for the second time that day, and slipped from the room.

Max didn't leave the offices of Chegarre and Associates immediately. He remained in the study, the old house creaking around him, the muffled sounds of revelry outside penetrating the covered window. He pulled the curtain back just slightly and watched as Ivory, wrapped warmly in her cloak, climbed into a carriage that was waiting for her in the crowded square. It was an expensive carriage, painted black and trimmed with fine lines of red. A pair of perfectly matched greys shifted and tossed their heads, as if in a hurry to leave the disorder of the square behind. There was no indication to whom the carriage belonged, other than someone quite wealthy.

Another peer with a problem he needed help sweeping under the proverbial Aubusson.

The carriage door snapped shut, and the equipage lurched forward. People scattered out of the way of the horses, and within minutes the carriage had been swallowed by the crowds, disappearing from sight altogether at the corner. He sighed, letting the curtain drop. He fully intended to wait, regardless of her ridiculous orders. It didn't matter how long it took, he would be waiting here when she came back home. He'd been telling her the truth when he told her he'd learned how to be patient.

He moved to the desk and retrieved the bottle of whiskey that was still on the floor, as if seeking proof that the time he had spent with Ivory had not been a figment of his imagination. As if to ascertain that the pleasure and the happiness they had shared had been real. He picked up his coat next, tossing it over the back of a chair. Her abandoned petticoats were still in a crumpled ball near the side of the desk, and he reached for them, the fabric sliding through his fingers.

She was impossible. And difficult. And infuriating. He'd been telling her the truth when he said he'd never known a woman like her. Yet for all her courage, she was like a skittish, feral creature, shying away when someone got too close. Holding herself distant when pressed too hard.

He was folding the petticoats when he became aware of a movement in the doorway. He didn't even have time to react before he found himself shoved up against the bookcase, rough hands fisting into the front of his shirt.

"Where is she?" a furious voice demanded.

Max stiffened. "Mr. Lavoie," he said, holding on to his temper by the barest of threads. "To what do I owe this pleasure?"

"Where is she?" Lavoie demanded again, his eyes dropping to the ball of linen Max still held in his hands. "Is she here?"

Max shoved Lavoie back with an effort, startled at the man's strength. "I must assume you're looking for Miss Moore."

"And I must assume you know where she is, given that you're holding her undergarments in your hands." His voice was cold and furious, but the underlying edge of urgency in his words had Max's gut dropping. "Is she here?"

"No," Max said slowly. "She just left. There was a carriage waiting for her."

"And you just let her go?" Lavoie snarled, his hands clenched. "You bastard."

Max felt anger rise, and he embraced it because it was better than the fear that was circling. "I am not her keeper. I do not control where she goes or what she does."

Lavoie swore. "She didn't tell you."

"Didn't tell me what?"

Lavoie glanced down at the petticoats still in Max's grasp and rubbed his hands over his face. "Of course she wouldn't tell you. Foolish, foolish woman. Jesus." He backed up a step, as if not trusting himself near Max. "Was it a black carriage that picked her up? Red trim?"

Max frowned. "Yes. But how did you know—"

"Because tonight, at my club, I heard rumors that Ivory Bellafiore was back in London. That she would be giving a very...private performance this evening at a house on the outskirts of London for one very lucky man."

Max felt his heart stutter even as his blood ran cold.

"How is Lady Beatrice faring, now that she is safely at home?" Lavoie asked, accusation rife in each syllable.

Surely Lavoie wasn't suggesting that—

"That was King's carriage that came to fetch her, Your

Grace. To take her back to Helmsdale House. You tell me why."

Max was shaking his head in denial. "She told me she negotiated my sister's release."

Lavoie's eyes slitted into angry shards. "She certainly negotiated, didn't she? She traded herself for your sister."

"She wouldn't have done that. She'd never even met my sister before. Beatrice means nothing to her."

"For a smart man, you are quite stupid," Lavoie snapped. "It wasn't your sister she did it for."

Max backed up a step, feeling the bookcase bang painfully into his shoulders. He'd been so happy to have Beatrice home that he hadn't insisted on knowing the truth behind Ivory's vague words. And later, on the study floor, he'd let her evade his questions, because he'd been too busy kissing her.

She'd traded herself for Beatrice's release. And she had done it for him. Why? Because she felt for him what he felt for her? An insane euphoria warred with guilt and fury and fear.

He would get her back. No matter the cost.

His first thought was to recall his crew and force his way into Helmsdale. But his men were scattered across London and it would take much too long. He needed to think of something else.

"Tell me how to get into this auction."

Alex shook his head. "I think you've done quite enough."

"I am uninterested in your opinions, Lavoie." Max leaned forward. "How do I get in?"

Alex crossed his arms unhappily. "You don't. King employs a veritable army to patrol both the perimeter of the property and the house. He's a paranoid bastard. You need an invitation to get in. There is no other way."

"Do you have one?"

"Do you think I'd still be standing here if I did?" Lavoie snapped.

Max reached for his coat and yanked it over his shoulders. "So that was a no."

"Yes, that was a no. I don't have one." Alex paused. "Where are you going?"

"To find someone who does."

"I'm coming with you."

"Good," Max said, already halfway out the study door. "You can drive."

⁓

The Lion's Paw was packed at this time of night. The air was stifling with the heat from so many bodies crowded into a small space. Added to the heat was the heavy scent of wet wool, ale, and grease. A steady din made hearing difficult.

Max plowed through the press, his eyes searching the faces. He caught a glimpse of a familiar one, its owner laden with a heavy tray stacked with tankards of ale. In a smooth movement, he stepped into her path and lifted the tray from her arms.

"Where's Gil?" he shouted.

The pretty redheaded serving girl scowled. "I'm working," she complained, reaching for the tray.

"Where's Gil? Tell me and I'll get out of your way."

She rolled her eyes. "In the back. Where else?" She retrieved her tray and plunged back into the crowd.

Max edged toward the back of the tavern and pushed

through the door of the back room, only to be greeted with the barrel of a pistol.

"Gentlemen knock first," Gil admonished. The barrel of the pistol didn't waver.

"I am not a gentleman. And you can put that gun away. You're too busy tonight to clean up a body."

"You're starting to sound like the duchess, Captain Harcourt."

"I've been told."

The gun dropped slowly. "What do you want?"

"An invitation to King's auction."

A shapely eyebrow arched. "And what on God's green earth would make you think that I have one?"

"Because not all of those invitations were delivered. And if one of your messages cannot be delivered into the hands of the recipient, it comes back here."

"And how do you know this?"

"I pay attention."

"*Hmph.*" Gil looked at him. "And even if I had one of these invitations to give you, why would I?"

"Name your price."

A second brow rose. "I think I've heard that from you before."

Max stared at her, waiting.

The woman pursed her lips, smoothing back a stray lock of deep-red hair, considering. "A share in your ship and its cargoes. The rising demand for cotton intrigues me."

Max felt his jaw slacken slightly. Of all the things he'd thought that this woman might demand, that had not been one. He cleared his throat. "Done."

Her mouth made a perfect O. "Done? Just like that? Bloody hell, but I should have asked for the entire ship."

"But you didn't." Though he would have given it to her if it had meant getting to Ivory. "We can work out the specifics of our new partnership a little later. You have my word. But right now I need an invitation."

"In a bit of a hurry, Captain? Afraid a pretty piece of canvas is going to get snatched up before you can get there?" she mocked.

Max felt every muscle in his body tighten. He had considered making a plea to this woman on Ivory's behalf, but he didn't know her well enough to be certain that she would be sympathetic, and Alex hadn't been sure either. Better Gil be left with the knowledge that he was a selfish bastard than that Ivory had sold herself. "Something like that."

Gil's lips twisted, but she drifted over to a small table in the corner. From the edge she plucked a square of folded paper sealed with a blood-red wax impression. "It's your lucky day, Captain," she said with a sardonic twist to her mouth. "This was returned by my boys." She glanced down at the name. "Viscount Rollins will not be needing this tonight, nor any other night. It would seem he snapped his neck after his horse went one way over a hedge and he went the other yesterday afternoon."

"Tragic," Max muttered, taking the proffered invitation. He broke the wax seal and unfolded the paper, revealing a heavy engraved card on the inside. It looked like an invitation to a coronation rather than an auction.

Gil had returned to the table and now came back with a domino mask that would cover the entirety of a man's face. Empty eyes stared up at him. "The invitations are delivered with one of these."

"That is positively ghastly." Max took it from her hands.

"King's bidders are all equal. Those masks strip everyone of identity, allowing only money to reign supreme. And when you're buying things you're not supposed to have, I suppose anonymity is helpful."

Max supposed that made sense in a strange, twisted way. "Is King aware of the viscount's recent demise?"

"I don't see how he would be. The invitation was returned to me, not him." Her forehead creased. "How did you know that there were invitations returned?"

"I guessed." Max shoved the invitation deep in his coat pocket, his hand already on the door. "I've learned from the best."

Chapter Thirteen

When Ivory arrived, the carriages of the men who would be attending the auction had yet to descend upon Helmsdale House, though she had no doubt they would not be far behind. She was led past the ballroom with all its treasures and shown into one of the upstairs chambers. It was a suite meant for a queen. There was a massive hearth with a roaring fire, chasing away the chill from even the farthest corners. A large bed dominated one side of the main room, with beautiful silk bed-curtains in shades of rose and blue. The walls were covered in cream-colored paper etched with swirling leaves, and the pattern was repeated in the embroidered cushions scattered across the bed. Just off to her left a deep hip tub steamed, with soft towels stacked neatly beside a selection of scented hard soaps. On a small table by the door, a bottle of wine had been opened, its contents waiting to be tipped into the delicate glass that was surrounded by an assortment of cheeses and small cakes.

Ivory's first instinct was to refuse it all. But then, what was the point? It had been her choice. She had known exactly what she was doing when she had agreed to this.

There was little point in wasting a perfectly good tub of hot water just to feel sorry for herself. She undressed, leaving her clothes draped over the bed, and wandered into the dressing room, where she climbed into the steaming water. She sank down, closing her eyes, feeling a residual ache in places she had long forgotten about, reawakened on the floor of her study. She wondered what Max was doing now. Hopefully he was at home with his aunt and his sister, where he belonged.

She stayed in the tub until the water cooled and then soaped and rinsed herself quickly before stepping out and toweling herself dry. She returned to the bedroom, only to find her ordinary clothes were gone, having been replaced by undergarments so fine they were almost transparent, and stays with satin ribbons. There were silk stockings, a pair of embroidered slippers, and a complement of jewelry that would get people talking. And lying beside that was a gown meant to stop conversation altogether.

It was the color of twilight, a deep indigo that changed hue as she moved around it. The bodice dipped indecently low, and the skirts fell away from a wide band meant to hug her ribs and graze the undersides of her breasts. She ran a hand over the fabric, hardening herself against the regret that was welling up in her chest. She had performed like this too many times in her life. She knew exactly how the script would play out once the last note had faded.

She had never felt more alone than she did at that moment.

A knock came from the door, and a maid who was roughly the same size as King's guards stuck her head in the room. "Can I help you dress, miss?" she asked, and it wasn't really a question.

Ivory sighed, reaching for the chemise.

He didn't have a plan.

That, for a man who meticulously plotted courses and made preparations for worst-case scenarios, was terrifying. He was making this up as he went, and there were only two times in his life that Max could remember having been so unnerved. Both of those times, he had found himself on the deck of the *Odyssey* as she wallowed on an oily ocean, the air around him heavy and thick and electric. Powerless to do anything but watch as the skies turned black and the clouds roiled and stacked as they advanced toward him.

The ballroom at Helmsdale House was not so different. He'd been searched when he entered the house—an efficient invasion of his personal space as two guards made sure he was not carrying weapons. The lack of a means with which to defend himself left him feeling further exposed and vulnerable. He was armed now only with his wit.

An eerie silence pervaded the ballroom, broken only by the hushed whispers and murmured conversations of men. In the center of the expansive ballroom, a massive square rug had been laid, and this muted any steps that might normally have echoed off the gleaming wood floor. The men already gathered in the ballroom were dressed in dark, somber attire that gave no indication of personality or preferences. Each faceless man wore the black domino that King had provided, and it lent a disturbingly sinister air to the room.

There was no sign of Ivory. Or any other female, for that matter.

Around the edges of the ballroom, glass cases, easels, and pedestals had been assembled, displaying their wares. The chandeliers had all been lowered, and the light bathed each treasure in a soft light. Max fell in with the rest of the guests, drifting around the edges of the room, his hands clasped behind his back. Every once in a while he paused to study a piece, as though he were considering its worth, before moving away again.

He stopped in front of a vibrant painting of a beautiful woman reclining against a tapestry of scarlet, a white swan arched between her thighs and resting its head on her naked breast. It was erotic and masterful, and he knew he should recognize it, but there were a hundred different thoughts zinging through his brain and none of them involved art.

Max leaned closer and read the small card resting at the bottom of the canvas, which read *Leda and the Swan*. Flanking the painting was a looming bronze statue, a triumphant David with one foot resting on the head of a vanquished Goliath. The small card at the base of the pedestal simply read *David*.

"An admirer of Michelangelo, are you?" The question came from behind him.

Max straightened abruptly, turning to find a man standing behind him, his hand resting casually on an inlaid ebony walking stick, rubies glinting from his fingers. He was dressed in the same impeccable black evening attire that every other man in the room wore and was probably about Max's age, red-gold hair cut and styled and falling artfully over his forehead. He was regarding Max with pale-blue eyes, and he could have been any one of the guests at the auction, except this man was not wearing a mask.

"Yes. These are exquisite," Max answered evenly, knowing instantly whom he was addressing.

"They are, aren't they?" Those pale eyes appraised him. "This is a fine piece here," he said, gesturing at the sculpture. "Bronze, not marble, which makes it especially rare. As is the painting. Did you know that this canvas was found in a brothel in Rouen?" he mused with distaste. "Can you imagine? Michelangelo relegated to decorating the walls of whores?"

"No."

King gave a slight shrug. "Ah well, this is what happens when the mob is allowed to rule. Ignorant French peasants stripping the grand châteaus and palaces, happy to trade such treasures for a barrel of damp gunpowder." He smiled a cold smile. "The revolution has been wonderfully profitable."

"Indeed."

King's eyes narrowed. "Who are you?" he asked abruptly.

Max had known that even with the mask, he would still be noticeable. No doubt King had an idea who each man in this room was. He certainly knew who had been invited. And who had not.

"Maximus Harcourt." Let King do with that what he might.

There was silence for the space of a heartbeat. "Alderidge."

Max gazed back at him. "Yes."

"How did you get in here?" It was said with mere curiosity.

"The same way everyone else did. Through the front door."

"I see." King drummed his fingers on the handle of his walking stick, his eyes taking in every inch of Max's appearance. "I must confess, your presence here tonight is most unexpected. Startling, even." Yet King didn't look startled. He looked almost...amused. "Your sister is no longer here, you know, Your Grace."

"I know."

"I do hope she has learned her lesson. Some men can simply not be trusted."

Max kept his stance impassive through sheer force of will.

"Why are you here?" King asked. "Have you come to kill me for the role that I played in Lady Beatrice's... misadventures?"

"No. Not tonight."

"Hmmm. The duchess said you were an arrogant ass. You don't disappoint."

"Miss Moore shouldn't be here."

King's mouth twisted. "Ah. So you've come to ride to her rescue. The duchess makes her own choices, Your Grace. As she did this afternoon when we came to our agreement regarding the release and safe return of your sister. Whatever infantile guilt you might be harboring regarding the duchess's actions on your behalf will find no purchase with me."

Max concentrated on drawing air into his lungs in measured breaths.

King sighed impatiently. "She doesn't need to be rescued, Your Grace. This is nothing that she hasn't done before."

"It is something she should never have had to do again. For anyone." Max took a menacing step toward King and immediately three guards closed in on them.

King's fingers stopped their drumming on the handle of his walking stick as he waved his men off.

"How much?" Max said quietly.

"I'm afraid you don't understand, Your Grace. This is an auction. Where everything is available to the man who simply wants it the most. I cannot make side deals in shady corners. My reputation would be in tatters." He paused. "I will, however, allow you to stay, provided you don't disrupt my soiree. If it makes you feel better, you will have your chance to ride to her rescue at the end of the evening, provided you don't squander all your money on the beauty and craftsmanship that surrounds us now. For the impossible will become quite possible. At least for a clever man."

"Why would you do that?"

"Because it amuses me."

Max eyed the guards still hovering behind King and considered his odds. They weren't good. It would be impossible to help Ivory if he was dead. "I want to see her."

That surprised a bark of laughter from King. "And why do you think I would ever grant you such a request?"

"Because then I would not kill you one day for your role in my sister's...misadventures."

King gazed at Max with shrewd speculation. "How very dramatic."

Max waited.

"Oh, very well. I will allow you two minutes. Two minutes to say whatever it is you need to get off your chest, make whatever apologies you think will make you feel better." He stepped aside, gesturing for Max to precede him. "I do so love the dramatic."

⁓

Ivory stood in front of the long mirror, running her hands down the elaborate silk dress. It had been a long time since she had looked like this. It had been a long time since she had done what she was about to do.

"You're quite stunning."

Ivory's eyes snapped to the doorway in the mirror. King was standing there, leaning casually on his walking stick.

"There are almost a hundred men downstairs who are positively quaking in excitement over the possibility of an appearance by Ivory Bellafiore. It will be a wonder if they can even concentrate on their bidding."

Ivory watched King in the mirror, not turning around.

"Oh, come now, Duchess, don't be so sullen. You think I'm going to auction you off like a piece of common art to the first old man with more money than hair?" He closed the door and crossed the room, coming to stand directly behind her, his eyes meeting hers in the glass. "You deserve so much better than that."

Ivory stared at him.

He stroked the length of hair that fell down her back, still damp from the bath.

Ivory frowned and stepped away.

King dropped his hand. "If someone is going to take you home tonight, he must prove himself."

"What does that mean?"

"You'll see. It might be possible no one even does. It might be me who ends up enjoying your company this fine evening, and I have to admit, Duchess, the idea has a certain appeal."

"I don't understand. Why would you do this?"

"Because it amuses me."

Ivory felt a rush of anger. She turned to face him. "Whatever game you're playing here, King, know that I've met my end of the bargain. Lady Beatrice and her family are off-limits. Forever."

"Of course they are. I agreed to that." He looked annoyed. "The situation that we currently find ourselves in is—"

"Business, King. Nothing more. You were in possession of a child—"

"Bah. She was hardly a child. She was eighteen. I was told you were thirteen when your pa sold you. And you turned out all right."

Ivory closed her eyes. She couldn't even begin to understand his twisted logic.

"You have a visitor."

Ivory's eyes snapped open. "What do you mean, a visitor?"

"Apparently you have some unfinished business that needs to be addressed before we can proceed this evening. You have two minutes. I trust you can resolve any outstanding issues in that time."

Ivory looked at him in utter confusion. What kind of ploy was this? "Who?"

King turned and strode to the door, then pulled it open. "Two minutes," he said, and vanished into the hall.

Ivory was still staring after him when Max stepped into the doorway.

～

"Max?" It came from the far side of the room, shock making it barely audible.

He shoved the door shut behind him and crossed the room in desperate strides, coming to an abrupt halt in front of her. He stared, a little breathless at the vision before him. She was dressed in an elaborate blue silk gown, her skin flushed and glowing. Her hair was pulled back from her face and then left to tumble down her back almost to her waist in a glorious mahogany curtain, making her look a little like a medieval princess.

"Max, what are you doing here?" she gasped.

"What does it look like? I'm storming the Bastille. Albeit not exactly how I pictured it. I have no weapons, no army, and I'm dressed in evening clothes."

She blinked. "Oh God. You came here for me?"

"Of course I came here for you. What the hell kind of question is that?"

"A good one."

"Wrong. The better question is what are *you* doing here."

She didn't flinch. "I can take care of myself, Max."

He closed the distance between them, unable to help himself. He caught her face in his hands and brought his mouth to hers, the gentle, reassuring kiss he had intended suddenly unraveling into a desperate, demanding one. He wondered who needed his reassurance more, she or he. She swayed against his body, and he pulled her closer, as if he could shield her from everything unpleasant that had been and might yet come. They stood that way for a long moment before he pulled back slightly, searching her eyes.

"What have you done?" He brushed his fingers down her cheek.

"What I had to."

"I won't let you do this."

"You don't have a choice, Max. This was my choice, and I would make the same one again."

Max fought the urge to simply pick her up and throw her out the window. Surely there were some bushes she might land in. Or perhaps the impact would finally knock some sense into her head.

"The windows are locked. Though I suspect that is more of a precaution to keep people out than to keep them in."

"What?"

"You were looking at the windows. Were you planning on throwing a chair through the glass? Knotting the bedsheets and climbing out?"

"Sounds reasonable. We're getting out of here." He grasped her arm.

"I can't leave."

"Of course you can. Over my dead body will I allow you to be reduced to an . . . entertainment for those men downstairs."

"That's just the problem, Max."

"I beg your pardon?"

"My presence tonight ensures the safety of Beatrice and your aunt. And you."

"What does that mean?"

"It means that King isn't stupid. It means he made sure innocent people would get hurt if someone stormed the Bastille."

Max swore. "Then I'll take Beatrice and Helen out of London—"

"And live the rest of your lives looking over your shoulder? Max, it's done. Beatrice is home. Your family is once again whole and secure and safe. Don't make it all for nothing by doing something stupid."

"I let you go. That was stupid. And I'll do whatever it takes to remedy that. There is nothing that I have that I wouldn't give for you. Nothing."

Ivory was looking at him, emotion welling in the dark depths of her eyes. "I'll be fine," she whispered.

"You shouldn't have to be *fine*, Ivory. You should be free. Protected from things that you survived once and that you shouldn't have to survive again." He brushed his lips across her forehead. "I want to do that for you."

A loud rap made him jump. "Your two minutes are up." King's muffled voice came through the door.

She leaned forward, kissing him hard and swiftly. "Max, I—"

The door swung open, and King stood there, his hulking entourage at his back.

His pale eyes went from Ivory to Max and back. "I trust you two have resolved your issues?"

Max stared stonily back, silent.

"Good to hear it." He stepped back from the door. "Like I said, Your Grace, you're welcome to stay so long as you behave. My men will attend you to make sure that you have everything you need." The threat was pointed.

Max clenched his fists behind his back.

King turned to Ivory. "Time to go, Duchess," he said. "Your audience awaits."

Max had come for her.

He had somehow discovered what she'd done and had somehow gotten into this house. Had somehow negotiated with King for the most precious two minutes of her life. Even though his efforts hadn't changed the inevitable outcome, no one had ever done something like that. She'd relied on herself and her wits so long, knowing that no one was ever coming to rescue her from anything. But Max had.

Maybe it was out of guilt or a sense of duty or remorse. But maybe it was for another reason entirely.

And as she waited downstairs for the auction to conclude, she held on to that *maybe* as tightly as she could. She was still holding on as she was led into the ballroom, now cleared of its treasures.

Each sculpture, each antiquity that she had glimpsed when she'd first arrived had been whisked away, no doubt packed carefully in a straw-filled wooden crate and shipped to wherever it was destined to disappear again. The only thing left was a looming bronze statue of David that it would require an army of muscle-bound men to remove.

Around a massive square rug, men had gathered, and though Ivory had been prepared for it, the faceless, shifting crowd sent a shudder through her. They waited, like a horde of masked executioners, a strange undertow of excitement churning throughout the room. Knowing that whatever was going to happen next would be different. King was about to present these jaded, cynical buyers with something novel. Something that they could compete for. It was this that she hated. This bleak feeling of exposed vulnerability that reduced her to a thirteen-year-old girl who had learned hard lessons about how one survived when one started with nothing.

Beside her, King was smiling. Or smirking. It was difficult to tell which.

"You are going to make me famous, Duchess," he whispered under his breath so that only she might hear. "You are my most incredible coup yet."

⁓

Max first became aware of the absolute silence that had fallen when he began to hear his own pulse pounding in his ears. He turned toward the door, and everything around him dimmed.

Ivory was walking toward him, or at least in his general direction. She looked neither right nor left, her gaze fixed firmly on something that only she could see. Her face was composed and serene, and she might have been strolling through Hyde Park on a Tuesday afternoon, so unconcerned did she appear. She looked exotic and flawless and . . . untouchable.

King was walking by her side, clearly enjoying the spell with which he had captivated his audience. Guards were ushering men to the edges of the ballroom, and King led her to the center of the rug, stopping and turning, making sure he had the attention of all of his guests. He need not have worried. Every man in the room was riveted.

"Thank you for your patience, gentlemen," he said. "But I had promised you something impossible and perfect, and that, my friends, takes some time, as you all know."

There was a subtle murmur of amusement throughout

the crowd. Max was imagining ways in which this man might meet his end.

"I give you Miss Ivory Bellafiore," King pronounced with all the pomp of a royal herald. "A jewel that even the most illustrious opera houses of Europe have failed to produce these past years." He let that point settle over his buyers. "Miss Bellafiore has agreed to sing for us tonight," King continued. "And should you wish a more...private performance later, one man may have that chance."

Another murmur rippled through the crowd, and this one carried the sharp edge of excitement and avarice. All these men, staring at her as if she were just another desirable object to be owned. As if they could buy her and put her in a pretty glass case so she could be taken out and admired when it suited.

Max focused on keeping his breathing even. He needed to keep his wits about him.

"Miss Bellafiore," King said, taking a half step back.

Ivory's eyes swept across the masses of masked men, all watching her expectantly. Max could barely breathe.

She found him where he stood, as still and as silent as the others around him. Her eyes held his, and she began to sing, no instruments or music or accompaniment, just her voice echoing throughout the ballroom, soaring up to the ceiling and swirling around each person in the room.

He had never seen her perform on a stage. He had never seen her at the royal opera houses, never heard her voice lifted up in the manner that had secured her legend. She sang in Italian, and his was rusty at best, but it didn't matter that he didn't understand each word. She drew him in and set his blood on fire. She was otherworldly and he couldn't look away.

When her voice had died away, there was utter silence in the ballroom. And then King stepped forward again, clapping loudly, and the men suddenly exploded into applause. The crowd was pressing forward now, as if wanting to touch such perfection, but King's men were keeping them back, well off the square rug. Max watched King carefully. He was looking around, satisfaction shining from his visage at the feat he had achieved. King had known how brilliant Ivory's performance would be because he had known she would do nothing to endanger Max's family. And he had known that after such a performance there was not a man among them who would be immune to her enchantment.

King held his hand up, and the room quieted. "Two thousand pounds," he said, and once again the silence was absolute. "Two thousand pounds will secure you a single chance to enjoy Miss Bellafiore's charms for the remainder of the evening, should you prove yourself worthy."

A hum of speculation rose.

Max was grateful for the mask, for it concealed his expression. What the hell was King doing? He'd been working under the impression that Ivory would be auctioned just like every other piece that had gone before. And there was not a man in this room who would be able to outbid him. But now...

"My men are circulating. You may give your promissory note to one of them should you be so inclined."

Judging from the flurry of sudden activity, almost everyone was inclined.

A half dozen of King's guards, each carrying a wooden box filled with what looked like smooth wooden sticks almost the length of a broom handle, had entered the ballroom sometime during the performance. Men craned their necks, waving their notes as King's guards came around. A note was collected from each client, and in exchange for two thousand pounds, each man was given a stick.

Max deposited his own promissory note in the hands of a beefy guard and was left holding on to the same sort of stick as the rest of the men. It was a hardwood, perhaps oak, smooth, with blunted ends, and thicker than he'd first thought. It looked more like a piece of long, stout kindling than a weapon, though used in the right manner, it would inflict some damage. Idly Max wondered how much damage he might inflict on King before he was dragged off of him and shot. Or stabbed. It would accomplish nothing, he knew, but it would certainly make him feel better, if only for a minute.

Max hefted the wood in his hand. For the life of him, he couldn't begin to imagine what it might be for. His eyes darted around, but everyone else seemed equally perplexed. Perhaps it was a lottery. Perhaps they were to mark each stick and toss it into a pile from which it might be drawn. Perhaps—

"Has everyone been seen to who wishes to enter?" King called out. The guards had withdrawn, and a ring of men stood around the rug, each clutching a piece of wood. Another silence fell.

"Very good." King turned slowly, appraising the audience that surrounded him. He was now holding a golden chalice of some sort in his hand, an object wrapped in pristine white cloth resting inside. Very slowly, giving everyone a chance to see, he unwrapped the object, revealing an emerald the size of a chicken egg. Beneath the overhead light from the chandeliers, it glittered and glowed.

Around him men shifted in renewed interest.

"The rules are simple, gentlemen," King said, bending to place the chalice and its emerald in the very center of the elaborate rug. "The first man to retrieve this jewel without touching the rug upon which it rests with any part of his body will win not only the stone, but Miss Bellafiore's company for the remainder of the evening."

Max stared at King. Seven men could lie end to end across the square rug without reaching its edges.

"You have only one chance, so strategize wisely," King continued. "I have given you a tool which you may use. You may find it helpful. Or you may not."

Max transferred his gaze to Ivory. She was still watching him, her dark-brown eyes calm and steady. But she was pale. So very, very pale.

Beside her, King offered Ivory his arm. "Come, Miss Bellafiore. Let's find a good seat from which to watch the entertainment, shall we?" He was smirking again. She took his proffered arm, her eyes leaving Max's even though her expression didn't change, and silently followed King to the far end of the ballroom. A dais of sorts had been set up, and two guards appeared bearing chairs, which they placed before King and Ivory.

The bastard was enjoying every minute of this, Max thought, gritting his teeth against the anger that rose. King and his queen. Presiding over his greedy, scrabbling subjects. Already men were pressing in, dropping to their knees on the floor at the edges of the carpet, straining forward helplessly with sticks that were much too short to reach anything. As men lost their balance, or their sticks fell, guards moved forward and ushered them away, their chance squandered. A trio of men were tying their sticks together with their cravats, presumably partnering to share in the spoils. Yet their longer pole drooped and fell, and still failed to reach the emerald. More men, seizing on the idea, suddenly became allies, and longer staffs were fashioned, lengths decorated with linen knots. Max watched as a group extended its pole, the wood swaying and dipping, and the end nudged the edge of the chalice. There was a collective intake of breath but then the pole fell apart, and King's guards once again swooped in.

Other men, not willing to align themselves with partners, moved in, throwing their sticks at the chalice, hoping to knock the emerald closer to the edge of the rug, where it might be reached. Two hit the chalice, the last knocking the cup over and spilling the emerald onto the rug, but the jewel remained unreachable.

Up on his throne, King was watching with undisguised delight. As if the childish, desperate antics of these men, brought quite literally to their knees by their greed, were inexorably proving that King was the superior being. Max considered him, his mind racing. Perhaps he had never intended Ivory to go home with any of these men, and would claim her company for himself. Perhaps he'd never had any intention of allowing Ivory to leave Helmsdale tonight. And for King's planning he was thousands and thousands of pounds richer, and it had cost him nothing aside from the two hundred pounds that he'd paid for a terrified debutante. It had cost Ivory much, much more.

The crowd around the rug was almost gone now, men retreating and muttering and seeking out more liquor in which to drown their failings. The guards had refilled their wooden boxes, reclaiming the tools that had failed. A few men were still pacing the edge of the rug, seeking a strategy that had eluded the rest. But eventually they too resorted to cartwheeling their sticks across the rug, trying to sweep the emerald closer to the edge. Max had hung back, not wanting to be caught in the surging, pushing crowd. He wandered around the perimeter, coming to stand at the edge closest to King and Ivory. He was aware he was the only one now left in the ballroom who still had a stick in his hand.

"Your Grace," King said from his perch. "Have you reconsidered?"

"No."

"Then whatever are you waiting for?"

Max turned to look up at King briefly before turning away. He couldn't look at Ivory. He needed to concentrate. "I was waiting for the hordes to subside," he said evenly.

"It was rather hectic, wasn't it?" King was drumming his fingers on the arm of his chair and sounded utterly pleased with the observation. Max could feel the weight of his gaze on the back of his neck, and it sent unpleasant prickles across his flesh. "I noticed you did not bid on either of the Michelangelo pieces earlier," he commented.

"No, I did not." King was probing again, Max knew, hoping to catch him in a lie. So he told the truth. "I took your advice. Saved my money for a chance at something far more valuable."

"Indeed. Well, whether that was good advice remains to be seen, Your Grace. You might yet leave here empty-handed. Look around you. All of these are educated, intelligent men. Yet they have failed to solve this puzzle."

"Mmmm." Max was beginning to appreciate the value of Ivory's non-answer answer.

"Why do you think you are better than any of those who have failed before you?"

"Because I am better. And I will not fail."

King's fingers stopped their drumming. Max smiled faintly and stepped closer to the edge of the rug. The emerald lay slightly off center now, the chalice on its side, the rim gleaming in the light. Max let the tip of his stick drop to the floor and jammed it under the edge of the rug. He levered it forward, and the carpet curled, rolling up on itself. He moved down the entire side, working the tip of his stick under the edge, constantly pushing the carpet into a thicker and thicker roll.

Around him he became aware of voices, exclamations mixed with grumbles and the occasional laugh.

Entertainment indeed.

He was sweating now, the heavy rug rolling faster and more easily now that it was started. King was standing on his dais, and men were once again pushing in. Max kept his movement steady and sure, until the rolled edge of the rug bumped the overturned chalice. Very slowly he bent down and, reaching over the thick cylinder of carpet, careful not to touch it, he simply plucked the emerald from where it lay.

"Well done," King said, his voice echoing through the ballroom.

Max curled his fingers around the stone, feeling the cut edges press into the flesh of his palm. Casually he slipped it into the inside pocket of his jacket. He couldn't tell if King was impressed or infuriated.

"Thank you," he said, striding toward the dais. He stopped, his eyes going to Ivory. "Miss Bellafiore," he said with a bow, "it would be my pleasure to see you safely from Helmsdale this evening." He chose his words carefully.

Ivory stood, picking up her skirts. Silently she made her way to the step off to the side and carefully descended.

Max held out his arm, and she slipped her hand into the crook of his elbow, her fingers resting lightly on his sleeve. He turned slightly, only to find that King had jumped down from the low platform and was now standing in front of them, blocking their way.

"You told me he was an arrogant ass, Duchess." His voice was low. "You never told me he was clever."

"You never asked." She sounded remarkably composed.

King folded his arms over his chest, his gaze going to Max's. Max met King's pale eyes without flinching.

"Well, enjoy your knight-errant, Duchess," King said with a slight twitch to his lips. "For he has certainly earned your favor this evening. I might even suggest you may find a use for his cleverness in the future, provided he doesn't sail away on you."

"I'll keep that in mind."

"You do that." He sniffed. "A pleasure doing business as always, Duchess." King abruptly turned and made his way through the ballroom, an entourage of guards at his side.

Max was already pulling Ivory toward the doors, unwilling to stay in the house a moment longer. They burst through the front door, both of them sucking in deep breaths of cold air. He yanked off his mask, catching Ivory's hand in his, terrified to let it go. Terrified that if he did, she would somehow slip away from him again. He headed toward the long line of carriages, picking out the sleek lines of Alex's equipage. There was a man pacing near the horses, bundled in warm clothes. He saw them coming and rushed forward.

"Jesus, Your Grace, that took you long enough," Alex snapped, his eyes raking Ivory from head to toe, his lips curling slightly at her gown. "I was about five minutes away from driving this thing right through that front door."

"Alex?" Ivory blinked. "What the hell are you doing here?"

"A great many things I never thought I'd do," grumbled Alex. "Freeze my tail off. Drive a carriage. Trust this oaf to extract you from a monumentally stupid decision you should never have made." He took Ivory by the shoulders and held her from him, as if searching for damage.

"Let's discuss later, shall we?" Max urged. *Much later.*

"Will someone be shooting at us soon?" Alex inquired, glancing around uneasily, letting Ivory go and climbing up onto the driver's seat.

"No. At least I don't think so. I won Miss Moore fair and square." Max wrenched the carriage door open and handed Ivory up into the interior. Her voluminous skirts made it awkward, and he half pushed her and the fabric ahead of him.

"You *what*?"

"Just go," Max ordered, climbing in behind Ivory. The carriage lurched into motion, and Max pulled the door shut behind them, plunging the interior into blackness. In a heartbeat he had Ivory in his arms, pressing her head against his shoulder.

"I can't say that I enjoyed any part of that evening," Max said into the softness of her hair. "Except maybe when you sang."

"Neither did I. Except maybe the look on King's face

when you rolled up that carpet. How did you know to do that?"

"How do you think we mend and dry out sails?"

Ivory uttered a choked laugh before it died. "I still can't believe you came for me." It was said with a touch of wonder.

"Of course I came for you. What you did was madness. You never should have done that," he said. "You never should have put yourself in that kind of situation—"

Ivory pulled back from him, and he wished he could see her face. "We're not having this conversation again, Max."

But Max wasn't done. "The thought of another man touching you—"

"Another man would never have touched me."

"Are you insane? Every man in that room wanted you, and not just to hear your voice. They would have taken you back to whatever hole they had crawled out of and then—"

She shifted, and he could hear the slide of silk. She fumbled for his hand in the darkness and grasped it, pressing what felt like a tiny glass vial into his palm.

"And then I might have urged him into bed. Brought him a relaxing glass of wine," she said in a low voice. "A *very* relaxing glass of wine. Or port. Or whatever my mark might be drinking. So relaxing, in fact, one might be overcome by sleep." Her fingers found the edge of his face, as if gauging his expression by touch. "I would see to his comfort, of course, then. Remove his clothes, rumple the bedsheets, discard the leftover drink. Even leave a note, expressing my gratitude and my admiration if I thought it was necessary. Men's egos can be fragile things. Especially if one cannot seem to remember what happened after one climbed into bed with Ivory Bellafiore. It's important to leave them an account of what they would like to believe."

Max swallowed, feeling the smooth glass in his palm, knowing what it would contain. "You would drug them."

"Yes." There was no apology in her voice.

Nor, he reflected, should there be.

"I learned my lessons early, and I learned them well. No one ever rode to my rescue. I survived by my ability to manipulate men."

Her fingers were tracing the edges of his jaw.

"And is this what you're doing now? Manipulating me?"

Her touch stalled. "No," she whispered. "You undo me, Maximus Harcourt."

He caught her shoulders then, moving one hand to caress her neck, with the other tracing her collarbone and the slope of her breast to the edge of her bodice. Beneath his fingers he could feel the rapid rise and fall of her chest.

"I will always come for you, Ivory Moore," he said, and bent his head, his mouth a breath from her own. She shivered, yet made no move to draw away. He brushed her lips with his, his restraint razed the second he felt her open up eagerly beneath him. He devoured her, unable to help himself, slanting his mouth over hers, his tongue exploring her heat. A reckless desire, unlike anything he had ever experienced, flooded through him, and any control he'd had left was eroding at a frightening speed. He slid his hands down her back, pulling her onto his lap so that she straddled him, shoving her skirts up over her thighs and hips. He pressed himself hard against her, letting her feel just how badly she undid him as well.

She had a hand between them and was yanking at the buttons to his trousers. He shifted back, allowing her more access, and in an instant she had her hand inside, stroking him as his erection sprang free from its confines. He ran his hands up the outsides of her thighs, pulling her up, feeling himself poised at her entrance. She was panting, and very slowly she guided him into her wet heat, accommodating him in a slow, torturous descent. They stayed frozen like that for a long moment, their breath harsh in the darkened carriage.

And then she moved, rocking her hips ever so slightly, and he claimed her mouth again, as much to muffle his groan of pleasure as hers. She was setting the pace, and it was deliberate and tormenting and unbearable and the most staggering ecstasy he had ever experienced. She suffused every one of his senses, and with this woman he couldn't think, could only feel. Feel the pleasure that she gave to his body. Feel the emotion that filled his heart every time he was with her.

She whimpered, losing her rhythm, her body trembling. He wrapped his arms around her, pulling her close, thrusting up into her, taking control where she had lost it. She wrapped her arms around his neck, her head buried against his shoulder, and he felt her tense as her body began to reach for release. He could feel the moment she came apart, her inner muscles convulsing, her arms tightening around him, her mouth pressed against the side of his neck. Letting himself loose to the mercy of his own pleasure, which was roaring through him, he drove into her, his muscles clenching as he pulsed and claimed her as his own.

She made a move to slide from him, but he caught her, unwilling to release the physical connection between them. Remembering what had happened the last time they had made love and she had withdrawn. "Don't go yet," he whispered in her ear. "I would have you with me."

She stilled in his arms and then leaned forward, kissing him unhurriedly. "I am with you, Max."

I would have you with me for always, he had wanted to say. Wanting the impossible.

Chapter Fourteen

Alex had given her a round tongue-lashing.

It was mostly her failure to involve him and ask for his help that he'd had an issue with, and he'd reminded her repeatedly that she wasn't immortal or magical or untouchable. That even though he was well aware she was able to look after herself, she'd put herself in a position that was unacceptable. He had even gone so far as to mutter that she'd been damn lucky Alderidge had been there, even if that statement had been followed up by a string of curses implying that that very same man had been the root of the problem to start with.

Elise had been less vocal but had hugged her tightly and promptly disappeared belowstairs. Ivory had found her later cleaning her rifle, something she did only when she was upset and agitated.

Max had seen her home that night, and every night since then. Nights that had left her gasping and pleasured, fulfilled and content beyond anything she had ever dreamed possible. And those interludes of passion had been linked by hours of conversation, by their sharing thoughts and secrets and laughter the way lovers were wont to do in the shelter of privacy.

Though they never talked about the future. What might happen in a week or a month or a year. Perhaps Ivory was too selfish to force the issue. Or maybe she was too much of a coward. Or maybe she just didn't want to know.

Occasionally he would seek her out in the afternoon, if only so they could share a quick meal or a cup of chocolate or tea to warm themselves against the damp chill, and on these days the bizarre normalcy and tender intimacy that they embraced was enough to make her heart feel as if it might explode. Her feelings had gone far beyond physical desire and attraction. What now existed between them was something Ivory wasn't sure how to handle.

Which was alarming for a woman who knew how to handle everything.

On the other days, when she and Max were separated by work and by distance, she would find herself staring into nothingness, wondering what he was doing. Where he was. She found herself counting down the minutes until darkness fell and he slipped into the Covent Square house, and into her bed.

Ivory sighed, closing the ledger on her desk. She felt unsettled, and no matter how busy she tried to make herself, her mind wandered.

"There is someone here to see you, Duchess," Roddy said from the door, interrupting her trance.

Happy for the distraction, Ivory rose. "Who is it?"

"She says her name is Lady Beatrice."

"What?" Ivory nearly tripped over her hem.

"Should I show her into—"

Ivory was already pushing past him. What was Beatrice doing here? A hundred different scenarios were running through her mind, each worse than the last. She burst into the hall to find a young woman wrapped in a plain wool cloak, her face hidden by her hood.

"My lady," Ivory said. "What are you doing here?"

Beatrice turned, pushing the hood from her head. She looked directly at Ivory, and her eyes were bleak. "I want to hire you," she said.

"Whatever for?" God almighty, what had Beatrice done now?

"I want you to make him stay."

"I beg your pardon?"

"Max. He's leaving. I want you to make him stay. Do whatever you need to. Sink his ship, burn it to the waterline, have him kidnapped, I don't care. He won't listen to me. And he won't stay."

"He's leaving?" Ivory's heart fell to her toes.

"I thought he would have told you."

"No. He didn't." Yet deep down she had known he would leave. He had never told her otherwise. "The *Odyssey* is ready to sail?" She was trying to work out how much time she might yet have with him.

Beatrice flung her hands in the air in helpless frustration. "My brother says she'll be ready by the end of the week."

That came like a slap across the face. Ivory might not know what existed between them—there was no name, no label she could give to the bond that had been knit between them. But she did know one thing. And that was that it was far from over.

Beatrice was fumbling with a reticule. "I brought money—"

"Put your money away," Ivory snapped. The last thing she needed was Maximus Harcourt's money to deal with Maximus Harcourt.

"If anyone could keep him from leaving, it's you," Beatrice said miserably. "I tried to explain. But maybe if I hadn't done what I did, maybe if I had been—"

Ivory suddenly felt sad. "Your brother loves you very much, my lady," she said. "Don't ever doubt that."

"I just want him to stay. Just once. Just so that I can get to know him. Aside from Aunt Helen, he's the only family I have." She was twisting the strings on her reticule. "Can you make him stay?"

"I very much doubt anyone can make your brother do something he does not wish to," Ivory muttered.

But she would try. Because it wasn't just Beatrice who didn't want to lose him so soon after she had found him.

"Roddy!"

She was met with silence.

"Roddy, get in here. I know you're listening."

There was the sound of a very ungentlemanly curse, and the boy stepped into the hall. "There was no way you could have heard me."

Ivory ignored his complaint. "Fetch my cloak, if you would be so kind. We're going out."

The sun was sinking quickly, and taking with it whatever remnants of feeble warmth it had given. The *Odyssey*, now moored on the other side of the basin, was a hive of activity, men laboring across the decks and down in the holds as his ship was prepared for the sea, making the most of the dying daylight.

"A miss here to see you," one of Max's coopers said as he passed him, rolling a barrel in front of him. "Though she's got that set to her jaw ye don't ever want to mess with in a female."

"Where?" Max glanced up from the log of inventory and passenger manifests he was reviewing.

"On 'em docks. Don't say I didn't warn ye." The old sailor winked at him and carried on.

His eyes slid to the expanse between the *Odyssey* and the warehouses, picking her out easily because she was the only one who wasn't moving. His heart missed a beat, and his hands tightened around the papers he held. She was so beautiful it simply stole his breath.

He caught the attention of one of his quartermasters, and his papers were whisked away. He navigated his way onto the docks and headed down toward Ivory, rehearsing in his head everything that he planned to say to her. She waited patiently for him to reach her.

"Your sister wants to hire me," she said, before he could even open his mouth.

He stopped abruptly, startled. "What? Why?"

"She wants me to make you stay in London."

"What?"

"Are you leaving?"

Max found himself on the defensive. "Not right away. It will be the better part of the week before we leave the basin. Assuming the weather cooperates, of course."

"Mmmm."

Max shifted uncomfortably.

"She suggested I burn your ship to the waterline." Ivory's eyes traced the graceful, powerful lines of the Indiaman.

"What?"

"She also suggested that I have you kidnapped."

"Good God." Max rubbed his face with his hands. This was not how he'd pictured this conversation going. These were not at all the things he had wanted to say to Ivory.

"What did you tell her?" he asked wearily.

"I told her nothing. I came here to ask if you had planned to leave without saying goodbye."

"What? No! No, of course not." He reached for her hands and clasped her fingers tightly. "I was going to tell you tonight."

Her expression was unreadable.

He cursed softly. He hadn't intended to have any of this conversation here, but it seemed that Beatrice had forced his hand.

He took a deep breath. "I was also going to ask you to come with me."

It was her turn to look startled. "I beg your pardon?"

"Leave London. Come with me to India."

"As what?"

As mine. It was on the tip of his tongue.

"I don't know," he said instead. "We can think of something."

Ivory gazed at him sadly. "I can't."

"Why?" he demanded.

"My work is here. My life is here."

"Your life could be with me."

"It could." She twined her fingers through his. "If you stayed."

Max felt a flood of frustration. "And do what? Pretend to be a duke?"

He saw a flash of anger, though it was quickly snuffed by sadness. "Are you even listening to yourself? You *are* a duke. And a brother. And a nephew. Beatrice would give away every pretty thing you have ever given her if it meant you would stay. Trade every one of her ball gowns and dancing lessons and golden baubles for time with you."

"Beatrice wants the brother who's in the letters I wrote. In the adventures I spun. She'd be disappointed to discover that's not me."

"That's not fair. To either one of you."

"I think I'm the better judge of that." He was aware he was scowling. "I can't stay."

"You won't stay," Ivory corrected. "You won't *try*."

Max stepped away from her, her fingers slipping from his and an impotent fury rising. She sounded exactly like Helen now. But Ivory knew better. She understood that he did not fit in here. He never would. "You're a fine one to talk."

"What do you mean?"

"Why won't you leave this Mr. Chegarre?" he demanded. "What does he hold over you?"

Ivory closed her eyes.

They had never discussed him after that night at King's. His name had never once come up. Max now wondered why. "Do you love him?" The thought cut fast and deep and hard.

Slowly she opened her eyes. "You don't understand."

She didn't deny it. Max felt something die inside. "You're right. I don't."

"I've built a life here for myself by myself. I don't belong to anyone anymore. I can't be dependent on you for my existence. I can't rely on others to live. I won't give that up."

None of that made any sense, but what did make sense was that she was choosing Chegarre over him. After everything, after what he'd thought they had, what he'd thought might be possible, she was choosing another.

"Then you should go. For it seems I can't give you what you want. I can't give you what Chegarre can give you." Max had never felt as wretched in his life as he had uttering those words.

"Max, you don't understand—"

"I want you to be happy. So go. Please." A weight settled in his chest, compressing his heart. "You have made your choice. And I have made mine."

Ivory watched him, her skin almost luminescent in the fiery glow of the setting sun. Her hands dropped from his, and she stepped back. The loss of her touch was a physical pain.

She was searching his eyes. "I'm so sorry," she whispered.

"Me too." God, he didn't want to draw this out any longer. "Goodbye, Ivory."

"Goodbye, Max."

She turned away, pulling the hood of her cloak up over her head, and in a minute she was lost in the crowd and confusion.

And Max felt…nothing. He felt utterly, completely empty. As if everything that had defined him had drained away, leaving nothing but an outer shell that could still walk and talk and give orders to a crew. He boarded the *Odyssey*, though somehow the ship didn't seem to welcome him as it once had. As if the very timbers were judging him and the choices he had made.

He shoved his hands deep into his pockets against the cold air, not knowing if he would ever truly be warm again. His fingers found the edge of a small card, long forgotten. He drew it out, smoothing the paper with his thumb, running his finger over the neatly printed words. Chegarre & Associates. When she had given this to him a lifetime ago, he had told her he hoped that he would never see her again. And now he was getting his wish. He had lost her to a man he had never even met.

But she was never really yours, was she?

He made a sound of anguish, and his fingers twisted, tearing the card. The last rays of golden light caught the edges of the small paper pieces as they fluttered to the deck at his feet, the printed letters swirling into an untidy pile. Max stared down at them, a strange sensation crawling through him.

Unfeelingly he bent, rearranging the pieces where they had fallen, turning over the few that had landed facedown.

Chegarre & Associates.

There was an *H*. And an *E*. And an *R*.

Max thumped to his knees. He rearranged the rest of the letters and sat back hard, burying his face in his hands. A dizzying array of emotions was crashing through him, leaving him disoriented and unsteady. He tried desperately to identify everything that was filling his chest and pressing into the back of his throat. Admiration and wonder for the woman who had slipped into his life. Relief and regret, aimed at himself; though they were selfish emotions, they were no less powerful for it.

There had never been a Mr. Chegarre. The only one who

had ever spoken of *Mr.* Chegarre had been Max, because for some insane reason he had made an insane assumption based on...nothing. There had never been another man competing for Ivory. She hadn't chosen another man.

She had chosen herself. When Max had forced her hand, had acted like every man who simply wanted to own her, to possess her on his own terms, Ivory had chosen Ivory.

Chegarre was not a man. Chegarre was nothing but an anagram.

Chegarre & Associates.

Her Grace & Associates.

Chapter Fifteen

The package arrived a week after Ivory left Max at the docks.

When she had left him standing in front of his ship, she had fled, tears blinding her eyes. Roddy, who had been waiting unseen somewhere, had appeared and simply slipped his hand into hers, silently leading her in the direction that would take them home. She had wiped angrily at her eyes, furious for allowing herself to feel this much when she had known better. She had known he would never allow her to possess him any more than she herself could be possessed. They were too much the same, she and Max. Both unwilling to be caught in a cage that was not of their making. She didn't fit into his world any better than he fit into hers.

So when Roddy came into the study with the bulky package wrapped in plain paper and tied neatly with red ribbon, Ivory was brooding miserably.

"What is it?" she asked dully.

"Dunno," Roddy answered.

"Well, who delivered it?"

"One o' Gil's boys." He placed it on the desk in front of her. "You want me to open it?"

Ivory shrugged listlessly. "Go ahead."

Roddy grinned. "I love opening presents," he said, attacking the bow with his small fingers.

"I know."

The ribbon fell away, and he turned the package over, peeling away the paper. A swath of velvet suddenly spilled out, a pure midnight blue, trimmed with satin of the same hue.

Ivory stared, transfixed. "Stop," she said.

Roddy looked up at her. "What is it?" he asked.

Ivory stood and bent over the desk, her fingers hovering over the pool of blue. Very carefully she picked it up, the fabric slipping and revealing a wide collar of silver fur.

"It's a cloak," she said into the silence.

"For a bloody queen?" Roddy asked, his brows hovering near his hairline.

It was exactly how he had described it that day. Blue velvet, edged with satin, trimmed with what Ivory could only imagine was silver fox. She was afraid to even guess what this meant.

"There's something else," he said, reaching into the paper, his eyes wide.

Ivory saw the flash of green even before Roddy gaped at the emerald he now held in his hand.

"Are you working for the prince again?" he asked, turning the large gem over in his small fingers.

"No," Ivory said.

"Then who's it from?" the boy demanded.

Ivory could only shake her head. "Well, there's a letter," Roddy piped up helpfully, bending to pick up the folded paper that had fluttered to the floor as he opened the package.

Ivory took it and hesitated, almost afraid to open it. A letter that would indicate that this gift was a gesture to assuage whatever guilt he was feeling at his departure? Perhaps he had sent his sister the same. Or was it something else?

"You need me to open that too, Duchess?" Roddy asked, watching her with a puzzled expression.

"No." This was ridiculous. She unfolded the paper, finding two sheets. Very slowly she began reading. She read both pages twice and then refolded them precisely and neatly.

"What's it say?"

Ivory cleared her throat. "Please head over to the Finish, Roderick," she said evenly. "And see if you can find the Harris brothers. I have some work for them, this evening, should they be interested."

"They're always interested," Roddy opined.

"There is also a job available for you."

The boy grinned. "I'll get my coat."

She glanced down regretfully at the beautiful velvet. She would not wear this where she was going. "Fetch my cloak while you're at it. I'm going out."

⌒

The *Odyssey* was long gone but the *Azores* still waited patiently in her moorings. Ivory waited equally patiently on the docks in front of the Indiaman while the captain was fetched. She shifted the heavy basket in her arms.

"Miss Moore," Captain Black called, standing on top of the portside railing, grinning down at her. With his tricorne and his beard, he looked like a character from a novel. "It's really you. I thought they were making it up." He disappeared, only to reappear a minute later on the docks.

"To what do I owe this utterly delightful pleasure?" He bowed, sweeping his antique hat from his head.

"I brought you dinner."

"Dinner?" He straightened so fast he almost lost his balance.

Ivory gestured at the basket she held. "I believe I owe you dinner as part of our bargain. The information you provided to Captain Harcourt did indeed assist us in retrieving his sister."

Black blinked at her before breaking into another wide grin. "Clever and honorable. I do so love a woman who keeps her word."

"I suspect you love a lot of types of women."

"True." He gallantly took the basket from her.

"And is your word still good?" she asked.

"I beg your pardon?"

"You once offered me your favor. Is that still the case?"

"Of course it is." His eyes narrowed. "What do you need, Miss Moore?"

Ivory smiled at him. "Let's discuss that over dinner, shall we?"

The Earl of Barlow was in a foul mood.

He sat hunched over his cards, watching the coin he had brought dwindle away into nothing. Again. He scowled, mentally cataloguing what remained in his estates that might yet be sold. He hated dealing with that smug bastard King, who sorted through his family's heirlooms like a country wife at a market, picking only the choicest offerings and discarding the rest like so much refuse.

Though King had taken the Harcourt girl off his hands, and as far as he knew, that problem was long gone. Barlow had been so sure she would agree to anything he asked when he had found her half naked and fleeing from her house. Her dowry would have been the answer to all of his problems, and he could have played the hero, saving her from ruin. She should have been eternally grateful to him. But just as with this card game, nothing had gone as he had planned.

Instead her brother had shown up, and after his first abortive attempt, Barlow had known there would be no negotiation on that front. And the girl had proven to be a truculent madwoman who'd refused to see reason. And then it had been too late. He hadn't been able to let her return home. And he'd been too squeamish to kill her himself. So he'd done the only logical thing and offered her to King.

But the two hundred pounds he'd gotten for his trouble was almost gone, the remnant sitting in front of him forlornly. He scowled again as he caught sight of Alexander Lavoie. The man was leaning up against the wall of his club overseeing the crowd like the merciless scavenger he was. Picking clean the carcasses of men, and becoming filthy rich for it.

Disgusted, Barlow pushed himself away from the table, sweeping what little was left back into his hand and then into the small purse at his waist. There was no point in

remaining. The stars were not aligned for him tonight. Barlow fetched his coat and stepped out into the night. He
hunched himself against the chill and began the long walk
home. He hadn't gone more than two dozen steps when a
boy crashed into his side.

"Beggin' yer pardon," the urchin said, before hurrying
off in the opposite direction.

Barlow swore and jammed his hands inside his coat,
only to realize with mounting horror that his pocket watch
and his purse were no longer on his person. He spun, and
the boy was still visible up ahead on the pavement. How
dare the little wretch take what wasn't his? With a shout of
anger, Barlow took after the thief. The boy turned and saw
him coming, then darted into an alley that led down in the
direction of the river.

In a blind rage Barlow followed, only to be brought up
suddenly by the sight of three hard-looking men, each with
a sword gleaming dully in the moonlight. The thief was
standing behind them, watching him with interest.

Barlow swallowed hard, fear rising.

"Thank you, Roderick," the tallest of the men said.
"We'll take it from here."

Barlow awoke slowly, his head pounding.

One of those thieves had hit him with the hilt end of
his sword, and the last thing he remembered was an ex-
plosion of pain before everything went dark. He blinked
in the dim light, trying to focus, but his head was still
spinning and the floor seemed to tilt beneath him. He
was lying on his side, and he realized he no longer had

his coat. In fact, he no longer had his clothes. Instead he was dressed in rough peasant clothes, layers of scratchy material that made his skin crawl. He sat up, only to be pitched sideways.

He waited for the ground beneath him to stop moving, but it continued to pitch and roll, and it took Barlow a good minute to realize that this was not an effect of the blow to the head. The ground *was* moving beneath him. He jerked up again, wincing at the pain in his head and the queasiness that roiled through his stomach.

A shaft of light suddenly pierced the dimness, and a figure was framed in silhouette.

"Ah, my sleeping beauty awakes," a man said. Barlow peered up. The figure had something perched on his head, a long feather swaying in the gusts of air that were now swirling around them.

"Am I on a ship?" Barlow asked with mounting horror.

The man laughed. "Can't get much past you, can we?"

"I can't be on a ship," Barlow croaked.

"You'll be pleased to know I've made you a bos'n's servant," the man continued, as though he hadn't heard him. "You may get started immediately."

"Do you know who I am?" Barlow demanded. There had been some mistake. He wasn't sure where he was. But he certainly wasn't where he should be.

"Yes. I just told you. You're my boatswain's servant." He pronounced each syllable slowly and loudly.

Barlow hauled himself to his feet, belatedly realizing his boots were gone too. "I am the Earl of Barlow," he said as loudly as his aching head would allow. "And I demand to speak to the man in charge."

"Well, that would be me," he was told cheerfully. "You

may call me Captain Black. Or just Captain works equally as well."

Barlow blinked. "Did you not hear me? I am the Earl of Barlow."

"Yes, yes. You keep saying." The man paused, stroking his beard. "Unfortunately, no one onboard cares. The only thing they'll be caring about is how fast you learn your duties. If you aren't up to snuff by the time we reach the Cape, I've told my men they can feed you to the sharks." He paused, considering Barlow. "I'll give you another hour or two to rest before we begin your education. You still look a little peaked."

The ship heaved beneath his feet, and Barlow fell to his knees in despair.

"Mind the rats down here, though," Black said. "They can get a little cheeky. I'll be back for you shortly." He turned to go, but then stopped. "Oh, and one more thing."

Barlow peered up at him blearily.

Black smiled. "On behalf of Lady Beatrice and himself, Captain Harcourt sends his best regards."

Chapter Sixteen

The Edward East clock in her drawing room chimed the hour, and it echoed down the hall and into the study where Ivory sat behind her desk.

In front of her she had a single sheet of paper, laid out precisely in the center of her desk. The sound of the chimes had barely faded when Roddy appeared in the doorway.

"The Duke of Alderidge is here for his appointment," he said.

Ivory's heart pounded, and butterflies swarmed through her stomach. "Please send him in, Roderick."

The boy vanished and, within a minute, was replaced by the broad figure of Maximus Harcourt. He was dressed as he had been the very first time she had seen him, in rough breeches and boots, a worn linen shirt, and a faded waistcoat. His hair was loose, brushing his shoulders, and he hadn't shaved in a number of days. He looked just like a pirate. He looked perfect.

"I do hope I am on time," he said.

Ivory's fingers were clenched in her skirts. With an effort she uncurled them and gestured to the empty chair in front of her desk. "You are indeed. Please, be seated."

Max approached the desk and settled his bulk into the chair. His eyes went to the papers on her desk. "I see you got my letter."

"I did. I also received the cloak. It's beautiful."

"I had it made for a beautiful woman."

A silence fell as they watched each other across the desk. God, he was breathtaking. And he was here, in her study. Not heading into the Atlantic winds.

"How did the Harris brothers fare?" he asked, breaking the deafening silence.

"Quite well. Though they weren't entirely sure what to do with an emerald of that size."

"I have faith that they will figure it out. I would think it will be sufficient to keep them from harassing anyone else for a very long time."

"It should be," she agreed. "I will take care to remind them of that from time to time."

"And Captain Black? I hope he was not difficult."

"He was not."

"I didn't think he would be. He is utterly besotted with you."

"Mmmm."

Another silence fell.

"Is it adequate?" he asked finally.

"I beg your pardon?"

"My list of references." He gestured at the papers that sat between them. "I'm a good hand with a blade, and have an excellent working knowledge of cannon, although you probably don't need to deal with heavy armaments that often. I'm quite comfortable with heights. Ropes and rigging and the like. I can speak three languages well, another less so, but enough to order an ale. I have excellent connections within the British navy and the East India Company. I suspect that within the month, those connections will have extended into the House of Lords. Once I start attending, that is."

"Max—"

"I have more recently discovered that I am adept at redressing corpses and staging accidental deaths. I've learned the value of clever restraint and careful patience, but then again, I learned those things from the best."

"What is this, Max?" Ivory asked.

He gazed at her. "Isn't it obvious? It's an application."

Ivory was struggling to draw a full breath. "An application?"

"Yes."

"For what?"

Max leaned forward, his clear grey eyes trained on her. "For Chegarre and Associates."

"You want me to give you a job?"

"I want more than a job, Ivory. I want whatever you're willing to give. Whatever you wish to be. I want you under any terms you set."

Oh God. A kernel of hope was lodged deep in her heart, and with each of his words it sent tiny tendrils reaching warily through her chest.

"But what about the *Odyssey*?"

"It left without me." He ran his palms over his thighs and shrugged. "She'll be back in two years."

She bit her lip, fighting for composure. "Beatrice must have been thrilled."

"She was. I have found myself the reluctant, if sudden, owner of a number of invitations to events that she seems to think her brother should escort her to."

"Mmm. And Lady Helen? How did she react?"

"Lady Helen departed yesterday from Liverpool on a packet ship destined for Boston. She took with her a companion, two trunks, and a terribly awkward case of purple orchids. It would seem she has some unfinished business there."

"I see."

"Do you?" Max stood, coming around the side of the desk and dropping to a knee in front of her. "I am willing to try to be a duke. And the brother that Beatrice deserves. But I can't do that if I don't have somewhere I belong. And I belong with you."

Ivory could feel the emotion rising in her throat and burning the backs of her eyes. She reached out and touched his face, and he caught her hand and brought it to his lips.

"Yes," she whispered. "You do."

"Does that mean you have a place for me?"

"I've had a place for you since the day you charged into my life like a Smithfield bull in a china shop," she said a little unsteadily.

He closed his eyes briefly, squeezing her hands. "I thought I'd lost you."

"As it turns out, I haven't gone very far."

"I love you, Ivory Moore. I hope you know that."

A joy unlike anything she had ever experienced burst through her. "I love you too."

"Don't ever change to please me. Promise me that."

"I promise."

Max stood and pulled her to her feet. He bent and kissed

her, a sweet, tender kiss. He drew back slightly and reached for the blue velvet cloak draped over the back of her chair. Very deliberately he spread it over the surface of the desk.

"I never should have asked you to choose between Chegarre and me," he said, straightening.

"About that—"

"It will never happen again. That is my promise to you."

"Max, there is something that you should know—"

"Indeed. Like how beautiful Chegarre looks in blue velvet? Or how much better she'll look naked in blue velvet?"

Ivory stilled. "You knew."

"I didn't know. And it almost took me too long to figure it out." He was pulling at the pins and ties of her dress. "But now that your secret is mine, I intend to use that to my every advantage." Her dress fell away, and his hands were on her, his heat burning through the thin fabric of her chemise.

It was getting harder to think. "How?"

"First I'm going to kiss you," he said, his mouth a breath away from hers. His fingers were easing her chemise off her shoulders. The linen slipped to the floor, and Max caught her at the waist, then set her gently on the velvet-covered desk. "And then I'm going to make love to you." He glanced at her desk with a slow smile. "I've wanted to do this for a long time."

Ivory looked up at him, catching his face in her hands. "Then do it."

"Are you giving me orders again, Miss Moore?"

She looked up at him, drowning in the love shining from his eyes. "Yes."

Did you miss Kelly Bowen's
Lords of Worth series?

To save an innocent girl, Gisele Whitby
needs a daring man to help her with her
cunning scheme. But when she meets
Jamie Montcrief, the rogue in question
may foil her plan—and ignite her
deepest desires . . .

Please see the next page
for an excerpt from the first book,

*I've Got My Duke
to Keep Me Warm.*

Chapter One

Being dead was not without its drawbacks.

The tavern was one of them. More hovel than hostelry, it was plunked capriciously in a tiny hamlet, somewhere near nowhere. Her mere presence in this dismal place proved time was running out and desperation was beginning to eclipse good sense.

Gisele shuffled along the filthy wall of the taproom, wrinkling her nose against the overripe scent of unwashed bodies and spilled ale. She sidestepped neatly, avoiding the leering gaze and groping fingers of more than one man, and slipped into the gathering darkness outside. She took a deep breath, trying to maintain a sense of purpose and hope. The carefully crafted demise of Gisele Whitby four years earlier had granted her the freedom and the safety to reclaim her life. True, it had also driven her to the fringes of society, but until very recently, forced anonymity had been a benediction. Now it was proving to be an unwanted complication.

"What are you doing out here?" The voice came from beside her, and she sighed, not turning toward her friend.

"This is impossible. We'll not find him here."

Sebastien gazed at the sparrows quarreling along the edge of the thatch in the evening air. "I agree. We need a male without feathers. And they are all inside."

Gisele rolled her eyes. "Have you been inside? There is not a single one in there who would stand a chance at passing for a gentleman."

Sebastien brushed nonexistent dust off his sleeve. "Perhaps we haven't seen everyone who—"

"Please," she grumbled. "Half of those drunkards have a dubious command of the English language. And the other half have no command over any type of language at all." She stalked toward the stables in agitation.

Sebastien hurried across the yard after her.

"The man we need has to be clever and witty and charming and courageous and . . . convincingly noble." She spit the last word as if it were refuse.

"He does not exactly need to replace—"

"Yes, he does," Gisele argued, suddenly feeling very tired. "He has to be all of those things. Or at least some of those and willing to learn the rest. Or very, very desperate and willing to learn them all." She stopped, defeated, eyeing a ragged heap of humanity leaning against the front of the stable, asleep or stewed or both. "And we will not find all that here, in the middle of God knows where."

"We'll find someone," Sebastien repeated stubbornly, his dark brows knit.

"And if we can't?"

"Then we'll find a way. We'll find another way. There will—"

Whatever the slight man was going to say next was drowned out by the sound of an approaching carriage. Gisele sighed loudly and stepped back into the shadows of the stable wall out of habit.

The vehicle stopped, and the driver and groom jumped down. The driver immediately went to unharness the sweat-soaked horses, though the groom disappeared inside the tavern without a backward glance, earning a muttered curse from the driver. Inside the carriage Gisele could hear the muffled tones of an argument. Presently the carriage door snapped open and a rotund man disembarked, stepping just to the side and lighting a cheroot. A well-dressed woman leaned out of the carriage door behind him to continue their squabble, shouting to be heard over the driver, who was leading the first horse away and calling for a fresh team.

Gisele watched the scene with growing impatience. She was preoccupied with her own problems and annoyed to be trapped out by the stables where there was no chance of finding any solution. Still, the carriage was expensive and it bore a coat of arms, and she would take no chances of being recognized, no matter how remote this tavern might be.

She was still plotting when the driver returned to fetch the second horse from its traces. As he reached for the bridle, the door to the tavern exploded outward with enough force to knock the wood clear off its hinges and send a report echoing through the yard like a gunshot. The gelding spooked and bolted forward, and the carriage lurched precariously behind it. The man standing with his cheroot was knocked sideways, his expensive hat landing somewhere in the dust. From the open carriage doorway, the woman began screaming hysterically, spurring the frightened horse on.

"Good heavens," gasped Sebastien, observing the unfolding drama with interest.

Gisele stood frozen as the unidentifiable lump she had previously spied leaning against the stable morphed into the form of a man. In three quick strides, the man launched himself onto the back of the panicked horse. With long arms he reached down the length of the horse's neck and easily grabbed the side of the bridle, pulling the animal's head to its shoulder with firm authority. The horse and carriage immediately slowed and then stopped, though the lady's screaming continued.

Sliding down from the blowing horse, the man gave the animal a careful once-over that Gisele didn't miss and handed the reins back to the horrified driver. The ragged-looking man then approached the woman still shrieking in the carriage and stood before her, waiting patiently for her to stop the wailing that was beginning to sound forced. He reached up a hand to help her down, and she abandoned her howling only to recoil in disgust.

"My lady?" he queried politely. "Are you all right? May I offer you my assistance?"

"Don't touch me!" the woman screeched, her chins jiggling. "You filthy creature. You could have killed me!"

By this time a number of people had caught up to the carriage, and Gisele pressed a little farther back into the shadows of the stable wall. The woman's husband, out of breath and red-faced, elbowed past the stranger and demanded a step be brought for his wife. Her rescuer simply inclined his head and retreated in the direction of the tavern, shoving his hands into the pockets of what passed for a coat. He ducked around the broken door and disappeared inside. He didn't look back.

Gisele held up a hand in warning.

"He's perfect," Sebastien breathed anyway, ignoring her.

Gisele crossed her arms across her chest, unwilling to let the seed of hope blossom.

"You saw what just happened. He just saved that wretched woman's life. You said courageous, clever, and charming. That was the epitome of all three." Sebastien was looking at her earnestly.

"Or alternatively, stupid, lucky, and drunk."

It was Sebastien's turn to roll his eyes.

"Fine." Gisele gave in, allowing hope a tiny foothold. "Do what you do best. Find out who he is and why he is here."

"What are you going to do?"

Gisele grimaced. "I will return to yonder establishment and observe your newfound hero in his cups. If he doesn't rape and pillage anything in the next half hour and can demonstrate at least a tenth the intellect of an average hunting hound, we'll go from there."

Sebastien grinned in triumph. "I've got a good feeling about him, Gisele. I promise you won't regret this." Then he turned and disappeared.

I am already regretting it, Gisele thought dourly twenty minutes later, though the lack of a front door had improved the quality of the air in the taproom, if not the quality of its ale. She managed a convincing swallow and replaced her drink on the uneven tabletop with distaste. Fingering the hilt of the knife she was displaying as a warning on the surface before her, she idly considered what manner of filth kept the bottom of her shoes stuck so firmly to the tavern floor. Sebastien had yet to reappear, and Gisele wondered how much longer she would be forced to wait. Her eyes drifted back to the stranger she'd been studying, who was still hunched over his drink at the far end of the room.

She thought he might be quite handsome if one could see past the disheveled beard and the appalling tatters currently passing for clothes. Broad shoulders, thick arms—he was very likely a former soldier, one of many who had found themselves out of work and out of sorts with the surrender of the little French madman. She narrowed her eyes. Strength in a man was always an asset, so she supposed she must count that in his favor. And from the way his knees rammed the underside of the table, he must be decently tall. Also an advantage, as nothing caught a woman's attention in a crowded room like a tall, confident man. Beyond that, however, his brown hair, brown eyes, and penchant for ale were the only qualities easily determined from a distance.

It was the latter—the utter state of intoxication he was rapidly working toward—that most piqued Gisele's interest. It suggested hopelessness. Defeat. Dejection. Desperation. All of which might make him the ideal candidate.

Or they might just mark him as a common drunkard.

And she'd had plenty of unpleasant experience with those. Unfortunately, this man was by far the best prospect she and Sebastien had seen in weeks, and she was well aware of the time slipping past. She watched as the stranger dribbled ale down his beard as he tried to drain his pot. Her lip curled in disgust.

"What do you think?" Her thoughts were interrupted by Sebastien as he slid next to her on the bench. He jerked his chin in the direction of their quarry.

She scowled. "The man's been sitting in a corner drinking himself into a stupor since I sat down. He hasn't passed out yet, so I guess that's promising." She caught sight of her friend's glare and sighed. "Please, tell me what I *should* think. What did you find out?"

Sebastien sniffed and adjusted his collar. "James Montcrief. Son of a duke—"

"What?" Gisele gasped in alarm. She involuntarily shrank against the table.

Sebastien gave her a long-suffering look. "Do you think we'd still be here if I thought you might be recognized?"

Gisele bit her lip guiltily and straightened. "No. Sorry."

"May I go on?"

"Please."

"The duchy is . . . Reddyck, I believe? I've never heard of it, but I am assured it is real, and the bulk of its lands lie somewhere near the northern border. Small, but supports itself adequately."

Gisele let her eyes slide down the disheveled stranger. "Tell me he isn't the heir apparent."

"Even better. A bastard, so no chance of ever turning into anything quite as odious."

Gisele frowned. "Acknowledged?"

"The late duke was happy to claim him. Unfortunately, the current duke—a brother of some fashion—is not nearly so benevolent. According to current family history, James Montcrief doesn't exist."

Gisele studied the man uncertainly, considering the benefits and risks of that information. Someone with knowledge of the peerage and its habits and idiosyncrasies could be helpful. *If* he could remain sober enough to keep his wits.

"He hasn't groped the serving wenches yet," Sebastien offered.

"Says who?"

"The serving wenches."

"*Hmphh.*" That might bode well. Or not. "Married? Children?"

"No and no. At least no children anyone is aware of."

"Good." They would have been a difficult complication. "Money?"

"Spent the morning cleaning stalls and repairing the roof to pay for his drink last night. Did the same the night before and the night before and—"

"In other words, none." Now that was promising. "Army?"

"Cavalry." Sebastien turned his attention from his sleeve to his carefully groomed moustache. "And supposedly quite the hero."

She snorted. "Aren't they all. Who says he's a hero?"

"The stableboys."

"They probably had him confused with his horse."

"His horse was shot out from under him at Waterloo."

"Exactly."

Her friend *tsk*ed. "The man survived, Gisele. He must know how to fight."

"Or run."

Sebastien's eyes rolled in exasperation. "That's what I love most about you. Your brimming optimism."

Gisele shrugged. "Heroes shouldn't drink themselves into oblivion. Multiple nights in a row."

Sebastien leaned close to her ear. "Listen carefully. In the past twenty minutes, I have applied my abundant charm to the chambermaids and the barmaids and the milkmaids and one very enchanting footman, and thanks to my masterful skill and caution, we now possess a wealth of information about our new friend here. The very least *you* can do is spend half that amount of time discovering if this man is really as decent as I believe him to be." He paused for breath. "He's the best option we've got."

She pressed her lips together as she pushed herself up off the bench. "Very well. As we discussed?"

"Do you have a better idea?"

"No," she replied unhappily.

"Then let's not waste any more time. We need help from some quarter, and that man is the best chance we have of getting it." Without missing a beat, he reached over and deftly plucked at the laces to Gisele's simple bodice. The top fell open to reveal an alarming amount of cleavage. "Nice. Almost makes me wish I were so inclined."

"Do shut up." Gisele tried to pull the laces back together but had her hand swatted away. "I look like a whore," she protested.

Sebastien tipped his head, then leaned forward again and pulled the tattered ribbon from her braid. Her hair slithered out of its confines to tumble over her shoulders. "But a very pretty one. It's perfect." He stood up, straightening his own jacket. "Trust me. He's going to surprise you."

She heaved one last sigh. "How drunk do you suppose he is?"

"Slurring his *s*'s. But sentence structure is still good. I'll see you in ten minutes."

"Better make it twenty," Gisele said slowly. "It will reduce the chances of you ending up on the wrong end of a cavalryman's fists."

Sebastien's dark eyes slid back to the man in the corner in speculation. "You think?"

Gisele stood to join the shorter man. "You're the one who told me he's a hero. Let's find out."

⁓

Jamie Montcrief, known in another life as James Edward Anthony Montcrief, cavalry captain in the King's Dragoon Guards of the British army and bastard son to the ninth Duke of Reddyck, stared deeply into the bottom of his ale pot and wondered fuzzily how it had come to be empty so quickly. He was sure he had just ordered a fresh drink. Perhaps the girl had spilled it on the way over and he hadn't noticed. That happened a lot these days. Not noticing things. Which was fine. In fact, it was better than fine.

"You look thirsty." As if by magic, a full cup of liquid sloshed to the table in front of him.

Startled, he looked up, only to be presented with a view of stunning breasts. They were full and firm, straining against the fabric of a poorly laced bodice, and despite the fact that they were not entirely in focus, his body reacted with reprehensible speed. He reached out, intending to caress the luscious perfection before him, only to snatch his hand back a moment later when sluggish honor demanded retreat. Mortified, he dragged his eyes up from the woman's chest to her face, hoping against hope she might not have noticed.

He should have kept his eyes on her breasts.

For shimmering before him was a fantasy. His fantasy. The one he had carefully created in his imagination to chase away the reality of miserable marches, insufferable nights, unspeakable hunger, and bone-numbing dread. Everything he had hoped to possess in a woman was sliding onto the bench opposite him, a shy smile on her face. And it was a face that could start a war. High cheekbones, a full mouth, eyes almost exotic in their shape. Pale hair that fell in thick sheets carelessly around her head and over her shoulders.

He opened his mouth to say something clever, yet all his words seemed to have drowned themselves in the depths of his drink. He cursed inwardly, wishing for the first time in many months he weren't drunk. She seemed not to notice. Instead she cheerfully raised her own full pot of ale in a silent toast and proceeded to drain it. At a loss for anything better to do, he followed suit.

"Thank you," he finally managed, though he wasn't sure she heard, as she had somehow procured two more pots of ale and slid another in front of him.

"What shall we toast to now?" she asked him, her brilliant gray-green eyes probing his own.

Frantically Jamie searched his liquor-soaked brain for an intelligent answer. "To beauty," he croaked, cringing at such an amateurish and predictable reply.

She gave him a dazzling smile anyway, and he could feel his own mouth curling up in response. "To beauty then," she said. "And those who are wise enough to realize what it may cost." She drained her second pot.

Jamie allowed his mind to slog wearily through her cryptic words for a moment or two before he gave up trying to understand. Who cared, really? He had a magnificent woman sitting across the table from him, and another pot of ale had already replaced the second one he had drained. This was by far the best thing that had happened to him in a very long time.

"What's your name?" Her voice was gentle.

"James. James Montcrief." Thank the gods. At least he could remember that. Though maybe he should have made an effort at formality? Did one do that in such a setting?

"James." His name was like honey on her tongue, and her own dismissal of formality was encouraging. Something stirred inside him. "I like it." She gave him another blinding smile. "Why are you drinking all alone, James?" she asked.

He stared at her, unable, and more truthfully, unwilling to give her any sort of an answer. Instead he just shrugged.

"Never mind." She tipped her head back, and another pot of ale disappeared. Idly he wondered how she still remained sober while the room he was sitting in was beginning to spin. She tilted her head, and her beautiful blond hair swung away from her neck, dizzying in its movement. "You have kind eyes."

Her comment caught him off guard. He did not have kind eyes. He had eyes that had seen too much to ever allow any kindness in. "I am not kind." He wasn't sure if he mumbled it or just thought it. Inexplicably, a wave of sadness and loneliness washed over him.

"What brings you here?" she asked, waving a hand in the general direction of the tavern.

Jamie blinked, trying to remember where *here* was, then snorted at the futility of the question.

"Nowhere else to go," he mumbled. The accuracy of his statement echoed in his mind. Nowhere to go, nowhere to be. No one who cared. Least of all him.

"Would you like to go somewhere else, James? With me?" Her words seemed to come from a distance, and with a frantic suddenness, he needed to get out. Out from the tavern walls that were pressing down on him, away from the smells of grease and bodies and smoke and alcohol that were suffocating.

"Yes." He shoved away from the table, swaying on his feet. In an instant she was there, at his side, her arm tucked into his elbow as though he really were a duke escorting her across the ballroom of a royal palace. He could feel the warmth of her body as it pressed against his and the cool silk of her hair as it slid across his bicep. Again he wished desperately he weren't so drunk. His body was dragging him in one direction while his mind flailed helplessly against the haze.

"Come," she whispered, guiding him out into the cool night breeze.

He went willingly with his beautiful vision into the darkness, dragging in huge lungfuls of air in an attempt to clear his head. He pressed a hand against his temple.

"Are you unwell?" She was still right beside him, and he was horrified to realize he was leaning on her as he might a crutch. He straightened abruptly.

"No." He concentrated hard on his next words. "I don't even know your name."

She stared at him a long moment as if debating something within her mind. "Gisele," she finally said.

He was regretting those last pots of ale. Thinking was becoming almost impossible. "And why were *you* drinkin' alone, Gisele?" he asked slowly.

The sparkle dimmed abruptly in her face, and she turned away. "Will you take me away from here, James?" she asked.

"I beg your pardon?" His mind was struggling to keep up with his ears.

She turned back. "Take me somewhere. Anywhere. Just not here."

"I don't understand." Blade-sharp instincts long suppressed fought to make themselves heard through the fog in his brain. Something was all wrong with this situation, though he was damned if he could determine what it might be. "I can't just—"

Jamie was suddenly knocked back, tripping over his feet and falling gracelessly, unable to overcome gravity and the last three pots of ale. Gisele was yanked from his side, and she gave a slight yelp as a man slammed her back up against the tavern wall.

"Where the hell have you been, whore?" the man snarled. "Like a damn bitch in heat, aren't you?"

Jamie struggled to his feet, fighting the dizziness that was making his surroundings swim. He reached for the weapon at his side before realizing he couldn't recall where he'd left it. He turned just in time to see the man pull back his arm to slug Gisele. With a roar of rage, Jamie launched himself at her attacker, hitting him square in the back. The man was barely half his size, and the force of Jamie's weight knocked both men into the mud. A fist caught the side of his head in a series of short, sharp jabs, only increasing the din resonating through his brain. Jamie tried to stagger to his feet again, but the ground shifted underneath him and he fell heavily on his side.

"Don't touch her," he managed, wrestling with the darkness crowding the edge of his vision. Usually he welcomed this part of the night, when reality ceased to exist. But not now. This couldn't happen now. He had to fight it. Fight for her. Fight for something again. He pushed himself up on his hands and knees. He looked up at the figures looming over him. Strangely, Gisele and her attacker were standing side by side as if nothing had happened. The buzzing was getting louder as Gisele crouched down beside him, and he felt her cool hand on his forehead.

"So sorry," he mumbled, his arms collapsing beneath him. "I couldn't do—"

"You did just fine, James," she said. And then he heard no more.

Fall in Love with Forever Romance

EXTREME HONOR
by Piper J. Drake

Hot military heroes, the women who love them, and the dogs that always have their backs. EXTREME HONOR is the first book in Piper J. Drake's high-adrenaline True Heroes series.

Fall in Love with Forever Romance

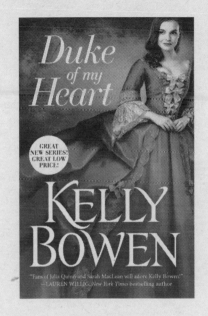

DUKE OF MY HEART
by Kelly Bowen

Captain Maximus Harcourt can deal with tropical storms, raging seas, and the fiercest of pirates. But he's returned home to a crisis and has only one place to turn. So now he's at the mercy of the captivating Miss Ivory Moore, known throughout London for smoothing over the most dire of scandals.

Max has never in all his life met a woman with such nerve. And such magnetic appeal...